CRIME IN OXFORD

A fiercely addictive mystery

CATHERINE MOLONEY

Detective Markham Mystery Book 15

Joffe Books, London
www.joffebooks.com

First published in Great Britain in 2022

Cover art by Dee Dee Book Covers

ISBN: 978-1-80405-090-3

To my darling Pa

PROLOGUE

Security guard Brendan Potter loved his Saturday morning shift at the Reynolds Museum in Oxford — or, to use its full title, the Reynolds Museum and Centre for Ethnographic Research. Saturday mornings were by no means popular with his colleagues, however. 'Nah, Bren,' went the popular refrain, 'weekends are for having a lie-in. Not traipsing round checking to see no one's nicked some poxy cooking pot or totem pole.'

But the museum held a rare charm for Brendan. Unenthused by history lessons at school, he was now entranced by these glimpses of strange peoples and vanished worlds.

Best of all was Polar Exploration in the Antarctic on the third-floor gallery, which he always saved till last. Seeing his interest in the new exhibition, Mr Kelleher, the museum's assistant curator, had told him all sorts of stuff; how the name 'Arctic' came from the Greek word for 'bear', because the continent was thought to lie under the star of that name, how the Elizabethans didn't really have a clue, so drew pictures of monsters at the bottom of their maps, how there was this Victorian bloke who got stuck in the ice and his crew ended up becoming cannibals . . .

As Brendan did his rounds, the names came back to him, and he rolled them round his mouth like an incantation,

1

displaying a retentiveness that would have astonished his long-suffering GCSE teacher.

De Gerlache . . . James Clark Ross . . . Sir John Franklin . . . Nansen . . . Amundsen . . . Captain Scott . . . Shackleton . . .

All those men with their blackened, blistered faces cracked by sunburn and frostbite. The ones who only truly came alive amongst icebergs and glaciers with the penguins and seals and whales, the stormy seas and danger . . .

Brendan had enjoyed watching Kate Winslet and Leonardo What's His Face in *Titanic* on that awkward date with Janice from HR. But those icebergs were child's play compared to the real thing and the sinister sheer mountains which shot out of the sea for thousands of feet.

He'd always thought snow was white and that was that. But Mr Kelleher said the photos in the display cases didn't give you an idea of all the colours, especially in summer when night never fell — every colour from violet to indigo and purple, like something out of a fairy-tale . . .

And the Brits were tops. That Norwegian bloke Amundsen might have made it to the South Pole first, but Mr Kelleher said he hadn't played a straight bat, and anyway Captain Scott and Oates and all that lot never cheated, won fair and square, and died like heroes every man jack of them.

The pictures of Captain Scott's grave never failed to send shivers down his spine. They called it a *cairn*, the snow-mound the rescue party piled on top of the three sleeping bags with the dead men inside after letting down the tent poles and canvas on top of them. They put a cross on top, but the museum director Dr Ashworth said ice was on the move so the bodies would eventually end up in the ocean and wash up somewhere. Brendan didn't like to imagine their tomb floating about. It didn't seem decent somehow. Then there was Oates and the other one, Evans, they didn't even have proper graves. He wondered what they looked like now . . . skeletons or ice-mummies?

Brendan knew what his mother would say.

No need to be morbid, son. Just stay focused on the job.

Mum was so proud when he was taken on at the museum. He knew she imagined him hobnobbing with professors and posh folk, and somehow he didn't have the heart to disillusion her.

Not that there was anything wrong with his job, he told himself, squaring his shoulders defiantly. Dr Ashworth said everyone had to start somewhere and no reason why he couldn't look for something on the management side provided he got some qualifications under his belt. A late developer, that's what he was. 'And none the worse for that.' He could hear mum's voice loud and clear.

Outside the Reynolds, it was a blazing hot July day, but the air-conditioned, dimly lit depths of the museum were unaffected and there was something almost delicious to Brendan in the thought of those snow-capped regions at the ends of the earth.

He passed a display on the Greenlandic Inuit, moving with studied casualness to the staircase that led to the third gallery and the polar regions.

And there it was. The latest exhibition, designed to pull in the punters.

Scott. Shackleton.

Photographs of men arrayed in stiff wing collars, gazing self-consciously into the camera lens, underneath poetic captions.

And how can man die better than facing fearful odds, for the ashes of his fathers, and the temples of his gods?

Brendan wasn't entirely sure what that meant, but he relished the way it sounded. Like the national anthem. Dr Ashworth said it was something to do with Ancient Rome, which seemed a bit weird because as far as he knew they hadn't got round to discovering the South Pole back then . . . Mr Kelleher explained it was about being ready to put yourself on the line for your country, which Brendan reckoned was a good thing.

He forced himself to walk slowly past cabinets featuring pictures of bergs and explorers, with their captions about

'Furthest South', latitudes and longitudes, heading for the section dedicated to Robert Falcon Scott.

Scott of the Antarctic.

Even the name had a thrilling ring.

As if even an obscure security guard could rise like Scott from midshipman to be the greatest ornament of the age.

It made his nerve ends tingle.

At the far end of the gallery in a mezzanine next to the lifts was what the curators called an 'art installation', based on some test the great Norwegian Roald Amundsen had devised in a whiteout blizzard. Apparently, he'd dug himself a cavity in the snow and then woken up to find it had turned overnight into a sarcophagus — a solid block of ice . . . a frozen coffin from which there was no way out!

Eventually, as in all the best action movies, Amundsen was saved at the last minute by his friend who spotted his reindeer-skin sleeping bag poking through the snow.

But Brendan couldn't dislodge images of the explorer scratching away in his icy coffin, struggling desperately to free himself. Sometimes at night, he woke in a cold sweat imagining that he too was a hair's breadth from death. It merged with dreams of Captain Scott and his companions entombed in their frigid carapace, floating onwards to the farthest sea.

An ice cube. Steamed up with the panicked cries of a man looking death in the face.

A mock-up. A piece of theatre designed to bring in the credulous public.

There it was, spot-lit at the end of the gallery.

An eerie rectangle condensed with exhaled human breath.

From an ice machine or one of those theatre contraptions, obviously.

Only something wasn't right . . .

It was meant to be a mannequin inside the display case. But the figure curled on its side in a foetal position was too life-like to be mistaken for a dummy.

Brendan swallowed hard then moved in for closer examination.

And recoiled.

He recognised those features, the teeth drawn back over the well moulded lips in a species of snarl.

Dr Timothy Colthurst. The 'up-and-coming man', as some called him sarcastically. The impetus behind the exhibition.

Suddenly, Brendan was fearful, the familiar shadowy galleries and alcoves — terra incognita.

He thought of those Elizabethan squiggles.

Hic Sunt Dracones. Here Be Dragons.

Brendan staggered back against the gallery railing and looked about him apprehensively.

All was quiet, and the outside world seemed a million miles away.

Twenty Thousand Leagues Under the Sea.

The recollection came out of nowhere. An English teacher banging on long ago about some fantastical conception of a Victorian novelist.

A hysterical giggle rose in Brendan's throat.

Freaking Captain Nemo, that's me. Oh my god, Mum. You're never going to believe this.

Transfixed, he stood there as if rooted to the spot, under some spell that held him fast.

Around him the galleries and exhibitions were inscrutable, silent.

Somehow, Brendan could not break the trance that held him. Afterwards he could not have said how long he stayed looking disbelievingly at the dead man pinioned in the ice.

Outside the Reynolds, carefree tourists and holidaymakers laughed and enjoyed the sun.

Inside the museum, the nightmare was only just beginning.

1. LETHAL BEAUTY

The morning of Sunday 25 July found DI Gilbert 'Gil' Markham sitting on a bench outside the Reynolds Museum, thoughtfully contemplating the brutalist architecture that was readily denounced by Oxford academics as an 'abomination'.

Personally, he rather liked all the solar-controlled glass, steel and concrete. It was the contrast with the quaint old English gardens that pleased him. He'd always thought those hedge-lined walks and arboreta had a peaceful tranquillity at odds with the building's rather sinister history.

For this was not the first time that murder had visited the museum, one of the killings in a previous investigation having cast its shadow over an exhibition on Neolithic Man.

Markham's thoughts turned to the previous day, a lazy Saturday when, for once, murder had been the furthest thing from his mind . . .

His partner, English teacher Olivia Mullen, with whom he had been enjoying a self-indulgent holiday in the Old Parsonage Hotel out on the Banbury Road, was frankly incredulous when he received the call about a suspicious death at the Reynolds Museum. Even Markham's assurance that the local CID had organised removal of the body failed to propitiate her.

'Oh *no*,' she groaned. 'Not another one. That place must be *jinxed*.' Then, biting her lip guiltily, 'I'm sorry, Gil. That sounds callous, but I just can't believe it's happened again.' *Surely a break from murder was long overdue*, she thought crossly. 'And let me guess, Sidney's tipped them off to have you take over this one, what with you being on the spot and "an Oxford man". Plus, it stops you stealing his thunder back at the ranch.' These observations were uttered through clenched teeth, Olivia being no fan of DCI Sidney ('Slimy Sid' to the troops), Markham's boss back in Bromgrove, whom she regularly likened to Judas Iscariot for his jealousy of the younger man.

'Oh, I reckon Sidney's mellowed,' Markham had pointed out mildly. 'And to be honest, with the Ivory Tower brigade, it doesn't hurt to have one of their own working the case.'

She conceded the logic of this, doing her best not to sigh too gustily over the rapidly diminishing perspective of hazy lazy days with Pimm's and punts.

'So what's next then, Gil?'

'The SOCOs are sending some pictures over, and I can do a preliminary recce tomorrow. The victim's an academic — Dr Timothy Colthurst from Sherwin College. Specialised in polar studies apparently.'

'What do you know about polar exploration, Liv?' he asked as they had tucked into their room service meal of seafood salad followed by strawberries and cream. 'Captain Scott, Shackleton and all that lot.'

She took a hefty gulp of Chablis. 'Let me see, I think it goes something like this. In the early nineteen hundreds, Scott led an expedition in his ship the *Discovery* which didn't reach the South Pole but got closer than anyone else . . . Then Shackleton — who'd been on the first trip but ended up getting sick and had to be pulled along on a sledge — went out in *his* ship called the *Nimrod*. There was some bad blood between the two of them over that, because he followed Scott's route after promising he wouldn't butt in on his territory. Anyway, he got even further and beat Scott's record by three hundred odd miles—'

'Didn't make it to the Pole, though?'

'No, he's famous for turning back when he was almost there to make sure he brought his team back safely after they ran into trouble.' She chuckled. 'Told his missus he reckoned she'd prefer a living donkey to a dead lion.'

Markham smiled. 'I like his style.'

'Then Scott had another crack at it . . . Led an expedition in the *Terra Nova,* but the Norwegian Roald Amundsen got there first. Scott's team all died when they weren't that far from help.' She forked up some crispy calamari and chewed appreciatively. '*Mmm*, this is seriously good . . . where was I?'

'Scott and Co expiring before they made it back to camp,' Markham prompted.

'Oh yes. Captain Oates was one of them, remember?'

'Ah . . . the chap who fell on his sword because he was slowing the rest down. Walked out into a blizzard, said he was just going out and might be some time.'

'That's the one.' Olivia frowned. 'Mind you, his old mother always said Scott talked him into it.'

'*What*, as in pressured Oates to do it?' Markham was startled. 'That's a new one on me.' He took a long draught of wine, watching her flushed animated features admiringly. With her pallor, waterfall of long red hair and sparkling grey-green eyes, she was the epitome of a Rossetti heroine, though the overall effect was somewhat belied by cropped trousers and baggy tee shirt. 'Where did you hear that story? I mean, I don't remember coming across it in my *Boys' Book of Heroes*.'

'Oh, these days it's terrifically fashionable to debunk types like Scott and Shackleton,' she replied, deflecting the question as was characteristic of one who wore her learning lightly. 'I wanted to do something on them with the history department at Hope.' The name of her school in Bromsgrove, popularly designated as 'Hopeless'.

'What happened?'

'Just the usual spoilsports . . . obsessing about it being outdated and imperialistic.'

'Well, Scott was hardly some chinless wonder,' Markham protested.

'My point exactly,' Olivia frowned. 'But the others didn't see it that way.' She chewed meditatively. 'In fairness, they're trying to make the curriculum more inclusive — less "stale white male" — so I can see where they're coming from. But you know me when it comes to cramping kids' imaginations. I hate watering down the adventurous stuff.'

He grinned, imagining the scene in Hope's staffroom.

'I seem to remember watching some film starring John Mills,' he said. '*Scott of the Antarctic*. Stiff upper lip and all the rest of it. Lashings of heroism.'

'I played that card for all it was worth,' Olivia told him with a sardonic gleam in her eyes. 'Said that it opened up a boundless world of possibility for kids with low aspirations. I even insisted it was a part of our history that shouldn't be glossed over. Come to think of it, that's probably what did for me.'

'Well, he's not exactly flavour of the month right now,' Markham pointed out, amused.

'I couldn't help myself,' she burst out. 'Scott and Shackleton and the whole lot of them believed in something bigger than themselves. They had fantastic *guts*, real deep-down courage like you hardly ever see these days.' She warmed to her theme. 'They took everything the Pole could throw at them — sunburn, scurvy, snow blindness, diarrhoea, frostbite, gangrene — but never gave in, even when they had the option of taking opium tablets to end it all. And anyway,' she went on indignantly, 'Shackleton was this maverick Irishman, not a moustachioed Colonel Blimp or one of the Ha! Ha! poshos. When he and his crew ended up marooned at some godforsaken place called Elephant Island after another trip across Antarctica went wrong, he just said, "Okay boys, now we go home!".'

'I'm definitely warming to Shackleton,' Markham commented. 'There's something appealing about the understatement.'

'They were all like that. Oates is a scream. Wrote to Mommie Dearest that employers would be keener to take on a man who'd been to the Pole than someone who only got as far as the Mile End Road. Scott was just the same. In the last letter home, with his toes about to drop off from frostbite, he told his wife to get their son interested in natural history because it was "better than games".'

Markham laughed, the austere hawklike features softening in a manner that his subordinates rarely witnessed.

'You've really gone into this, haven't you?' he said affectionately. 'I can see that Scott and his buddies cast quite a spell.'

'Don't get me wrong, I know they made terrible mistakes — inadequate provisions, dodgy paraffin lamps so the fuel ran out, not using dogs and all the rest of it. But they were so brave at the end . . . Plus,' she pulled a wry face, 'reading their diaries about the strain of being cooped up cheek by jowl put me in mind of the snake pit at Hope.'

'*Ah.*' Markham could imagine it all too well. He polished off the last of his rollmops before asking, 'Couldn't you have got Mat Sullivan onside?' Sullivan was a Deputy Head at Hope and one of their oldest friends, the relationship having been cemented after a murder investigation at the school when he came briefly under suspicion.

'Oh, Mat was very keen. Loved all the derring-do and amazing stories.' She chuckled. 'Their clothes froze like suits of armour out there as soon as the heating ran out. It meant they held whatever shape they froze in. One poor bloke stopped to look sideways for a few minutes then found the neck of his hood had frozen solid and he was stuck in that position until they could unthaw him so he could look ahead again.'

Markham smiled. 'Couldn't the two of you have talked up the heroics and played down the Empire side of it?'

'God knows we tried. We knew the kids would lap it up. But that witch Judith Lipscombe wasn't having it.'

At this reference to Hope Academy's insufferably right-on assistant head, he began to see why Olivia's plans had never got off the ground.

'Lipscombe read history at uni,' Olivia explained, 'and she's got ideas for a million other projects that don't involve white male explorers . . . Projects that are more in line with the school's *caring*, inclusive ethos, *yada yada*. She took all her concerns to Call-Me-Tony.' Her voice resonated with scorn for the headteacher Anthony Brighouse, as she added, 'And you know what an invertebrate he is!'

'No Navy men on the curriculum this year then?' Markham smiled wryly. 'Just don't mention any of this to George. I know what he'd have to say about it . . .'

'George' was DS George Noakes, Markham's trusty sidekick to whom his thoughts now turned as he sat outside the museum savouring the warmth of the early morning sun.

Over their seafood supper the previous night, Olivia had observed that the passionate devotion of Captain Scott's men to their 'Skipper' ('It will be an honour to drop down any crevasse in the world with you', as one put it) was reminiscent of Noakes's dogged loyalty to his guvnor.

And it was true. The porky, bulldog-featured, monumentally tactless and uncouth sergeant was the absolute antithesis of the smooth careerists who mainly populated CID these days and the despair of his politically correct superiors.

After several fruitless attempts to have Noakes put out to grass, however, DCI Sidney appeared to have accepted that he was a fixture at Markham's side.

'Just keep him on a tight leash, Markham,' he instructed. 'The man's a walking PR disaster.'

For her part, Olivia adored 'Noakesy', appreciating the strangely romantic, almost poetic side of his nature, which he generally took good care to conceal from colleagues. He was intensely proud of being bagman to a DI of Markham's culture and refinement, even if he didn't understand all the 'big words' or the mystical streak in his boss's makeup. No intellectual, he nonetheless had an omnivorous curiosity about the world, startling his colleagues during a recent investigation by the way he enthusiastically hoovered up every crumb of information about a religious cult. There had even been a brief flirtation with Catholicism, though his Sunday school Methodist upbringing was too sturdily entrenched to see him go over 'to the dark side'.

When Markham had telephoned him in Bromgrove with news of the latest murder, the DS had been surprisingly knowledgeable about polar explorers. 'Them bloody Norskies never played fair,' he said of Roald Amundsen. 'An' Captain Scott was a hero . . . I remember this documentary. It said all these soldiers wrote to his missus after World War Two to say how knowing about him an' Oates an' the rest helped give 'em courage. She needed it herself, poor lass . . . travelling out to meet him when he was long dead.' While short on compassion for 'scrotes', Noakes had a tender chord that was readily touched. 'An' one of the other wives had given her fella a little silk flag to fly at the Pole when they got there, but the Norskies beat 'em to it.'

The knight-errantry of it all clearly appealed to the DS, possessing as he did an oddly chivalric strain in his own character that came out strongly in his relationship with Olivia. Her ethereal charms inspired in him an almost Sancho Panza-like devotion and reverence that were a considerable source of irritation to his formidable spouse.

Muriel Noakes was a snobbish, overbearing woman who had a marked partiality for her husband's handsome boss with his charming manners and old-world gallantry but regarded Olivia with a jaundiced eye. Of late, however, they had achieved some kind of truce, aided by glimpses of a softer, more vulnerable side to the woman who at first glance resembled a Sherman tank crossed with Margaret Thatcher (it being no coincidence that the eighties, as the heyday of the Iron Lady, were Muriel's favourite era). Unlikely as it seemed, she and Noakes had met on the amateur ballroom circuit and showed a surprising chemistry on the dance floor. Markham had never succeeded in fathoming the precise dynamics of the marriage, but Noakes was fiercely proud of his 'missus' and a doting father to their perma-tanned beautician daughter, Natalie. Undoubtedly the biggest crisis of Noakes's life was the discovery during the infamous Bluebell investigation that Natalie was not in fact his biological daughter but the result of his wife's brief affair in her teens. It had almost cataclysmic consequences for his police career and partnership with Markham, but he hung on to his job and the two men came through the storm stronger than ever — even though neither man ever alluded to it again. How typical of their relationship that such personal matters went largely unspoken. Noakes knew that Markham was a victim of childhood abuse, but he never sought to pry, conveying a wordless sympathy that required no explanation.

As Olivia had once put it, in some people's opinion George Noakes might have very little displayed in the shop window, but the goods inside were pure gold.

Technically, Noakes was enjoying some well-earned leave, but had made it clear he was 'up for' this investigation. Markham suspected this was more to do with a desire to escape the list of DIY tasks earmarked for his attention than any sudden enthusiasm to revisit the city of dreaming spires.

The DI had been amused at the eagerness with which his bagman suggested scrambling a team to join him in Oxford.

'You know Burton'll want a piece of the action,' Noakes insisted. 'I mean, Oxford an' the museum an' Captain Scott . . . She'll think she's died an' gone to heaven.'

DI Kate Burton, currently based in London, and Noakes had started out as adversaries; the earnest, politically correct university graduate guaranteed to turn the chip on his shoulder into a great big boulder. But over the course of many investigations, Markham's protégée and the grizzled veteran had gradually learned to appreciate each other and become friends. A psychology graduate now engaged to a criminal profiler at Bromgrove University, Burton shared Noakes's addiction to true crime documentaries, though she had never managed to win him over to the merits of her beloved *Diagnostic and Statistical Manual of Mental Disorders* which accompanied her everywhere. Aware that the DS had christened her fiancé 'Shippers' on account of his startling resemblance to the serial killer Dr Harold Shipman, Burton had unbent sufficiently from the po-faced detective of yore to find the nickname endearing rather than otherwise. Having come through many tight corners with Noakes — including being rescued by him at the eleventh hour — she also secretly liked his protective attitude towards her even when expressed in terms that would have the diversity personnel reaching for their smelling salts.

Like Noakes, she was always hungry for knowledge and Markham had no doubt that this investigation with its tie-in to the age of polar exploration would strongly appeal. Her capacity for hard work and loyalty to him — qualities she shared with the DS — made her inclusion a no-brainer. He should be able to square it with DCI Moriarty at Southampton Row provided Sidney was on board.

And where Burton went, no doubt DS Doyle would wish to follow. The lanky ginger-haired youngster had moved with Burton to Southampton Row and was much missed by his former colleagues in Bromgrove — none more so than Noakes, his mentor in relation to football and matters of the heart alike. The two men invariably enjoyed meeting up for a 'drinkathon' on Doyle's regular forays home, so it would be quite like old times to reunite them . . .

Markham glanced at his watch. Quarter to nine. He was due to meet the museum's director Dr Clive Ashworth shortly, the Reynolds being closed to the public after the previous day's shocking discovery.

Right on cue, a hulking fresh-faced young security guard emerged from the building and approached his bench. With a reassuring smile, the DI introduced himself.

'If you'd like to follow me, I'm to show you round,' he said before adding nervously, 'I'm Brendan Potter, the one who found him yesterday.'

14

The DI found himself warming to Potter and imagined that Noakes would feel the same way about the youngster who so obviously idolised the great Antarctic explorers, even if they *did* lack the winning touch. Gentle questioning about the polar exhibition and its strange art installation showed how strong was the spell cast by this land of the midnight sun.

'You can see why they weren't able to stay away,' Brendan said. 'There's no place on earth like it. And Captain Scott was the *best*. Eight thousand men volunteered for his second expedition . . . *Eight thousand.*' Shyly he added, 'The man who sponsored him had the same surname as *you*. Sir Clements Markham.' The DI wasn't sure whether or not he should regard this coincidence as a good omen but received the information with a ready smile.

The interior of the museum was neo-gothic and as traditional as any orthodox heart could desire, with coffered ceilings, iron wrought spiral staircases and massive oak cabinets. As though the designer of the exterior had been sacked and the architectural status quo restored. The mismatch gave the place a unique quirkiness, and its cool depths had the quality of a mysterious aquarium.

Markham's eyes were drawn to some black and white photographs of strangely shaped bergs, grottoes, tunnels, colonnades, and snow-covered ships resembling Christmas cakes, like some wondrous sculpture park that lay under a dark enchantment.

Following the detective's gaze, Brendan had told him, 'The black and white photographs mean you don't get any idea of the colours . . . But they wrote about it in the diaries, and about the rocks and birds — skuas and giant petrels and things. I don't know much about the science,' the youth added modestly, 'but it wasn't just a race to the Pole. Captain Scott discovered all sorts. He was collecting specimens right till the end. And Shackleton's lot were the same.' His voice trailed away as he gestured to the art installation now surrounded by screens. 'How did Dr Colthurst die, sir?' he now asked, tentatively.

Markham thought back to his brief conversation earlier that morning with the pathologist Dr Merrick.

'I understand he was most likely attacked elsewhere—' Dr Merrick had in fact said 'bludgeoned,' but Markham refrained from using the word — 'and then lifted into the replica ice box.' He had almost said 'coffin' but, observing his stricken interlocutor, stopped himself just in time.

A look of relief washed over Brendan Potter's broad freckled face. 'I was afraid he'd been put in there alive and then suffocated, sir . . . you know, screaming and scratching — only no one came.'

Markham repressed his shudder at a scenario that sounded like something out of Edgar Allen Poe.

Entombed alive.

At least Dr Timothy Colthurst had been spared that.

'Did you have much to do with Dr Colthurst?' he asked the security guard.

'Well, he was a research don at Sherwin, but ever so down to earth . . . no airs and graces.' Not toffee-nosed, his mum would have said. 'Polar exploration was a big thing with him. He had lots of stories about what it was like man-hauling — that's pulling sledges,' he added kindly. The DI's lips quirked at Brendan's unconscious tone of condescension to the uninitiated. 'And all about the ponies, how Scott hated having to kill them and called one of the camps Shambles Camp cos they had to finish off so many. And—' he broke off suddenly, embarrassed. 'Sorry, Mr Markham, you don't want to be hearing all this.'

Letting his tongue run away with him, mum would say.

'Not at all.' The tall dark policeman with the steady gaze was kind. 'It helps to have a picture of Dr Colthurst. He sounds likeable,' Markham added with a pang.

Any man's death diminishes me.

'He was round here quite a lot. When him and Dr Ashworth and Mr Kelleher got started about explorers, they could go on for hours. They each had their favourite . . . Dr Colthurst's was Henry Bowers. "Birdie", they called him cos he looked a bit like a penguin.'

'Why did Dr Colthurst particularly admire Mr Bowers?' he asked, intrigued.

'Well, Bowers was just this short-arse . . . Sorry,' he blushed, 'I mean he was a bit diddy, five foot four or something. But Scott called him a "marvel" cos he was so tough. Never say die.' The boy's face crumpled. 'Only he did.'

'He sounds an amazing character.'

'Yeah, he was. Dr Colthurst said when he was dying, he wrote to his mum last thing so she wouldn't fret.' Devoted as he was to his own mother, this had made a powerful impression on Brendan. 'Told her he was just going to sleep in the cold. *Imagine* that. I mean, he was a bible basher, so likely that helped him cos he knew everyone'd meet up in heaven and all that, but even so . . . Him and Dr Wilson — that's the other bloke they found dead with Scott — wouldn't even make a dash for the last depot in case they didn't make it back and the captain was left on his own.' Brendan screwed up his face in recollection. 'And Bowers told his mum that best of all was dying with his two mates, cos they were the tops.'

Something about the earnest open face brought a lump to Markham's throat. He sent up a silent prayer that Brendan Potter would never lose his shining faith in the capacity of friendship and courage to overcome all odds.

In his mind's eye he imagined the pathologist superintending the removal of the murdered academic. Dr Merrick — or 'Jigsaw Man', as Noakes had nicknamed him during the Sherwin College investigation from his habit of discussing victims in terms of bones and body parts, 'like a bleeding Rubik's cube' — had not been particularly forthcoming in their earlier telephone conversation. 'At a preliminary estimate, I would say death occurred around 10 p.m. on Friday night, Inspector, but don't hold me to that.''

Brendan said agitatedly, 'There should be something on CCTV, Mr Markham . . . It's a brand-new system. Everything gets picked up in the control room.'

These words echoed in Markham's head as the security guard disappeared to fetch the director.

He knew all about the state-of-the-art technology introduced at the museum in the wake of the previous murder investigation.

Somehow, he reflected, the killer must have found a blind spot . . .

Dr Clive Ashworth — the new director who had taken over after the last incident at the museum — came panting up and ushered Markham into his well-appointed ground floor office that had been okayed for use by the SOCOs.

The predominant impression was acres of teak and mahogany with a magnificent view of massed fritillaries and roses through the floor to ceiling window that took up the whole length of the room. Oil paintings on the wall portrayed various doughy bald grandees whom Markham took to be benefactors and academics. Learned and ugly. He could only imagine what Olivia would make of it . . .

Dr Ashworth was a short man with sparse silver hair, spectacles and a little pointed beard who put Markham in mind of Lenin. But his manner was amiable enough, with nothing of the despot. 'I'd be glad to show you around the polar exhibition, Inspector,' he volunteered.

'That's very good of you, sir. I suggest that we postpone a guided tour until tomorrow when my team should be available to accompany me. It would certainly be useful to meet the principal museum staff as well . . . those who had the most contact with Dr Colthurst.'

'Of course, Inspector.'

As he had feared, it transpired there were blind spots not covered by CCTV.

'Only three,' Dr Ashworth confirmed in his slightly squeaky voice. 'One next to the staff locker room and the other two on the second and third floor next to the lifts . . . The risk assessment indicated it was alright, and anyway after last time we never thought—'

'That lightning could strike twice,' Markham finished gravely.

The director's face was troubled.

'We've worked hard to move on from . . . last time,' he said.

'I imagine the notoriety initially brought a certain cachet,' Markham observed wryly.

'Ye-es. But the council wasn't happy about that.'

'Ah, of course, I remember now . . . Oxfordshire County Council owns the museum, so it's a public resource, though there are close ties to the university.'

'Correct. Sherwin College sponsors the polar exhibition, hence Dr Colthurst's involvement.'

Markham requested a list of personnel and information on the current museum exhibitions, deciding that it was almost time to call it a day. The poor man was no doubt anxious to salvage what was left of his weekend and the DI himself fancied a stroll with Olivia. She had suggested they take a turn in St Sepulchre's Cemetery out in Jericho — 'It's so peaceful, Gil, all butterflies and briars' — and the prospect suited his mood. Out there with nature, far away from the police tape and white-suited SOCOs, he would be able to commend Dr Timothy Colthurst to God while recalling all those other murder victims whose footfalls echoed down the pathways of his memory.

Dr Ashworth was back with a handful of glossy handbooks and brochures, Markham's gaze dropped to the gilt lettering of the topmost booklet.

'*They that go down to the sea in ships, that do business in great waters see His wonders in the deep,*' he read, looking up enquiringly at the director.

'That was the psalm underlined in Dr Edward Wilson's little prayer book when his body was found in its sleeping bag next to Scott. In the margin next to it, he wrote, *All is ready for us.*'

As he left the museum heading for Jericho, Markham found himself hoping that Dr Timothy Colthurst too was in safe harbour out of the swing of the sea.

2. WEIRD WHITE WORLD

Kate Burton, predictably, was enthralled by the museum's polar exhibition when the hastily scrambled 'Gang of Four' assembled there first thing on Monday morning.

Markham was struck by how well she was looking, the glossy chestnut bob more geometric and edgy than he remembered, and the turned-up features — snub, tip-tilted nose and chipmunk cheeks giving her an endearingly squashed up look — vibrant with wellbeing.

Noakes and Olivia always maintained that Burton had long harboured a serious crush on him, and of late Markham intuited a jealous insecurity in his partner on that score which had surprised and unsettled him, causing him to wonder if Olivia was aware of something that he hadn't cottoned on to. Privately, he admitted that Burton's retrenchment of hero-worship had caused a pang, but he wryly put that down to his own punctured vanity as much as anything else. And it was good to see his former protégée so happy with Professor Nathan Finlayson — a man whom he liked and respected — even if Noakes *did* insist, 'You'd only have to crook your little finger an' Shippers would be history'.

Now secure in her position as a DI at Southampton Row, her dress sense too had evolved, and she was the epitome of executive chic in a mint-green two-piece accessorised with a brown leather briefcase containing the essential notebook and reading glasses.

DS Doyle too looked well content with life and was clearly delighted to be included in the team for the museum murder. Always a snappy dresser, he had opted for the preppy button-down look with navy gingham shirt, fawn chinos and deck shoes.

Noakes, needless to say, had fallen wide of the mark in his attempt to muster a sartorial ensemble suitable for the student city, ample paunch spilling over baggy beige combat trousers bizarrely topped with fuchsia polo shirt and flapping navy cardigan. Markham was amused to note the mildly appalled sideways glances Burton and Doyle shot the DS before looking down with renewed complacency at their own attire. The only thing in favour of his batman's horribly mismatched clobber was that Noakes had eschewed crocs or sandals and was sporting his usual George boots. Perspiring heavily on arrival at the museum, florid face the same hue as his shirt, the DS was grateful for the air-conditioned depths of the Reynolds, his complexion gradually subsiding from beetroot-red to something less suggestive of a coronary waiting to happen.

Having ascertained that his three colleagues were satisfied with the accommodation he had arranged for them at Malmaison, the Victorian prison converted into a boutique hotel on Oxford's New Road, Markham introduced them to the museum's director who offered to show them around the polar exhibition since they had time before they were to meet the museum's administrator.

Having seen the disturbing pictures of Timothy Colthurst's corpse in situ, they were by no means loath to postpone discussion of how the man had met his end.

Noakes was as delighted as Burton by the stunning black and white pictures of the Arctic landscape, though Doyle commented uneasily that the bergs looked like tombstones in a cemetery. 'A kind of spooky ghost world,' he commented.

'Interesting that you should say that, Sergeant,' Dr Ashworth told him. 'When he was trekking over mountains and glaciers in South Georgia, Shackleton said he always had the feeling of there being an *extra* presence — one more person than could actually be counted.'

On hearing this, Doyle looked more uneasy still.

Noakes meanwhile was pouring delightedly over a display case devoted to polar expedition dogs and ponies. 'Says here they named one of the ponies Weary Willie,' he chuckled delightedly. 'An' would you believe it, two of 'em that ended up going to the bottom of the ocean were called Davy an' Jones!' Doyle joined him at the large glass cabinet, glad to be distracted from thoughts of ghosts. '*Blimey,* it says here that Amundsen shot twenty-two of his dogs somewhere called the Butcher's Shop.'

'Unlike Amundsen, Scott was an animal lover,' came an amused voice behind them. 'Mind you, getting the beasts over by ship was a nightmare. On one trip, there were nineteen ponies housed immediately above the sailors . . . kept peeing on them, so they spent most of the time drenched in urine.'

The director brightened at the sight of a tall bespectacled colleague dressed in light-coloured chinos and cream linen jacket. Lean and rangy with curly black hair, he had an air of ironic detachment that reminded Markham of Mat Sullivan.

'Ah, greetings Jonjo,' Dr Ashworth greeted him. Then, turning to the detectives, 'This is our assistant curator, Mr Kelleher,' he said before introducing Markham's team to the newcomer.

'Christian names, John Joseph, but everyone calls me Jonjo,' the other said with a grin. 'Not very donnish, but somehow I get away with it.'

'Are you responsible for the polar exhibition then, Mr Kelleher . . . or, sorry, is it *Doctor* Kelleher?' Kate Burton was punctilious about getting handles right.

Another grin. 'No, you were right first time. Never got round to finishing my PhD. . . . kept getting distracted and going off at a tangent,' he said ruefully.

'He's being modest,' the director put in. 'With a first-class MA on the role of the Royal Geographical Society in Arctic exploration, we counted ourselves lucky to snap him up before academe got hold of him.'

It was clear the two men enjoyed a good relationship. As though by mutual consent, they refrained from mentioning the recent tragedy while Markham and his team moved round the exhibits.

'Behold how good and joyful a thing it is: brethren to dwell together in unity!' Burton murmured, peering at the caption above a series of portraits along the wall.'

'Captain Scott inscribed that at the front of one of his journals,' the assistant curator told her. 'Given the tricky mix of personalities, it was about as appropriate as Margaret Thatcher quoting St Francis at the door of 10 Downing Street,' he added with a chuckle as Burton gazed at the trim slight figure with receding hair attired in naval uniform.

'God, this bloke's a bit of a runt,' Noakes declared, from further along the line of pictures.

'Ah, that's Henry "Birdie" Bowers, one of the two men found with Scott at the end,' Kelleher told him. 'A racist and a complete "hater" by all accounts, but devoted to Scott. The one next to him is Dr Edward Wilson. He and Birdie were committed Christians while Scott was an agnostic. But they all had total faith that what they were doing *counted*.'

As the DS nodded his approval, Markham reflected that this was a fair description of Noakes himself.

'And there's Oates,' Doyle said, regarding the muscular handsome figure with the steely gaze and close-cropped hair. 'They never found his body, did they?'

'No, but a memorial was erected where he was thought to have walked out into the blizzard,' Kelleher said. 'His nicknames were "Soldier", because he was army, and "Titus" for Titus Oates, the man who plotted a conspiracy to kill Charles the Second.'

Absorbed, the group moved further along, listening attentively to their affable guide. 'The last two are Dr Edward

"Bill" Wilson and Petty Officer Edgar "Taff" Evans . . . Dr Wilson was found in his sleeping bag next to Scott, but Evans — like Oates — has no known burial place. He fell into a coma — frostbite, hypothermia, mental collapse, no one's quite sure — and they just had to leave hm. He was the only non-officer . . . it was devastating for him when they found out Amundsen had beaten them to the Pole, because he was hoping that fame and fortune from being first would allow him to buy a little pub and settle down.'

Noakes scrutinised the working-class bloke with interest. 'Poor sod,' he said. Then, 'That Amundsen were a right sneaky bastard,' he added venomously, with a contemptuous glance towards a nearby portrait of a hawk-faced man who looked like a modern-day Viking, 'pretending to focus on the North Pole when all the time he planned to go south.'

Before the DS had any chance to embark on a xenophobic rant, Burton drew their attention to the photograph of a woman in a sack-like dress with an intelligent face and hair piled high on her head. 'It says Scott's wife was a sculptor,' she said, examining notes on the adjacent plaque.

'That's right,' Kelleher said. 'She was a feisty lady. Oates wrote about her getting into arguments with the other wives — said two of them had a magnificent battle and it was a draw after fifteen rounds.'

As the detectives laughed, Markham could see the director was visibly pleased at the way his assistant curator had brought the exhibits to life, Ashworth's rather fidgety, prissy manner giving way to a more relaxed demeanour.

The two men were an effective double act, the director taking over as they moved down the line towards the section devoted to Sir Ernest Shackleton.

'He was different from Scott. More of an adventurer than your officer type, though he had worked his way up through the merchant navy.' Ushering them to a long low table with newspaper cuttings under glass, 'That's the advert he put out before the *Endurance* expedition.'

'"Men wanted for Hazardous Journey,"' Doyle read aloud. '"Small wages, bitter cold, long months of complete darkness, constant danger, safe return doubtful."' The young DS chuckled. 'Great sense of humour,' he said appreciatively.

Ashworth laughed. 'Oh, "Shackles", as they called him, was the buccaneering type. He had heart problems but just shrugged it off. The last thing he said to his doctor was, "You're always wanting me to give up things, so what is it I ought to give up now?" The doctor replied, "Chiefly alcohol, boss, I don't think it agrees with you." Shackleton died a few minutes later. He was only forty-seven.'

Markham was surprised to find the museum director a natural raconteur, quite different now from the man he had first encountered in that over-the-top office.

'Scott's wife couldn't stand Shackleton,' Ashworth went on. 'Even said she'd happily assist at his assassination.'

There was an awkward silence at the reference to homicide before Markham stepped in. 'Wasn't that because Shackleton moved in on what Scott saw as being his patch?' the DI enquired.

'Well, to be honest, in the circumstances Shackleton didn't have much choice,' the director replied, 'but according to the strange codes of chivalry in those days, it wasn't the done thing to break your word . . . Edward Wilson had been one of Shackleton's closest friends but never spoke to him again for doing that to Scott.'

'Shackleton was a kind of ghostly pace-maker for Scott,' Kelleher put in.

Doyle shifted uncomfortably at the mention of ghosts.

Seeing this, the assistant curator continued smoothly, 'In many ways they were very alike. Couldn't find contentment ashore . . . There was always that yearning for the Arctic.' Kelleher smiled at them. 'But I reckon Shackleton was much more *fun* than Scott . . . less *stodgy* somehow . . . There's this lovely story about him teaching his sisters signalling . . . When he sailed off with the *Discovery* on that first polar expedition with Scott, he brought out his white handkerchief then got one of the crew to bring him another and semaphored to each of them — in strict nursery order of precedence.'

'Was he religiously minded like Bowers and Wilson?' Burton asked.

'Not at all. He didn't like clergymen,' Kelleher replied. 'Called them sky pilots and only accepted one as chaplain because when the guy opened his attaché case, a woman's silk underwear and champagne cork rolled out.'

'Sky pilots, eh?' Doyle said amidst the laughter, with a mischievous look towards Noakes. 'That's what you call them ain't it, sarge?'

The other affected not to hear this sally.

'It says here Scott's crew could've topped thesselves with opium,' he observed, squinting at another noticeboard.

'Correct, Sergeant.' Kelleher grimaced. 'But they chose not to take that way out. Actually, in Oates's case, he wouldn't have been strong enough to feed himself opium tablets or even undo his clothing to speed things up.' Remembering what Olivia had said about the accusations levelled by the gallant soldier's mother, Markham wondered if one of Oates's comrades might have assisted the process. 'But he likely died within ten minutes or so of walking out into that blizzard,' Kelleher continued. 'You see, nerve-endings would have frozen from the outside in . . . and then he'd have been oblivious, probably travelling back in spirit to his home in Essex and leaving that weird white world behind.'

'It's like the surface of Mars or somewhere in outer space,' Doyle murmured gazing around.

'Treacherous too,' Kelleher told him. 'If a man fell through the ice pack and survived, the hole he fell through would drift away faster than he could catch up to it . . . It meant he'd be trapped on the underside of the ice, clawing desperately to find a way out, staring up till everything turned black.'

It sounded to Markham eerily reminiscent of Timothy Colthurst's death throes.

As though conscious he had put his foot in it, the assistant curator turned to Doyle, 'You're right about there being something lunar about the landscape, Sergeant. The pressure ridges make it look almost Saharan.' Following the young detective's rapt gaze, he added softly, 'Explorers said the ice pack gave out cries like human moans . . . as though it was a child saying its first words.'

To Markham, wandering past the stunning photographs, the Arctic topography seemed at once sinister and curiously restful, mantled in the white silence of death, the medium he knew so well.

'Reckon they were crap at skiing.' Noakes's voice brought him back to earth. 'They look like bandy-legged crows with them poles.'

Kate Burton frowned. 'It's so ethereal,' she said almost reverentially.

Kelleher smiled at her. 'I suppose you could say so when you look at shots of the funny little crenellated townships they constructed out on the ice floes, but there's nothing ethereal about the diaries. The men are either grumbling about the grub-scoffing useless beggars who don't pull their weight or whingeing about fried penguin being inedible.'

'Fried penguin!' Noakes was appalled.

Kelleher enjoyed the reaction he had produced. 'Oh, believe me, that was haute cuisine compared with the usual hooch.'

'Hooch?' This was Doyle.

'A sort of stew . . . Basically they chucked everything in it,' Kelleher told them. 'From biscuits, raisins, curry paste and pemmican — that's powdered meat mixed with melted fat — to cocoa powder.'

Doyle's jaw dropped. 'Christ!'

'Oh, they dreamed endlessly of big feeds in their sleep, Sergeant — cakes and sirloins — night after night.'

The man was a born teacher, Markham reflected, enjoying this evocation of another world, though by the sound of it if Dante had witnessed the explorers at their worst, he might have found inspiration for another Circle of Hell.

'Being trapped out there must have tipped some of them over the edge,' the DI remarked.

'Yes indeed.' Kelleher's face was suddenly sombre. 'What they called "overwintering" could produce severe psychological side-effects. A sailor on one of the early expeditions developed delusions that the ice was alive — possessed by angry spirits that were coming after him.' He paused impressively to let this sink in before resuming. 'Of course, the ice could be a fairyland of light—'

'The Aurora Australis,' Burton cut in eagerly.

Noakes and Doyle exchanged glances.

Somebody's been swotting up.

Kelleher shot her an approving glance. 'Correct. And there was a spectrum of rainbow colours to gladden the heart of any artist — aquamarine, pink, orange, mauve, indigo . . . Plus there were spectacular illusions like the Four Suns.'

Noakes's piggy eyes widened on hearing this. 'But ain't it dark for six months of the year out there?' he asked, recalling a programme he'd seen on the Discovery channel.

'Indeed,' Kelleher nodded in his unpatronizing manner. 'Lack of light often accelerated the emergence of mental symptoms.'

'I've heard of folk going screwy like that . . . SAD or summat,' Noakes confirmed sagely.

'Seasonal Affective Disorder.' Burton could never resist translating an acronym.

'Yes, that's one reason why explorers like Scott and Shackleton set great store by arranging theatricals,' Dr Ashworth told them.

'Theatricals . . . You mean like musicals?' Noakes boggled at the notion of Oklahoma on ice.

'It was an essential distraction,' Kelleher explained. 'Shackleton in particular was always looking out wigs and dresses.' He winked mischievously. 'Some of the men made very fetching leading ladies.'

Doyle smothered a grin at the expression on Noakes's face. He could tell the older man didn't at all care to hear his naval heroes associated with cross-dressing and 'pervy' goings-on.

Aware of the portly policeman's disapproval, Kelleher steered them into safer waters.

'It was important to keep the men from becoming depressed,' he said easily. 'Scott even got up an expedition newspaper . . . anything to stave off mental breakdown.' Face serious, he added, 'It could make the difference between a happy crew and the threat of mutiny.'

'Mutiny?' Visions of Fletcher Christian and Captain Bligh of the Bounty danced across Doyle's brain.

'Oh yes,' Dr Ashworth joined in. 'Shackleton had to face that down more than once, but he had nerves of steel.'

'When people live together in close proximity in a confined space, you can get collective outbreaks of semi-hysteria,' Kelleher went on.

Burton the psychology graduate was gripped.

'They found it happening in convents in the sixteen-hundreds,' she said earnestly. 'There was a Ken Russell film . . . *The Devils of Loudun* . . . with Oliver Reed.'

At this mention of the notorious hellraiser, Noakes looked as though he could guess only too well what kind of film that was.

Registering his boot-faced expression, she added hastily, 'Being in darkness half the year would play havoc with their body clock too.'

'Absolutely,' Kelleher replied, 'to say nothing of problems from scurvy which was poorly understood back then before the importance of Vitamin C became clear. Edgar Evans said he would follow Scott to Hell, but he could never have imagined the horrors involved in getting to the Pole — starvation, their teeth splitting from the cold, altitude sickness, disorientation and madness . . .'

'Of course, it wasn't all about coming first in a race,' Dr Ashworth told Burton in a confidential tone as they moved along the display cases. 'People forget that Scott's *Discovery* expedition was stunningly successful . . . They were the first to take aerial photographs and the scientists made all kinds of discoveries, found a leaf fossil that indicated Antarctica had been part of a super-continent with a tropical climate . . . The geological research was first-class.'

Noakes's expression clearly said, *Bollocks to geology*.

Doyle nudged the older man. 'Hey, there's some weird stuff about 'em in these old newspapers,' he said before reciting in sing-song tones, 'At the Pole, at the Pole, Britannia's pretty sure to reach her goal; Her ever-conquering legions, Will annex those distant regions, And make a new dominion of the Pole.'

'Not much cop at limericks, if you ask me,' Noakes grunted.

Markham recalled Olivia's colleagues deploring the jingoism of Scott-worshippers. Personally, knowing that the Great War was just beyond the horizon, he found the words almost unbearably moving in their desperate evocation of an epic pre-eminence so soon to be extinguished . . .

Time to leave the Antarctic for now.

Sensing the DI's change of mood, Dr Ashworth gestured towards the lift. 'Gentlemen,' a courtly little bow to Burton, 'and lady. Perhaps we should adjourn to my office. I've asked the museum's administrator Yvonne Garrard to arrange refreshments so we can discuss . . . recent events in comfort.'

Reluctantly, Kate Burton turned her eyes away from the glaciers and crevasses and summits, with ice floes like gleaming prehistoric shields.

As they walked to the lift, questions raced through her mind.

Did the polar exhibition hold a clue to Dr Timothy Colthurst's death?

And why pose him in that grotesquely theatrical manner, as though to re-enact some frightful ice-bound trauma of long ago?

Captain Scott's wife had wanted to assassinate Shackleton . . .

The word seemed to float in the still air of the galleries, like a malign prophecy.

What had Timothy Colthurst done to merit such a violent end? Was it a one-off, or was the killer engaged in working out a pattern to some predetermined end?

Even in the cool dim depths of the museum, she could not repress a shiver.

Then there was the spectre of madness. From what Ashworth and Kelleher said, it sounded as though insanity had stalked those polar expeditions. Was it possible some contagion had reached across the centuries to break out here in Oxford?

The others were waiting for her, Noakes and Doyle wearing expressions of the *Oh no, she's gone off on one* variety.

She quickened her pace to catch them up.

* * *

Yvonne Garrard, the museum's administrator, was waiting for them in the director's office and, after introductions were made, set about arranging coffee and biscuits for the group with a quiet, calm efficiency.

Markham put her at late fifties, with artfully silvered hair which fell in soft curls just past her shoulders, perfectly groomed with an excellent figure set off by a well-cut charcoal business suit. The DI believed Dr Ashworth when he called her his 'tower of strength'.

He didn't miss the faintly scandalised expression, swiftly suppressed, with which she greeted the news that they had been touring the polar exhibition, nor the propitiatory manner in which the director said, 'The detectives wanted to gain a feel for the set-up, Yvonne.'

'Yeah, soak up the vibes an' all that.' Noakes smiled at her. The DI had the feeling that his wingman had been dreading the appearance of a Mary Beard character spouting 'academic bullshit', but the down-to-earth competence — and provision of lemon curd biscuits — had reassured him. 'All that Arctic stuff's champion. Jus' wish we had more time for a closer look.'

The administrator smiled with genuine warmth at the policeman who looked the farthest thing imaginable from a hot-shot CID officer.

'We're very proud of it,' she said. 'It's an even bigger draw than the David Livingstone exhibition in spring.'

Noakes sniffed in the manner of one who would take the Antarctic over African jungles any day of the week.

'Of course, Jonjo deserves the lion's share of the credit,' she went on. 'He sweet-talked the British Library and all kinds of places into loaning us items.'

'I aim to please,' Kelleher said self-deprecatingly.

'Do you have valuable artefacts here, Ms Garrard?' Burton asked, wondering if Timothy Colthurst could have interrupted a burglary.

'Relics an' stuff?' Noakes prompted hopefully, remembering how the team's last investigation into a religious cult had featured just such treasured souvenirs.

'Well, certainly some pieces would be priceless to a collector,' she said uncertainly. 'The Apsley Cherry-Garrard belongings, for example . . . No relation,' she added before Noakes could ask the question.

Frowning, the administrator turned to Markham.

'Given that you said Dr Colthurst was . . . posed . . . in the art installation, I presumed this had to have been someone with a grudge.'

'We aren't ruling anything out at this stage,' the DI replied. 'But you're right, there was something very deliberate about the positioning of the body.'

'Almost like Shelley's Memorial,' she said.

Uh-oh, thought Noakes observing Kate Burton's sudden interest, Boffin alert.

And sure enough, Markham's fellow DI couldn't resist.

'That's a sculpture of the nineteenth-century poet Shelley depicting him after he was washed up drowned in

Italy,' she murmured. 'Actually, he ended up being cremated and his heart buried separately.'

It was just what Noakes expected of some long-haired Victorian poet. But he was quick to catch on. 'Mebbe that means Colthurst was murdered by some academic type,' he said darkly, the scornful emphasis eloquently conveying his distaste for the breed. 'I mean it's not likely your average Joe would come up with owt like that.'

'What kind of a man was Dr Colthurst?' Markham asked in the silence that ensued. 'Was he at odds with anyone that you know of? A quarrel, feud . . . something like that?'

The three colleagues looked uncomfortable.

'Tim was very popular with his students and everyone at Sherwin,' Dr Ashworth said after a pause. 'Somewhat flamboyant, mind you . . .'

'Flamboyant, sir?' Markham prompted.

The director cleared his throat. 'He had a rather colourful private life, his romantic relationships . . . caused a few ripples.'

Noakes pursed his lips.

God, you'd think he'd be too busy writing books and thinking big thoughts for that kind of caper. The missus was bang on the money when she said their Nat was better off not going to uni. One great big shagfest by the sound of it . . .

'Was there any relationship in particular that caused, er, controversy?' Burton asked delicately.

'Yeah, the one with Des Milner,' Kelleher replied as the director hesitated. 'Desmond Milner to be precise. Second-year undergraduate in Modern Languages at Plessington College . . . So no abuse of power,' he added laconically. Then observing the director's troubled expression, he said gently, 'Come on, Clive, it would've got out anyway . . . It doesn't mean they're going to clap handcuffs on Milner.'

Not yet anyway. But boyo had shot straight to the top of Noakes's shit list.

33

When it came to the subject of CCTV, Dr Ashworth hummed and hawed apologetically about the whole museum not being covered.

'So what you're saying is, the security here's duff,' Noakes broke in impatiently.

'Why aren't the lift areas covered?' Burton enquired politely.

'It wasn't thought necessary,' the director replied. 'And the facilities budget was tight . . . Plus we always positioned art installations next to the lifts as opposed to artefacts.'

'But surely what happened here last time justified some additional outlay,' Burton persisted.

Ashworth shrugged helplessly. 'The council's finance committee wouldn't wear it.'

Mindful of the need to liaise with the pathologist and settle into their incident room at Oxford CID, Markham moved on to the matter of alibis, eliciting the information that all three members of staff were single and home alone on Friday night, Ashworth in his flat on the Woodstock Road and the other two further out in Summertown.

'They were really shifty when you asked if Dr Colthurst had mixed it up with anyone,' Doyle observed afterwards as the team emerged blinking into the sunshine.

'Agreed,' his boss said quietly. 'But they need time to sleep on it . . . Hopefully we'll get more out of them tomorrow when Dr Ashworth gives us a list of Colthurst's main contacts.' Romantic and otherwise, he thought grimly. 'Obviously we need to review the movements of all museum staff, but I'm inclined to think Dr Colthurst was killed by someone in his intimate circle . . . someone he never for a moment suspected.'

Suddenly, Doyle remembered the director's words about that ghostly extra presence Shackleton had been convinced was following at his heels.

And for all the heat of the day, like Burton earlier, he gave a convulsive shiver.

3. DECEIVED WITH ORNAMENT

'This reminds me of the Bronte graveyard in Haworth, Gil,' Olivia said later the same day as they wandered through the long-lost monuments and hidden paths of St Sepulchre's Cemetery. 'Full of ghosts hovering above and beyond us all.'

Hearing this, Markham recalled the story of Shackleton's spectral follower. As he looked around him at the tranquil scene — the mossy graves and lichen-covered vaults — with the sub-dued gentle hum from Walton Street a reassuring reminder that life continued to roll round, mixed up with nature's rocks and stones and trees, such a notion seemed like a bad dream.

But Timothy Colthurst had been stalked and murdered in the very heart of the university city where artists painted and poets penned their immortal verses. The sound of bird-song, the drowsy buzz of insects and Markham's awareness that this ancient cemetery was the playground of rabbits and foxes couldn't banish the ugly reality of human malice.

Sensing his mood, Olivia drew him over to one of the modern benches arm in arm.

'Oxford's at its best this time of the year,' she said. 'Strange isn't it, the way buildings seem to become more beautiful the older they are . . . unlike people.'

Markham laughed at that. 'True, Liv, but I'm quite taken with the modernism of the Reynolds Museum — the glass and concrete . . . the *angularity* of the whole thing. And somehow it works with those romantic landscaped gardens. There's this sense of *continuity*, of something spanning the ages . . . uniting past and present.'

'True.' She was silent for a moment, gazing out at the tranquil scene before turning back to him, a mischievous twinkle in her eye. 'How was George? Did he succumb to the spell?'

'God, yes. Actually, he and Doyle were like children at the circus.' Markham smiled. 'I knew Kate would be up on it all.' He missed the slight tightening of Olivia's expression as he said this. 'But seriously, they were *entranced*.'

Olivia strove to hide her jealousy of the casually admiring reference to DI Kate Burton. Sometimes it felt as though she would never entirely conquer the banked-down resentment of a colleague who had admittance to a world from which she was barred.

Swallowing hard, she said, 'When are they re-opening the Reynolds by the way? I plan to queue up with Joe Public.'

'Should be Thursday or Friday,' he replied. 'I imagine footfall will be heavier than usual,' he added wryly.

'*Naturellement*,' she chuckled. 'Murder's gotta be a draw.'

Olivia saw his chiselled features stretch and tauten at this.

'C'mon,' she encouraged gently, 'how was it with the museum honchos? What were they like?'

'They seemed perfectly decent and bewildered,' he replied. 'The director, Dr Clive Ashworth, is a sort of Lenin lookalike — tugging away at his goatee beard — but he relaxed after a bit. Then there was his assistant curator, Jonjo Kelleher — a cross between that actor Stephen Mangan and Mat Sullivan—'

'*Jonjo?*'

'He owned up to John Joseph . . . opted for the snappier sobriquet at university.'

Olivia was thoughtful. 'Hold on a minute,' she said. 'Yep, I know who that is. He was at Manchester when I was there, the year above me. Come to think of it, I vaguely remember Colthurst too — life sciences or geography — big in the Environmental Sciences Society.' She shrugged.

'I didn't realise you'd crossed paths with them,' Markham said. 'Kelleher and Ashworth make a good team, full of anecdotes — they really brought the exhibition to life.'

'Talk about ghosts from the past!' Olivia was clearly struck by the coincidence. 'Downright spooky coming across former classmates . . . and with the whole polar connection thrown in.' She shivered. 'Almost like it's predestined. The planets aligning or something.'

It was a sensation Markham had occasionally felt during investigations, but never quite so strongly as in this Oxford mystery.

'Who else did you meet?' Olivia asked.

'There was the administrator, Yvonne Garrard. Very competent. I got the feeling she was a bit horrified at us, in the circumstances.'

'How come?'

'Well, taking the guided tour given what happened to Colthurst.'

'But I imagine you wanted to get inside his head, didn't you?'

Markham squeezed her arm.

'Precisely,' he murmured.

'And *did* it help, Gil?'

'To be honest, I don't know, Liv.' Markham's quiet sigh was almost borne away on the soft breeze that stirred the beech trees next to their bench. 'Apparently Colthurst was majorly involved in the exhibition . . . did his bit in terms of helping attract sponsorship and making it a success.'

'Despite the best efforts of the woke brigade bleating on about our evil imperialist past?' Olivia enquired sarcastically. 'Let's face it,' she went on, 'ever since Lytton Strachey did a hatchet job on Florence Nightingale, academics can't get enough of character assassination. They've been busy constructing Scott's wife as a scorned woman and his sponsor

Sir Clements Markham as some kind of Victorian Jimmy Savile . . .'

'*Really?*'

'That's not the half of it, Gil . . . There's a sizeable contingent obsessed with proving that Scott tried to persuade Bowers and Wilson to lie down with him and wait for the end.'

'As in some kind of assisted suicide?'

'Exactly.' She smiled ruefully. 'I don't believe it,' she added softly. 'His men *adored* him. Some bloke called Thomas Crean called him a born gentleman and said he loved every hair on his head. Even Oates told his old mum not to take any notice of his grumbles about Scott because he was having a hard time and didn't mean a word of it.'

'Methinks you've been doing some research, sweetheart,' Markham teased. 'I guess you haven't given up on the idea of organising a project at Hope.'

Olivia's eyes were dreamy as she gazed at a lozenge-shaped tombstone immediately in front of their bench.

'Scott was so *fine*,' she declared. 'He really left something behind in men's minds when he died. He was *the real thing*.' Olivia clutched Markham's hand, her delicate features flushed with admiration for the long-dead explorer, her grey-green eyes misty with fervour. 'He was just so incredible at the end, Gil. Scribbling away with that pathetic little stub of a pencil, telling his wife he knew he hadn't been a very good husband but hoped to be a better memory, desperately trying to comfort his mother, exhorting the Admiralty to "look after his people". Talk about *Exit Stage Left*,' she breathed, 'it was the exit of all time.'

Markham smiled. 'I suppose I should be jealous,' he observed mildly. 'Here's my girl in love with this heroic explorer. Or should I say explorers, *plural* . . . What about Shackleton?'

'Oh, he was incredible too. D'you know, he wrote in a letter to Winston Churchill that death was very little and knowledge very great.' She snuggled closer. 'He had all these groupies . . . One of them said life was humdrum for the most part till he gave her a glimpse through the magic casement.'

They contemplated the peaceful woodland scene before them.

Finally, Olivia said, 'Scott and Shackleton were out of the common way, mediating everything through the prism of literature. You can tell from the diaries what they were reading at any given moment — Wordsworth, Austen, Shakespeare . . .' Dreamily, she continued, 'Imagine it, out there in an Antarctic blizzard, huddled in their little tent reading the Bard. *The world is still deceived with ornament . . . How many cowards, whose hearts are all as false As stairs of sand wear yet upon their chins The beards of Hercules.*'

He looked at her. 'You think someone was pretending devotion to Dr Colthurst with murder in their heart, Liv?'

She shrugged expressively. 'Who can say? But from what you've told me, it feels extraordinarily *personal.*'

They remained some while in silence, lazily somnolent in the summer heat. In the distance, childish cries and whoops suggested a cricket match or school sporting fixture was in progress.

'So, what's next, Gil?'

'Bedding in with Oxford CID . . . Plus we're going to round up Colthurst's associates at Sherwin College,' he replied. 'I've got Kate checking out museum staff, but I agree with you — this has to be personal.'

She hesitated. 'Does that mean we're based here for the foreseeable?'

'It does . . . Sidney's coming down Wednesday to organise the press conference.'

'What about the team?'

'Happily berthed at Malmaison . . . As featured in *Lewis*, don't you know.' With no way of breaking it gently, Markham plunged on. 'There's a prayer service for Dr Colthurst on Thursday at Blackfriars and Muriel's coming down on Friday.'

Olivia took the news better than might have been expected.

'Okay, I reckon I can cope with afternoon tea at the Randolph,' was the phlegmatic response. Then with a grin, 'But you owe me a slap-up dinner when this is over.'

'You're on,' he agreed readily.

Afternoon shadows were lengthening, but the couple seemed disinclined to move.

'I just can't imagine being stuck out at the South Pole,' Olivia said finally. 'Watching your shadow crawling round and round all day long, with nothing but snow stretching out as far as the eye can see . . . only the swish of snow and the cracking of ice to break the silence.' She frowned. 'Enough to send anyone crazy.'

'You're forgetting the stench of rancid whale blubber, unwashed bodies and clothes unchanged for six months,' Markham put in wryly. 'To say nothing of bird and animal shit. *Happy* days!'

'Look, why the hell would anyone want to kill some obscure academic?' Olivia demanded, reverting to the investigation. 'It's true there's that whole cancel culture thing going on around British heroes, but Scott and Shackleton are up there with King Alfred and William the Conqueror . . . killing an academic seems a bit extreme, right?'

'The answer *has* to lie in Colthurst's rather complicated personal life,' Markham replied. 'I think he had a lot of love affairs and wasn't discreet about it. Though, as you say, we have to reckon with the anti-imperialist warriors.'

'*Amundsen says he won the Cup, Then why do our men guard it? Two lie prone, but one sits up. Over his hands there hovers a Cup,*' Olivia quoted so quietly he had to strain to hear her.

'That's rather beautiful,' Markham observed.

'Just this poem I found about Scott and his team,' she replied. 'But you're right, it makes them sound like the Knights of the Round Table or something. Even though they lost the race, they come out on top somehow . . . because they played a straight bat or whatever.'

'Someone in Oxford hasn't played a straight bat,' he said sombrely. 'And I mean to find out who.'

'They say Shackleton was obsessed with Robert Browning,' she said lightly. 'Took his battle cry from *Prospice*: "I was ever a fighter, so — one fight more, The best and the last!"' She met his eyes steadily. 'You're just the same, my love, dauntless to the bitter end.'

Markham's finely moulded mouth set in a determined line. 'Timothy Colthurst passed violently before his time. Whoever killed him — whether it relates to Arctic mythology or not — I will hunt them down like a dog . . . like one of those poor animals Amundsen slaughtered out on the ice pack.'

His voice was so implacable that Olivia flinched.

It sounded like an unbreakable vow.

* * *

Despite the comfortable hotel room, Markham slept badly, plagued by nightmares where he stood in an Arctic wasteland watching the shrouded body of Timothy Colthurst, lashed horizontally to an explorer's sledge, slide headfirst into a crevasse only for the sledge to whip upright at the last moment. It was as though, like Rasputin, the man simply refused to die. As he watched, the bindings fell away and Colthurst contemplated him steadily, lips drawn back in the snarl of his death throes, though it seemed to Markham they held a sneering contempt too. Stiffened by rigor mortis, the corpse stood to attention before sinking slowly into the black water below.

Try as he might, Markham could not dispel the phantom image of Colthurst suspended over the icy depths, floating about in a standing position like some ghastly revenant. Logic told him this was ridiculous. Colthurst ended up in an art installation, not the ocean. According to Dr Merrick, he was dead before featuring in that grotesque tableau, but the DI found himself unable to picture the academic's soul wandering through more congenial regions.

'The Antarctic's taken hold of you too, Gil,' Olivia observed sympathetically as he endeavoured to do justice to the Old Parsonage's magnificent full English the next morning.

'Well, it can't be Seasonal Affective Disorder,' he commented wryly, gesturing to the beautiful sunny morning unfolding beyond the bay windows of the Grill Room. 'Not on a day like this.'

Olivia chuckled.

'There's this condition called polar anaemia,' she said. 'Sent lots of the early explorers doolally. There was some ship's doctor who got the men to strip off in front of a coal fire and "bake". He had the right idea, but no one really understood the medical science back then.'

'From something Yvonne Garrard said, I gather Dr Colthurst was interested in that side of it,' Markham told her.

'Really, as in *madness*?' Olivia was deeply intrigued.

'Well, it was one strand of his research, apparently. By the sound of it, he aimed to corner the market in early twentieth-century concepts of winter-over syndrome or whatever it's called.' Markham toyed with his black pudding. 'Colthurst had lots of irons in the fire, though . . . he was planning a monograph on Roald Amundsen too.'

Olivia grinned. 'The one George called out for being a sneak.'

'And for massacring so many of his dogs,' Markham added drily. 'Noakesy couldn't get his head round that . . . Scott, on the other hand, had a hang-up about killing sled dogs hence the decision to use ponies.'

She nodded. 'Probably cost him the race to the South Pole. But at least he wasn't a butcher.'

'Indeed.' Markham reached for some toast. 'Amundsen died in a plane crash over the Norwegian Arctic when he was just fifty-five . . . part of a rescue mission for some Italians who were stranded. They never found a trace of him or the five crewmen.' Markham threw up his eyes theatrically. 'No doubt Noakesy would call it Karma.'

Olivia helped herself to a croissant, slathering on butter with gusto. 'No point worrying about calories on a jaunt like this,' she smiled across the table at him. 'I reckon that's probably just how a bloke like Amundsen would choose to bow out . . . suddenly, up there in the clouds, while embarking on some great chivalrous quest.'

'Hmm. For all the rivalry and one-upmanship, he and Scott were brothers under the skin. They had this almost masochistic urge that drove them on, so they could never have been content with ordinary life.'

'A different kind of insanity,' she agreed. 'And don't forget Shackleton.'

'Ah yes. Living on pack ice for nearly five months and then a seven-day crossing to Elephant Island in life-boats . . . followed by a seven-hundred-mile crossing through raging seas to South Georgia Island to get help . . . Talk about snatching victory from the jaws of defeat!'

She laughed. '*You've* been doing your homework!'

'Well, there's something pretty compelling about all this setting off to do battle with the forces of nature. Scott and Shackleton were certainly larger than life.'

'Apparently a fortune teller told Shackleton before his last expedition that he would die at forty-eight,' she said unexpectedly. 'He was superstitious about it . . . imagined the harbour bell was tolling his death knell when he set out for the last time. But he wouldn't turn around . . .' Despite the torpid warmth of the day and her pretty sundress, she suddenly looked pinched. 'D'you think Dr Colthurst had any inkling, Gil . . . saw death coming, but then it was too late . . . ?'

'The pathologist says he didn't know much about it,' Markham said gently, forcing back memories of his nightmare and the image of Colthurst's corpse bobbing like a cork on the ocean floor. 'There were no defensive injuries.'

She didn't appear much comforted by this reassurance.

'It has to be a man, surely,' she pressed, 'seeing as he was lifted into that ice-box thing.'

'Not necessarily.' Markham hesitated, lowering his voice as a pair of guests passed their table. 'The SOCOs found blood on a steel platform truck at the far end of the third-floor gallery . . . They think the body was bent over the shelves on the pallet and then brought up from the staff room on the ground floor in the lift. Merrick doesn't think it would have required great physical strength to slide it into the art installation . . . The staff room and lifts aren't covered by CCTV, so our killer was home and dry.'

She stared at him.

'God, how *horrible* . . . As if he was a *specimen* or something.'

'He was a slight man . . . underweight if anything,' Markham continued musingly. 'So a woman could have done it.'

'A spurned lover?'

'It's one possibility . . . On the other hand, university politics can be murky—'

'*I'll say*,' she responded with feeling. 'Remember the last time you checked out a murder here . . . the backbiting and intrigue made my snake pit at Hope look like Enid Blyton!'

'Or maybe the answer lies in the museum itself,' he said. 'By the by, when it opens again, be sure to look out for a lad called Brendan Potter. What he doesn't know about polar exploration isn't worth knowing.'

'Will do, Gil . . . In the meantime, I'm going to take a stroll round Christ Church and imagine myself hobnobbing with Auberon Waugh.' She watched him lovingly over the rim of her coffee cup. 'I suppose it's wall to wall interviews at Sherwin for you, though?'

'Well, mercifully the cast list isn't as large as it might have been due to this being the holiday season. Kate's narrowed it down to three this morning: Guy Hanbury, Emeritus Professor of Modern History, Maggie Rawson — a female postgrad Colthurst was supervising, and finally, Dr Marion Peary, Fellow and Tutor in Modern History. Essentially the college contacts who were still around last Friday. There's another tutor from Latimer College we're hoping to catch up with in the afternoon plus some ex-girlfriend—'

Olivia's ears pricked up. 'That sounds promising.'

'Noakesy seemed to think so,' Markham said drily, 'though he was also quite struck by the news that Colthurst was involved with a second-year male undergrad at Plessington College.'

'Liked to live dangerously by the sound of it,' she observed.

'Not one of his tutees apparently, but certainly sounds like he might've been skating on thin ice from an ethical point of view,' he agreed.

'Is the boyfriend on your list for today?'

'If we can track him down . . . He lives out on the Iffley Road, but no answer there and he's not answering his phone.'

'Prostrated with grief?' Olivia suggested cynically.

'You're worse than Noakes,' Markham said reproachfully.

'Oh, I've a long way to go before things get *that* bad,' she laughed, the joyous peal causing an elderly couple at a nearby table to smile indulgently. They probably imagined he and Olivia were honeymooners, thought Markham ruefully, when all the time it was violent death and sexual intrigue under discussion.

'Enjoy Christ Church but stay away from Deadman's Walk,' he said lightly, referring to the footpath that bordered Merton Field.

'Righto, guvnor,' she replied cheerfully. 'Now, are you going to eat that last croissant, Gil, or can I have it?'

* * *

To Markham's way of thinking, Sherwin College's stern gothic architecture — crenellated and turreted like some miniature fort — looked at its best in winter when romantically wreathed in the vaporous fog that invariably shrouded the city at that time of year. Clad now in abundant clinging wisteria, First Quad had an almost sheepish look, as though with the arrival of the holidays the ancient buildings had lapsed into dishevelment.

His old friend, the head porter Mr Stevenson — a staunch ally in Sherwin's previous murder investigation — was on leave, but a briskly efficient crop-haired young woman informed him that the team were waiting for him in the Fellows' Common Room.

'I can find my way,' he told her politely, forbearing to mention that he was an alumnus.

Deciding there was time to pay his respects to some old haunts, Markham peered in at the black and white chequerboard-tiled chapel in the front right-hand corner of First Quad.

There they all were: the twelve apostles on the oak screen at the far end, each one depicted in his own little choir stall with an iconic motif above — fishing net, money bag, martyr's palm, spear — the stained-glass panoply of saints glowing in their various windows, red-robed flowing-haired Mary Magdalene brooding in a mysterious cavern with symbols of death strewn at her feet like some ecclesiastical Lady of Shalott, Saint George bearing off his wimple-clad princess . . . and presiding above all from the rose window, a luxuriantly bearded God the Father with arm extended in a gesture more forbidding than benevolent.

The air felt somewhat stuffy, overlaid with scents of incense and beeswax, but the mahogany curlicues, marble seraphim and magnificent side-view mirrors mounted either side of the organ exercised their old fascination. The interior was narrow — almost boxy — with choir stalls a hand's breadth apart across the nave and a low wooden ceiling painted navy blue that was studded with what Markham thought of as little gold love knots, though the guidebook said they symbolised Christ the Morning Star.

Olivia had been wistful when they visited the chapel for the first time together. 'It's *gorgeous*,' was her verdict. 'All sumptuous and heavy and brooding . . . sinister too,' she had added eying the Magdalen. 'But way better than anything we had at Manchester. Our gaff had all the charm of a B&Q outlet.'

Now Markham wondered whether Timothy Colthurst too had ever found Sherwin's chapel sinister, ever felt as though God the Father was singling him out with that peremptory forefinger.

Reluctantly he tore himself away and headed for the Great Hall, which formed one side of the courtyard in Second Quad.

Just one peep at Gloriana, he promised himself, being particularly fond of the portrait of the Virgin Queen who presided over the dining room in a beruffed and periwigged splendour that cast the canvasses of lean faced cadaverous Elizabethan clerics quite into the shade.

Yes, there she was, the ashy pallor, russet pompadour and great rope of pearls more striking than ever beneath the golden apse emblazoned with Sherwin's crest. Fresh from his meditations in the college chapel, he could almost fancy she regarded him with a severity equal to that of the bearded Deity.

Seeing a young, whippet-thin college servant busily wiping one of the six tables that were ranged two by two in three long columns in the well of the hall, Markham decided not to linger and quietly withdrew before the dark-haired boy had a chance to notice him.

Wandering back towards the Fellows' Common Room in First Quad, he was struck by the silence. Probably the lull before Oxford's conference season got into full swing, he reflected. At any rate, it was good news if it meant they were spared having to dance attendance on the principal and fellows.

The clock tower chimed the hour.

Markham felt the usual tingle of anticipation that signalled the start of a murder investigation.

With a swift upward glance at the college ramparts, he stepped through a stone archway and turned to the well-remembered stout oak door on the right-hand side.

Time to begin.

4. THUNDERBOLT

Sherwin's Fellows' Common Room was one of the most delightful rooms in the college, with portraits of Elizabethan and Jacobean nobility presiding over its civilised appointments.

The crowning glory was a reproduction of the *Field of the Cloth of Gold* depicting a sumptuous open-air conference between the Kings of England and France in the sixteenth century.

On the team's last visit to Oxford, Noakes had been fascinated by the painting, regarding it like some grownup version of *Where's Wally*, delightedly scrutinising the miniature tents, castles and processions of beruffed manikins to see 'who were doing what'. The DS had been particularly taken with a pterodactyl-like dragon flying aloft in the top left-hand corner like some evil spirit bent on jinxing proceedings. Even Kate Burton's prosaic explanation that this was a nod to King Henry's Welsh lineage couldn't dispel the magical impression.

Standing in the doorway looking up at the picture, Markham suddenly recalled the fantastical drawings of dragons and mythical beasts with which Brendan Potter had told him the early cartographers filled up their maps to indicate unknown terrors at the edge of the world.

Here Be Dragons. The words resonated in his mind as though to transmit a warning . . .

But now there was a new attraction in town, he observed with amusement as he watched the team bent over a series of glass cases lined up along the opposite wall.

'Their faces are the colour of mulligatawny soup,' Noakes was telling his colleagues.

'Sunburn,' Burton replied.

'He's got your dress sense, sarge,' Doyle observed critically. 'Birdie Bowers . . . God, get that hat, the woolly balaclava and those mitts on a string round his neck. Hmm, bit titchy and chubby, though,' the young detective continued with some complacency, looking down at his own well-honed physique.

'Most likely him being a bit plump were all to the good,' Noakes observed, ignoring the observations on wardrobe. 'He'd have kept warm when the rest of 'em were perishing with cold . . . An' being shorter meant he'd find it easier in the tent.'

Doyle was determined to have the last word. 'Didn't do him much good in the end though, did it? Being short and tubby . . . He died just the same, along with the rest of them.'

Burton peered in. 'There's lots of quotes here about trusting in his Heavenly Father and not worrying about the future because the Lord would wipe all tears from their eyes.'

'He were a God squadder,' Noakes pointed out approvingly. 'Thass what gave him backbone.'

Kate Burton's voice was unwontedly gentle. 'Looks like he was devoted to his mum,' she said softly. 'Trying to keep her spirits up by telling her they'd have a glorious return and he was going to stick by Captain Scott no matter what.'

Watching his colleagues, so absorbed by this mini-museum that they were wholly unaware of his presence, the DI felt he was learning more about their characters than ever before.

Burton's voice was almost dreamy. 'Listen to this,' she quoted. '"No worry now — only living out one's full allowance of time under conditions that fulfil one's ideas of manliness . . . You may be sure of one thing that though I may not get to the Pole or make a splash in the public eye — I shall do much towards the honour of my mother who deserves something better than a rolling stone for a son.'"

Possibly Markham was the only one who knew the depth of Kate Burton's desire to make her parents — especially her father, who had opposed her entry into the police ('No job for a woman') — proud.

The DI advanced into the room.

'Well, I reckon this was no rolling stone,' he said.

His three colleagues turned to face him, the two men shuffling awkwardly as though they had been wrongfooted.

Doyle cleared his throat.

'It's an exhibition on Birdie Bowers,' he told the DI.

Markham nodded. 'Ah yes, the fifth man on Captain Scott's ill-fated expedition.'

Noakes frowned. 'Him an' Scott weren't always bezzie mates,' he said, 'cos there's stuff about getting into the skipper's bad books over instruments not working.' A shy glance at the DI. 'But they got over the hump an' it says here he wrote home that he were all for Captain Scott.'

Markham was touched. He knew that when Noakes referred to 'getting over the hump,' his wingman was also thinking about their own relationship which had so nearly foundered during the Bluebell investigation.

'No wonder Scott called Bowers a marvel,' he smiled.

'Yeah.' Noakes was studiedly nonchalant now, as though embarrassed at having been betrayed into a display of personal feeling. 'He might've been this little fat, flat-footed bastard with an ugly mug an' big hooter.' Here a baleful glance at Doyle. 'But he were so sure they were gonna reach the South Pole,' the DS continued. 'Kept writing home that they were on target to plant the British flag an' all that.' There was a curious catch in his sergeant's voice. 'Tramping away an' dragging them bleeding sledges for hundreds of miles when all along they should've been using huskies . . . At least they didn't end up beating the dogs to death or chowing down on 'em like the Norskies.'

Doyle shot his mentor a concerned glance.

'You're right, sarge,' he said. 'Bowers was one in a million.' The young detective was anxious to strike a happier note. Gesturing towards the glass cases, he added, 'Pretty incredible. He even rustled up a Christmas dinner with plum duff and all the trimmings.'

Noakes's mastiff face brightened. 'Yeah, imagine that,' he said admiringly. 'All scabby an' out of it with frostbite, but he still knew what was what.' As far as the DS was concerned, that meant a decent feed at Crimbo.

A voice came from the doorway behind Markham.

'They all took it in turns to do lectures in the hut at Cape Evans,' the newcomer said. 'When it was Birdie's turn, he did a talk on whether cocoa was preferable to tea during marches. Apparently it provoked a lively debate between the "tea-ites" and "cocoa-ites".'

Markham turned and saw a thin stooped figure with sparse grey hair and spectacles moving towards them. He noticed the figure was dragging one leg slightly.

'Guy Hanbury,' the cultured voice continued, and Markham realised he must be the first of their interviewees. 'I was Timothy Colthurst's mentor back in the day, but as you can see—' a rueful wave of the hand — 'he'd long since ceased to need my sponsorship.'

Introductions made, the group moved across to some comfortable armchairs near the richly carved oak chimney piece, a gargantuan flower display of gladioli and red hot pokers occupying the hearth beneath.

'Is that lot down to Colthurst then?' Noakes jerked a stubby finger towards the glass cases.

The Emeritus Professor of Modern History smiled kindly at the overweight detective whose ensemble appeared to give a nod to the worsteds and woollens of polar explorers, consisting as it did of a khaki green sleeveless tank top over British army camouflage trousers and the ever trusty George boots.

'Indeed, it is.' Hanbury chuckled. 'Not everyone was happy about a posse of Edwardian explorers invading our Tudor sanctum, but Colthurst won the day.'

'Bit of a self-promoter, was he?' Doyle enquired guilelessly.

'No more than any of us,' Hanbury retorted mildly. 'And it was good to tilt the balance away from Renaissance princelings in favour of the twentieth century.'

The urbane academic was easy and relaxed, sharing anecdotes about Birdie Bowers which enthralled his listeners, not least Noakes who was perfectly charmed to learn that Bowers had enshrined one of pony Victor's hooves at a polar depot in the hope of taking it back to England as a souvenir.

'Sounds an all-round decent bloke,' the DS told Hanbury.

'Well, Tim was certainly very taken with Bowers,' the other confirmed. 'The letters home are a revelation . . . It's incredibly poignant what he said about five of them being a pleasant little crowd and just the right number when exploring so far from home.' Seeing Noakes's interest, he added, 'Nothing came easy to Bowers. It was a case of good honest sweat driving him on.' He grinned, looking suddenly endearingly puckish. 'Had quite a way with words as it turned out, really brings the Adélie penguins to life, just like a cohort of Charlie Chaplins.'

'I saw 'em on *Frozen Planet*,' Noakes offered. 'Well cute.'

Before Noakes had a chance to build up a head of steam on the merits of David Attenborough, Burton brought them back to the matter in hand, establishing that the professor, a widower, had been working alone in his terraced house on the Marston Road the night of Colthurst's murder. 'I'm writing a book about Scott, Amundsen and Shackleton,' he said. 'These days, people are more open to accepting that they had very different backgrounds, qualities and objectives so we need to look at them in the round . . . understand how each of them can be recognised as a great man in his own right without detracting from the reputation of the others.'

'And Dr Colthurst was working on a monograph about Amundsen, is that right sir?' Burton pressed him politely.

'That's correct, for the Oxford University Press, but as far as I was concerned, the more the merrier. We bounced ideas off each other really. I was more focused on the group dynamics of the various expeditions whereas Tim was looking at one man.'

'Group dynamics, yeah.' Noakes appeared much struck by this phrase. 'The idea that Bowers an' Wilson could've saved their lives an' left Scott!' he exclaimed indignantly, though his startled colleagues were innocent of having made any such suggestion. 'Men like that couldn't do owt but stand by him right through.'

Hanbury nodded sadly. 'Bowers was quite philosophical about the risks,' he said. 'Confided to his diary that he knew how the smallest thing could upset the best laid plans . . . He was properly spooked when his mother and sister came to wave him off on the expedition with Scott, because there was this truckload of coffins on the platform alongside the train.' The academic shook himself as though someone had walked over his own grave. 'But you're quite right about his loyalty, Sergeant. Abandoning a comrade was an impossibility for explorers of that calibre. The last thing Birdie did before he died was scribble a note on the back of one of Scott's letters indicating where the rescue party would find Wilson's final letter to his wife.'

'The prof seems an alright bloke,' Noakes said after the professor had left them. 'For an intelleckshual.'

Burton and Doyle, proud possessors of degrees in psychology and criminal law respectively, exchanged wary glances at this reference to the anathematised breed.

'Full of stories, that's for sure,' Burton said. Then hesitatingly, 'I wonder if he wasn't a bit too keen to head us off from asking more about his relationship with Colthurst.'

For all that Noakes had relished the polar folklore, he was shrewd enough to recognise the truth of this. 'Prob'ly a bit chippy about the young fella overtaking him,' he conceded.

Just like Slimy Sid about Markham, he thought. 'But sounded like there were enough room for everyone . . . I mean both of 'em were working on their own book.'

'Colthurst had a publisher lined up, though,' Doyle pointed out. 'But Hanbury didn't say anything about his.'

Kate Burton scribbled a memo in her moleskin notebook to check it out.

'By the by, Kate, what about Dr Colthurst's next of kin?' Markham asked. The DI was well-known for never ducking a meeting with bereaved relatives.

'Only child, and both parents dead, sir. There's an aunt in a nursing home down south. Local CID are on it.'

At that moment, the crop-haired young woman who appeared to be manning the fort in the head porter's absence appeared with coffee and biscuits (chocolate Hobnobs, Noakes noted approvingly), allowing the detectives to regroup before their next interview.

'Thank God it's the holidays,' the DS grunted. 'I like this place better without that slimy principal an' bursar oiling around, getting under our feet.'

The DI was privately relieved about this, having no great desire to renew his acquaintance with their bêtes noires from the previous murder investigation at Sherwin.

'Cuts down the list of suspects too,' Burton said happily. She sipped her coffee daintily, perched on the very edge of her chair in the habitual manner which made Noakes wonder irritably why she never parked her bum four square like everyone else. 'I've asked Yvonne Garrard for a list of the museum staff and details of their shifts, guv,' she told Markham, 'but it doesn't seem like Colthurst had all that much to do with the hoi polloi other than telling them how he wanted the exhibits set up.'

There came a rap at the door.

Their next interviewee had arrived.

Maggie Rawson was a statuesque blonde with a flicky shoulder-length pageboy and side fringe, fleshy horsey face and the husky voice of a smoker. She would have been strikingly good-looking but for a prominent scar from some long-ago accident that she clearly disdained to camouflage with cosmetics. The postgraduate's turquoise-patterned tie dye dress flattered her curves, and the overall impression was that of a woman thoroughly at ease in her own skin.

She lost no time in setting out her stall.

'Someone else will probably tell you, so I might as well get in first.' There was defiance in her tone. 'Tim Colthurst was a total dog in the manger when it came to other people's research.'

'He was your supervisor, Ms Rawson?' Markham enquired smoothly.

'I switched to someone at Latimer,' came the blunt reply. 'Colthurst did bugger all supervision . . . if anything, I'd call him actively obstructive.'

The DI was curious to learn more. 'How so?'

'Always dodging meetings, ignoring emails . . . Kept trying to make me change direction.'

'What was your research field?' Markham asked.

'The Four Musketeers.'

'Eh?' Noakes did a double take. 'How come? That's fiction ain't it?'

'That was the title I planned on using,' she replied with a thin smile. 'I was looking at the four men who went with Captain Scott to the Pole — from their own time to the present day.' Her lips curled. 'And I wasn't going to do a hatchet job on their reputations with any fancy revisionist bollocks about a homosexual underground.'

Noakes blinked hard at this bluntness, but Markham was unperturbed.

'Was that Dr Colthurst's approach then, the psychoanalytical angle?'

She snorted. 'Anything sensationalist to make a splash and ensure he stood out from the crowd. Colthurst was the type who'd have reduced Christ to a failed carpenter.'

Markham could see that Noakes was liking this less and less.

Noticing the sergeant's affronted expression, the post-graduate appeared to recollect herself.

'Sorry, but seems to me it's a tawdry way of making a name for yourself,' she continued. 'Colthurst constructed the rivalry between Scott and Shackleton as having all kinds of homosexual undercurrents . . . sidelining everything they achieved, though obviously the trendy mob couldn't get enough of it. And he was at it again here.' She bit her lip. 'Part of me wonders whether he wasn't secretly ashamed of himself, so when I came along wanting to play it straight,' an ironic chuckle, 'he tried to undermine me.'

It was an intriguing hypothesis.

'Professor Hanbury seemed okay with the way Colthurst did things,' Doyle pointed out.

In that moment, the scar on her cheek stood out lividly in a lead-coloured streak.

'Don't you believe it.' Her tone was scornful. 'Colthurst backed off from helping the prof when one of his undergraduates committed suicide. Hanbury never forgave him.'

Burton leaned forward intently. 'When was this?'

'Three years ago. The family insisted Hanbury had bullied him.' A short bark. 'It was total crap. He had a major drug problem, and an investigation cleared the prof in the end. But you see, Colthurst hedged his bets, frightened of being damaged by association. Him and Hanbury patched things up, but I reckon it was never the same between them after that.'

Interesting that Professor Hanbury had omitted any reference to the episode, Markham thought. On the other hand, maybe it was still too raw and painful to talk about.

'How's it working out with your new supervisor at Latimer?' Burton enquired neutrally.

The woman's petulant expression softened. 'Oh, Freda Carrington's great. Doesn't do the great "I AM", if you know what I mean . . . She's interested in the psychological side, but doesn't make you feel she's got it in for cultural historians.'

'Wouldn't like to get on the wrong side of that one,' Doyle mused after she had left them.

'Yeah, don' look like she stands for any BS . . . I can jus' imagine her bashing Colthurst over the head,' Noakes agreed.

'She seemed honest enough to me.' Kate Burton's tone was stiff.

Noakes winked at Doyle before humming the tune from 'Sisters Are Doin' It for Themselves'.

Burton declined to rise to the bait.

'Right,' she said. 'Marion Peary's next.'

Noakes yawned.

'Not another bleeding academic jawing on about, what was it, revisionism and psychoanalysis,' he groaned.

Burton took a certain malicious satisfaction in informing him that Dr Peary was a fellow and tutor in Modern History.

A cough outside the door alerted them to the tutor's arrival, putting an end to Noakes's grumbles.

In the event, Marion Peary was so dry and colourless that she practically faded into the wood panelling.

Hiding behind long dark hair, outsize spectacles and heavy bangs, she spoke in a nervous monotone, as though afraid the walls could hear.

A difficult woman to read, Markham thought as Burton took her through the standard questions. The tutor reluctantly confirmed what Maggie Rawson had volunteered about the estrangement between Timothy Colthurst and his erstwhile mentor Professor Hanbury but didn't appear to consider the rift serious.

'I reckon that one had a crush on Colthurst,' Noakes said after the interview was over and the tutor had disappeared back to her books.

'What made you think so?' For all his lack of social finesse, the DS was quick to pick up on subtle vibes that escaped others and Markham had learned to respect his intuition.

Noakes jabbed two fingers at his own eyes.

'There was jus' summat,' he said musingly. 'A spoony look when you were talking about Colthurst and the exhibition . . . An' I reckon she'd been crying.'

Doyle mulled this over. 'But as far as Colthurst was concerned, Marion Peary was just a colleague, right?' The lanky youngster scratched his chin. 'I mean, he had something going with that male undergrad they told us about at the museum.'

'Yes.' Markham was thoughtful. 'If Dr Peary did have feelings for Dr Colthurst, it appears they went possibly unrequited.'

Noakes got to his feet and hitched up the dodgy camouflage trousers.

'Right, thass them three done.' He scratched his paunch in a manner which had Kate Burton fastidiously averting her gaze. Looking hopefully at his watch, the DS added, 'The lass on the front desk said we could pick up sarnies an' whatnot in the hall. Reckon I'm ready for that.'

When was he not, the DI thought resignedly.

'Can't stand that weirdy picture of Good Queen Bess they've got in there,' Noakes added as they headed for the door. 'But you can't turn down free grub.'

* * *

The long narrow refectory appeared less austere than in winter when the dark linenfold panelling, rows of supercilious portraits, wooden benches and draughty casements contributed to a less than cosy dining experience. Now, picked out by a shaft of sunlight and sitting well away from Gloriana, the team was quite comfortable. Excellent coffee and a platter of deep-filled baguettes were conjured up in no time, the group being waited on by the dark-haired college servant Markham had noticed earlier.

'Alex Mason,' the haggard looking but not unattractive youth introduced himself.

'Are you a scout then?' Noakes was rather proud of himself for remembering the old-fashioned term for the college housekeepers.

'Junior porter actually, sir, but I do a bit of everything in the holidays,' the other replied self-deprecatingly. He smiled shyly round the table. 'Is there anything else I can get you?'

'Nah, this is champion, lad. Great cheese and pickle.'

'Thank you. I'll tell Mrs McShane. The chutney's home-made, her gran's recipe.'

'Nice manners,' the DS said approvingly to his retreating back. 'Looks a bit famished, but I suppose that half-starved druggie look's all the rage these days.'

Kate Burton winced. *No point telling him to keep his voice down*, she thought ruefully. With Noakes, that was what passed for a compliment.

Despite her impatience to crack on with the case, she had to admit it felt good sitting companionably in the dusty sunlight of the hall. Her humous and salad baguette was unexpectedly tasty (she'd been expecting anaemic ham and a few limp lettuce leaves, with cotton wool bread curling at the edges), and for a few moments she could almost fancy they were a group of students with nothing more pressing before them than an afternoon boating on the river . . .

Then her eye fell on Noakes.

'Almost' being the operative word, she thought. That awful, mismatched clobber didn't exactly fit the idyllic image of college gondoliers!

Doyle had finished his roast chicken and salad. 'Who's up next then?' he enquired.

'A tutor at Latimer.' Burton was all business. 'Plus Colthurst's ex-girlfriend.'

'Oh aye.' Noakes's eyes gleamed. 'That should be interesting.'

'Obviously we're approaching this with an open mind,' the DI told him firmly. 'Whatever the nature of Dr Colthurst's private life, it may have nothing to do with his murder.'

Noakes looked distinctly dubious on hearing this.

'Don' forget the lad Colthurst were sh— involved with,' he said heavily.

Doyle suppressed a grin. Those diversity courses hadn't been totally wasted, he thought. The old warhorse would be a fully paid-up member of the PC brigade in no time at all at this rate.

Markham turned to Burton. 'Any sign of the elusive Mr Milner?' he asked.

'Not yet, guv. I've asked St Aldate's to give me the heads up when he shows.'

'How's ole slab face then?' By which affectionate designation, Noakes meant Superintendent Ian Charleson of Oxford CID.

Burton grimaced. 'Onside, more or less. Actually, I think he's quite glad to leave this one to us. After last time, I reckon he didn't fancy checking out the museum.'

'Happy to give it to la-di-da Inspector Linley here, you mean,' Noakes guffawed, thumping the table with a sly look at his boss.

'Er, something like that,' she replied, flustered. 'At any rate Charleson's giving us an incident room.'

'So we can entertain Slimy Sid in style,' Doyle sighed. Then, blushing, 'Sorry, sir. That just slipped out.'

'It's alright, Sergeant.' Markham's tone was ironic. 'The DCI won't be up till tomorrow, a pleasure all the greater for being deferred.'

Suddenly, in the silence following the DI's remark, they heard footsteps pounding across First Quad and up the steps to the narrow wooden corridor which led to the Great Hall on one side and the college kitchens on the other.

Instinctively, the detectives jumped to their feet as one.

The acting head porter appeared followed by a frightened-looking Alex Mason.

'You need to come at once, sir,' she said breathlessly. 'There's a body out at Revenger's Folly. They're saying it's murder.'

5. REVENGER'S TRAGEDY

The team took Burton's car out to Ridley College which lay to the north of the University Parks with grounds running down to the river Cherwell.

Parking in the gravel forecourt at the front of the main building, they contemplated the gracious Edwardian red-brick facade, its pediments and classical lines softened by trailing clematis and roses.

Noakes scratched his head. 'Whass all this about a folly?' he demanded. 'Do they mean some sort of ruin like that clock tower thingy from last time?'

None of the team particularly cared to recall their previous visit to one of the university's picturesque landmarks, but Burton grasped the nettle.

'It's really just a vanity project from the 1800s,' she told them. 'The principal back then built an imitation gothic gatehouse to house his collection of geological specimens.'

Noakes's pudgy brows contracted, giving him the look of a constipated Shar-Pei. *Typical up-himself posho with more brass than sense*, he thought crossly on hearing this information.

The team headed through an arched passageway to the right of the great oak front door, Burton leading the way.

'It's called Ridley College after a bishop who was burned at the stake by Bloody Mary for being a Protestant and trying to put Lady Jane Grey on the throne,' she informed them, unable to resist a pedagogic opportunity. Then she caught herself up with an embarrassed cough. 'Sorry, sir,' she said, turning round to Markham. 'I forgot you already know all that.'

'Not at all, Kate,' he said kindly. 'I remember when I was a boy being fascinated by some pictures in *Foxe's Book of Martyrs* . . . those figures half hidden by piled up firewood, and little banners coming out of their mouths with holy sayings in Latin.'

'The other bishop being burned told Ridley to play the man and see it through,' she said eagerly.

Doyle shuddered. 'I remember now. Ridley was one of them in that mosaic we saw at Latimer College last time . . . a little wizened type like Rumpelstiltskin with his bottom half burned away.'

'They used green wood to drag things out and make victims suffer as long as possible. Sometimes friends of the victims would bribe the executioners to use explosives, so they'd die faster.' Burton was enjoying the impromptu history lesson. 'There was even a pregnant woman who gave birth in the flames, but they just chucked the baby in after her.'

Noakes threw Doyle a meaningful look. Trust Burton to tell them this straight after they'd had their sarnies. Bleeding morbid. He could just imagine her and Shippers poring over all the gruesome details. Most likely it was their idea of foreplay.

These images had the effect of quickening their steps so that they barely noticed the velvety lawns and dappled landscaped gardens where a lake framed perfectly reflected trees.

'What's with the daft name?' Noakes grunted, perspiring heavily as he puffed along in the rear, his territorial army getup bizarrely out of place in these manicured surroundings. 'Did they call it Revenger's Folly cos someone bashed the batty ole principal over the head with one of his rocks or summat?' As far as the DS was concerned, that was quite a feasible scenario.

Once again, Burton was pleased to display her knowledge. 'The story goes that the principal — Sir Somebody or other — stole from another collector and then took credit for the discovery. His rival took revenge by ambushing him in the folly one night and battering him to death with his own geologist's hammer. The killer tried to cover his tracks by staging a break-in but made the mistake of confiding in his mistress who spilled the beans when he refused to marry her . . . ended up being hanged.'

Noakes was incredulous. '*What*? All that for a bit of rock?'

'Geology was big business back then,' she explained patiently. 'Nathan says one of the reasons that Captain Scott's team all died was because they insisted on collecting geological samples on the way back from the Pole which cost them six or seven miles . . . Plus it meant they ended up lugging thirty pounds of stones on a sledge when their strength was running out. The rescue party dug the geological specimens out when they found the bodies.'

'Anybody with any sense would've dumped the lot,' Doyle observed.

'But don't you see, it was their *legacy*,' Burton insisted. Slightly pink in the face, she added, 'Nathan says their finds helped settle the debate about whether Antarctica and Australasia were joined at some stage.'

'Triffic,' Noakes grunted unenthusiastically. Only *she* could think some discovery about climate change was worth dying for.

'Anyway, that's how the folly got its name,' Burton wound up. Somewhat apprehensively she added, 'Apparently it's got its own ghost too.'

It bloody would have, Noakes thought sourly. Nothing like your own resident spook to get the cash registers ringing.

Doyle was evidently thinking the same way. 'Is it some kind of tourist attraction then?'

'No, I don't think so.' Burton rather enjoyed taking the wind out of her colleagues' sails. 'There's a staircase round the side which goes up to the roof and anyone can use it . . . Look, we're here.'

In front of them, nestled in a dell just a stone's throw from the serenely gliding river, was a greystone castellated gatehouse. Two storeys high, with twin turrets and a roof terrace from which fluttered a flag with the college's coat of arms, the lozenge-shaped mini-castle with its arched embrasures — three on the first storey and two beneath on either side of a vaulted entrance — resembled something out of a fairy story . . . were it not for the police tape and cluster of white-suited personnel huddled round screens on the ground in front of the building.

Dr Merrick detached himself from the group and came towards them.

Although the owlish medic, who could easily have passed for a postgraduate student, was as different as possible from bluff-featured pathologist 'Dimples' Davidson back in Bromgrove, Markham had warmed to him during the previous investigation on glimpsing genuine humanity behind the man's somewhat anaemic exterior. Despite the sobriquet of 'Jigsaw Man', Noakes, like the guvnor, felt the dead were in safe hands.

Now the DS demanded bluntly, 'Who've we got?'

'I believe the victim worked at the Reynolds Museum,' the doctor said, twitching his specs more firmly onto his nose. 'We ID'd her from credit cards in her purse . . . A Ms Yvonne Garrard.'

Noakes's jaw sagged. 'It *can't* be her,' he rumbled. 'She were giving us the lowdown on everything only yesterday, laid on lemon curd biscuits an' all.'

'I'm afraid there's no doubt about it,' he said gently. 'The couple who found the body recognised her.'

He gestured to two figures standing awkwardly next to a policewoman on the periphery of the scene: a tall gangling youth with a protective arm round his petite girlfriend who could not seem to stop shivering.

'How did Ms Garrard die?' Markham asked calmly. It was a quirk of his that whereas colleagues swiftly resorted to surnames, he invariably accorded victims the correct form of address. And woe betide anyone who displayed gallows humour in the vicinity of the dead, the DI's blistering salvoes in such an eventuality having passed into legend.

'It would appear the poor woman jumped off the roof.' The pathologist indicated a spiral stone staircase which wound around the right-hand turret. 'Broke her neck on impact,' he added quietly.

'This weren't suicide,' Noakes growled. 'No sodding way.'

'I need to get her to the John Radcliffe,' Merrick told them. Registering Noakes's furtive glance at the screens, he said gently, 'She was lying at an unnatural angle, so the broken neck was obvious right away. There's some blood at the corner of her mouth but no other external injuries.'

'Were her eyes open?' the DS asked almost pleadingly, as if Yvonne Garrard's expression at the moment of death might afford a guarantee of foul play.

'She was looking up at the sky,' the doctor replied.

At the sky or up at the face of her murderer? The unspoken question hung in the air.

In that instant the sun went in, and it seemed to Markham that the folly's arched windows loured at them as though the character of the place was forever altered by what had taken place there.

Then the moment was past, and the body bag went by on its trolley, everyone bowing their heads in respect as it headed towards an ambulance parked on the path which wound alongside the river.

'I want you and Doyle to take a statement from those youngsters who found the body please, Kate,' Markham instructed.

As she nodded in response, her mobile rang, the sound almost shocking in the silence of the copse.

'Desmond Milner's turned up,' she told Markham at the conclusion of the call. 'He's waiting for you at Plessington

College. And local CID have tracked down Colthurst's ex-girlfriend along with a colleague from Latimer.'

'Right,' the DI said briskly. 'Noakes and I will check in at St Aldate's and then do those interviews. When you're finished with the two who found the body, check out anyone who's still resident at Ridley and then fan out from the college . . . This is a romantic setting for a late-night stroll. If we're lucky, there may have been students wandering out here last night who noticed something.'

'Bloody creepy place,' Noakes muttered looking at the folly. ''S like them windows are *squinting* at us.' He rubbed beefy arms that were suddenly goose pimpled. 'Are we gonna look inside before we do the interviews?'

Markham wondered if the DS had intuited his curious reluctance to set foot across the gatehouse threshold.

'We'll get pictures from the SOCOs after they've secured the area,' he said quietly. 'Better give them a clear run for now.'

'Did you never come here when you were a student, guv?' Noakes was surprised, since Markham was notorious in CID for antiquarian interests — visiting old churches and National Trust properties — that, together with his Oxbridge education and air of cultivated refinement, made him somewhat of a rarity. Though he professed nonchalance on the subject, the DS was privately proud that his guvnor was 'a bit of an egghead' and basked in reflected glory.

'I believe this part of Ridley's campus was off limits to everyone but the fellows back then,' the DI replied.

Noakes sighed gustily. Typical of your la-di-da boffins wanting to keep the best bits to themselves, he thought.

With a last mistrustful look at the miniature stronghold, he followed Markham out of the dell.

* * *

'That Charleson's as chippy as ever,' Noakes observed an hour and a half later as they sat in the bursar's office tucked away in a corner of Plessington College's Third Quad.

'Well, I imagine there's a certain resentment of our being foisted on him just because—'

'You're a nine carat posho,' the DS finished.

'I was going to say just because I'm an alumnus,' Markham reproved him. 'And also, having handled the Sherwin College investigation, we're presumably more au fait with university protocols.'

'As in making sure the university comes out of it smelling of roses,' Noakes said sourly.

The DI was unperturbed. 'Something like that,' he replied equably.

Noakes turned his attention to the bursar's quarters. 'Nice little gaff he's got in here. Thank God he's off in Greece or wherever it is studying mouldy ole statues, so we don' have to be polite an' have a chat.'

Markham reflected wryly that small talk was not exactly a weapon in his wingman's social armoury but agreed that it was a relief not to have to deal with the college hierarchy.

'No polar stuff in here.' Noakes sounded disappointed as he gazed round the oak-panelled room which looked out onto a stunning array of terraced blooms wafting their heady scent in through half-open mullioned windows. 'Jus' them hook-nosed types with no eyes an' leaves on their heads,' he muttered disparagingly, eying various ornamental busts on plinths which seemed to form a guard of honour along the walls.

'I believe the bursar's an expert on Ancient Rome,' Markham grinned. 'Those are the emperors wearing laurel wreaths to symbolise their military triumphs.'

'Oh aye. I remember summat like that from *Gladiator*,' the DS sniffed. It was clear he didn't consider the victories of Marcus Aurelius and Co. a patch on the achievements of Birdie Bowers and 'Titus' Oates. 'Them lot,' he jerked a stubby forefinger at the Roman luminaries, 'were jus' greedy, wanted power an' to be king of everybody. But Captain Scott's blokes . . . well, *they* did it for their country an' to show what was out there, plus they looked out for each other no matter what. They were the real deal alright,' he concluded firmly.

'I'm inclined to agree with you there, Noakesy, but it's interesting to see another college's treasures.'

'This lot prob'ly cost a bomb,' the DS continued, casting a beady eye on the marble ware.

'Well, no doubt the bursar has access to antiques on loan from various collections.'

'*Hey,*' Noakes was struck by a thought. 'You don' reckon Colthurst an' Garrard copped on to the killer stealing from the museum, so he had to shut them up?'

Markham was ahead of him. 'I've asked Dr Ashworth and Mr Kelleher to carry out an inventory and check the museum's storage areas but, assuming Ms Garrard *was* murdered, somehow I don't think these killings are connected to missing artefacts.'

'*What* then, boss?'

Markham leaned back in the wing back chair and steepled his fingers together. 'I think it's possible Ms Garrard discovered something which led her to suspect the killer,' he said slowly.

Noakes whistled.

'You mean *blackmail* — as in she asked him for money in return for keeping shtum an' then he clobbered her?'

'We've seen it before, Noakes. People will go to great lengths to keep things hidden.'

The DS thought intently. 'D'you reckon she knew all the time she were having tea with us, cool as a cucumber?'

'As to that, I couldn't say. She didn't seem at all uncomfortable or anxious, which leads me to wonder if it wasn't until after we left that something or someone raised a red flag in her mind . . .'

'Dr Ashworth called the poor cow his "tower of strength",' Noakes mused. 'Kind of a sick joke that she ended up being pushed from one.' Sympathetically, he added, 'Sad that she ain't got no family to speak of. Well, other than them cousins out in New Zealand.'

'She seems to have been self-sufficient and happy with her own company,' Markham commented. Her immaculate flat had certainly offered no clues, being as free from clutter as the most ardent tidiness guru could desire.

'The kind who ends up swigging vodka every night an' gets eaten by Alsatians . . . like it says in *Bridget Jones*,' Noakes remarked gnomically.

The DI's lips twitched at his wingman's compassionate empathy for heroic failures, be they Captain Scott and his band of brothers or the twentieth century's icon of spinster-hood. It was at such moments that he felt he could never swap Noakes for the most sophisticated bagman CID had to offer.

'Lack of close family is probably the only thing Ms Garrard and Dr Colthurst had in common,' the DI went on. 'By all accounts his lifestyle was *unconventional*, whereas she appears to have been a well-respected manager who didn't make waves. Certainly, her flat doesn't point to there being any disorder in her private life.'

'Burton's had a gander at Timbo's rooms in Sherwin,' Noakes observed. 'She said they looked like a tip, but according to housekeeping they're always like that.'

'Hmm. Once they're processed, we might have a better idea of Dr Colthurst's personal affairs.'

As he said this, there came a knock at the door and the next minute Desmond Milner advanced into the room.

Slightly below average height with russet-gold hair, he was trim-figured and bore himself like an athlete. Alert grey eyes suggested he would be no pushover when it came to dealing with the police, and his cultured well-modulated tenor held an unmistakeable wariness as introductions were made.

If Milner was 'prostrated with grief', as per Olivia's cynical description, he maintained his composure, responding to questions in a dignified way. Milner had no alibi for either murder, having apparently been tramping round Oxford and eventually ending up in Christchurch Meadow.

'What, you've jus' been *walking around for four days*?' Noakes challenged him.

'Pretty much yes.' A vague smile. 'It's not *so* unusual, Sergeant. Charles Dickens used to average twenty miles a day.'

'You ain't Dickens.'

What was it with these arty-farty types? What normal twenty-something would come out with bollocks like that and expect to be believed? In the middle of a murder investigation too . . . For crying out loud!

Milner freely admitted that he and Dr Colthurst had been going through a rocky patch. 'Tim didn't want to be . . . exclusive . . . whereas fidelity was important to me.'

Afterwards, Noakes was sceptical. 'Talk about a cold fish.'

Markham was thoughtful. 'Self-contained but not necessarily cold.'

'Sounds like him an' Colthurst were splitting up. Then there's all that stuff about dossing outdoors to clear his head . . . I reckon he's planning to play the ole mental health card.'

'Yes, I clocked the reference to his GP. We need to tread carefully, Noakes, or Student Welfare will be all over us.'

Treading carefully not being his strong suit, the DS looked decidedly disgruntled on hearing this.

His mood was not improved by the interview with Timothy Colthurst's ex-girlfriend Evelyn Bennett, an alumnus of Sherwin who now worked as assistant manager at Blackwell's Bookshop on Broad Street.

Petite and with what he called 'one of them teeny-tiny voices', he observed afterwards that she reminded him of a Disney princess. Certainly the diminutive stature, rippling dark hair and porcelain complexion added up to an attractive package, conveying a feminine allure and vulnerability that many men would have found seductive.

Surprisingly deep-voiced, she insisted that the split with Colthurst had been perfectly amicable and, like Milner, barely reacted when Markham mentioned Yvonne Garrard's name.

'Yeah, she rings a bell . . . Think I may've seen her around for book-signings and that kind of thing,' she said.

Markham thought he detected a flicker in the striking green eyes at the mention of Desmond Milner, but it was gone so quickly he couldn't be sure he hadn't imagined it.

'Tim went for those fey types,' she said airily. 'Sometimes they found it hard when he moved on.'

'*Love em an' leave em*,' Noakes put in.

His sarcasm was wasted on the Disney princess.

'Yeah, something like that. Tim liked to keep everything *light* . . . Couldn't bear to be tied down. Didn't like *scenes*.'

Scenes.

She sounded the voice of sweet reason, but Markham wondered if her choice of words didn't disclose more than she had intended. Was it possible that Evelyn Bennett had turned termagant when Colthurst decided to call it a day?

As with Milner, there were no alibis to speak of. The night of Colthurst's death, she had apparently been at a party in Headington, but it was the kind of event where 'people drifted in and out' so there was no one to vouch for her being present the whole time. As for the previous evening when Yvonne Garrard nosedived from the roof of Revenger's Folly, she 'stayed in to wash my hair'. Given the length and luxuriance of her mane, this didn't sound as far-fetched as it might have been in the mouth of another suspect.

Their final interviewee, Freda Carrington was the complete opposite of the Pocket Venus, being a tall raw-boned woman with ruddy cheeks and bird's-nest hair, the mousy locks being scraped back in a messy chignon that was partly falling down. She had an engagingly unpretentious manner and reminded Markham of nothing so much as a farmer's wife.

Despite being a fellow and tutor of Latimer College, with a distinguished publications record to her credit, she was far from the typical Oxbridge academic. Charitably, when pressed about Colthurst's deficiencies as a supervisor and Maggie Rawson's claims that he had undermined her, she refrained from overt criticism and talked vaguely about there being a 'personality clash'. Likewise, she was discretion personified when it came to the story of Professor Hanbury and Colthurst having fallen out over the latter's failure to support his mentor during the disciplinary investigation that followed a student suicide. 'Tim may have been afraid of making things worse for Guy by putting his oar in,' was as far as she was prepared to go. Markham thought he could detect that Freda Carrington had reservations about Colthurst and wondered what these were.

Again, as far as alibis went, hers were unsatisfactory given that they depended on the corroboration of her husband, a tutor at Oxford Brookes University. It turned out that Dr Carrington knew Yvonne Garrard by virtue of events at the Reynolds — 'a first-class administrator . . . did a marvellous job on the Margery Kempe exhibition' — but she displayed no particular self-consciousness when talking about the museum and was warm in her praise of what she called the 'troika' of Clive Ashworth, Jonjo Kelleher and Garrard.

'Okay, what've we got so far?' Noakes reviewed the list of suspects after the door closed behind her. 'There's Clive Ashworth an' that bloke Kelleher at the Reynolds. Seem straight up the pair of 'em an' no issues with Colthurst that anybody knows about. Then there's Prof Hanbury . . . nice ole git, even if he kept shtum about that disciplinary stuff. Maggie Wossname, the scary blonde who hated Colthurst's guts cos he didn't dig her take on the polar blokes—'

'Maggie Rawson.'

'Yeah, her . . . Plus the boyfriend "Des".'

Noakes pulled a face and Markham frowned at him so the DS hurriedly continued.

'Then there's the Disney princess . . . Ethel . . .'

'Evelyn Bennett.'

'Right. An' that nice lass who don' look like a teacher type at all.'

'Freda Carrington.' Markham thought for a moment. 'You've forgotten Marion Peary.'

Noakes gaped at his boss.

'The history tutor you thought might have been keen on Colthurst?' Markham prompted.

'Oh yeah . . . the depressing one,' Noakes frowned. 'With the face like a smacked arse,' he clarified in case of any doubt. Then he threw up his boxer's hands. '*Jesus*, none of 'em fits.'

Markham famously disliked profanity but, listening to the roll call, he felt an invocation to the heavenly powers might not be entirely inappropriate.

'None of them looks particularly promising,' he agreed.

Noakes's stomach rumbled.

Pre-empting the inevitable, the DI said, 'I suggest we adjourn to Browns, Sergeant.'

The DS's face brightened. He hadn't counted on a trip to the famous brasserie so early in the investigation.

'There's the press conference tomorrow,' Markham reminded him. 'And the DCI will need to be briefed.'

All the more reason to fuel up with one of their burgers, Noakes reasoned. Somehow, with one of those under his belt, even the prospect of Slimy Sid lost its terrors.

'I'll tell Burton an' Doyle to meet us there,' he said reaching for his mobile. 'Even though Burton jus' likes that vegan shit,' he added sorrowfully.

Outside, the day was darkening. As they prepared to leave the bursar's office, Markham's thoughts returned to the folly where Yvonne Garrard had been found. Suddenly he remembered a play he had studied at school, *The Revenger's Tragedy* . . . Was revenge the key to these murders, he asked himself. And if so, revenge for what?

He looked back at the sightless classical busts whose exquisitely moulded lips seemed tightly closed upon timeless secrets far beyond the reach of ordinary mortals. Whatever secrets belonged to Dr Timothy Colthurst, he *had* to bring them into the light.

The clock was ticking.

6. PRESSURE

Wednesday, 28 July promised to be a scorcher, though as he paced up and down behind St Aldates Station, Markham doubted there was any chance of fine weather distracting the local newshounds from a potentially juicy scandal involving Oxford's academic community, nor from rehashing all the details of the previous murder investigation at Sherwin College.

His thoughts turned to the previous afternoon when the team had sat in Browns evaluating developments . . .

'The summer hols in Oxford are one big Slow News Day,' Burton observed. 'Stands to reason the journos will want to make the most of this,' she added philosophically.

'Yeah, but at least most of the uni big wigs are away . . . swanning about abroad an' that.' Noakes had little time for *abroad* and would thoroughly have approved of the Cecil Rhodes dictum that Englishmen happen to be the best people in the world. As far as the DS was concerned, Scott's team exemplified the superiority of the national character and his patriotic soul thrilled to the notion of their agonising march to the Pole. No dogs, no smart alec shortcuts, just plonking one frostbitten foot in front of the other till they reached their goal.

Doyle interrupted this nostalgic train of thought. 'Even so, the DCI won't be happy unless we can put a lid on it.'

'An' how're we supposed to do *that*?' Noakes demanded tetchily. 'Now that it looks like Garrard was murdered.'

Dr Merrick had moved quickly, informing them that there were traces of alcohol and lorazepam in Yvonne Garrard's system. And Burton's trawl of Ridley College had proved fruitful when a pair of student lovebirds came forward to say they had seen *two* figures on the gatehouse tower shortly before the time of death, which the pathologist had put at around midnight. Bruising on Garrard's upper arms was also consistent with her having been gripped forcefully at some point.

'We keep it safe and inconsequential,' Markham said. 'Talk about one death that we're treating as murder and the other as potentially suspicious. Nothing about Dr Colthurst's private life and the bare minimum about how his body was found. Obviously details about the art installation will have leaked — museum staff were bound to talk — but we keep it as unsensational and low-key as possible.'

Admittedly difficult when the flamboyant academic had been found curled up in the foetal position inside a replica ice block, he reflected wryly.

'At least the super'll know how to handle 'em,' Noakes said with some relish. 'Jus' remember what Charleson did last time when he found that tosspot from the local rag wandering round the station claiming he were looking for the toilet.' Noakes had his own running feud back in Bromgrove with one Gavin Conors of the *Gazette*, tempers running so high at one point that it had ended in fisticuffs. 'One thing you can say for ole misery guts is, he won't pander to the media.'

Markham supposed it was some small comfort in the circumstances.

'Jigsaw Man ain't saying categorically that Garrard was murder,' Noakes mused. 'But he's ninety percent certain.'

Over the brasserie's legendarily good burgers — Burton for once passing on the vegan option (or 'bird-seed crap', as

Noakes called it) — they reviewed suspects and alibis, the consensus being that no one stood out.

Once they had hoovered up the last of their triple-baked fries, Markham ordered a round of flat whites and the group examined photographs from the interior of Revenger's Folly.

''S like them prison cells in the Tower of London.' Noakes sounded disappointed as he looked at the prints of bare mortared walls and grey paving stones. 'Nowt to write home about.'

Markham suppressed a grin. Knowing Noakes, he would doubtless have liked to see evidence of bygone dons using the place as a private dungeon.

'Those recesses are where the geologist principal kept his treasures — in cast iron safes,' Burton explained. 'The place isn't furnished now, it's more a sanctuary for owls and wildlife and things—'

'An' murderers.' As ever, Noakes was determined to have the last word.

Markham broke the uncomfortable silence that followed this pronouncement.

'Anything from Dr Colthurst's rooms in college, Kate?'

His fellow DI wrinkled her nose. 'They were pretty chaotic,' she said disapprovingly. In Burton's book, tidiness was next to godliness. 'He seemed to have lots of projects on the go. Notes on Amundsen and other explorers.' She looked embarrassed then plunged in. 'Plus a bunch of stuff on queer theory—'

'Whass that?' Noakes scowled before answering his own question. 'Oh don' tell me, it's like that Maggie woman said, he were planning to show all of 'em who went to the Pole were at it with each other.'

Burton cleared her throat. For all her political correctness, she understood that Captain Scott and his gang had laid claim to Noakes's heart in some wholly unexpected manner. It echoed the sergeant's enthusiasm for a long-dead saint in their recent investigation of a religious cult and reminded her that there were hidden depths to the colleague whom Sidney dismissed as 'Markham's useful idiot'. Over the years, she had learned to see beyond the apparent philistinism to a quixotic chivalry that lurked beneath. For all his occasional obnoxiousness, Burton had secretly become very fond of her irascible colleague and felt a curious reluctance to tarnish his reverence for the polar explorers he regarded as heroes for their sheer grit and stoicism in the face of overwhelming odds. In truth, it occurred to her that theirs was a very Noakesian creed.

'Dr Colthurst seemed to be looking at Sir Clements Markham — he's the man who sponsored Scott and Shackleton — as a closeted homosexual,' she said carefully. 'Drawing parallels between his adulation of muscular naval types and the cultivation of same-sex relationships in Ancient Greece.' As Noakes and Doyle gaped, she became somewhat flustered. 'Way over my head,' she said, 'but it looked like he was majorly into the gender studies side of things.'

'*Jesus*,' Doyle said before catching Markham's eye. 'Sorry, sir, but can't they leave *anything* alone these days? I mean, why do they always have to make it all about sex?'

'Sex sells,' Burton opined sagely. 'In a crowded academic market, it's one way to stand out.'

'It's a valid enough academic perspective,' Markham pointed out. 'And we can't draw negative inferences about Dr Colthurst and his lifestyle on the basis that he belonged to a specific school of thought.'

'What about Amundsen?' Noakes demanded. 'Is *he* meant to have been queer too?'

'Well, from what was on the computer, it looked like Colthurst was out to make something of Amundsen's closeness to another explorer, Frederick Cook, who started out as a ship's doctor.'

Seeing Noakes's face turn the colour of corned beef, Burton consulted her notebook. 'Colthurst seems to have cornered the market in psychoanalytical studies of polar explorers, starting with his MA dissertation and then the PhD, which he turned into a book for OUP. *The Icemen: Antarctica's Hidden Story.*'

Noakes snorted with derision, leading Markham to interpose hastily.

'Did you find out if Professor Hanbury had any takers for his book, Kate?'

'According to Dr Ashworth, the prof was let down by Piatkus who originally commissioned it, and had no luck finding another publisher.'

So Hanbury had a double motive to resent and dislike Timothy Colthurst.

'Going back to Dr Colthurst's computer, was there anything significant on there, Kate . . . other than his interesting take on the exploring community?'

'Not so far as I could tell, guv.' She gave an exasperated sigh. 'And there was no phone with the body.'

'There's the prayer wotsit for Colthurst tomorrow,' Noakes mused. 'Mebbe one of 'em will let their guard down . . . That Milner looked close to the edge,' he added hopefully.

'The pinstriped mob won't want us coming down hard on a student,' Doyle cautioned. 'Especially not if he and Colthurst were . . . having a thing. And you know what Sidney's like.'

Markham did, all too well. Where Town and Gown were concerned, the DCI was firmly on the side of the latter. Olivia harboured dark suspicions that Sidney was angling for some kind of 'cushy little Oxbridge number' post retirement — say, visiting professor of criminology — but Markham believed it was more likely his boss's reverence for academe derived from self-consciousness about a comprehensive school education and undistinguished university record. Together with a lurking social insecurity which made him antipathetic to Markham, the DCI was always going to align himself with the Establishment. This pronounced tendency in Sidney made Markham feel strangely compassionate towards him, so that when others sounded off about 'brown-nosing sycophants', he wondered if they weren't doing the man an injustice. Certainly, in the team's last investigation, Sidney had risen above his innate prejudice in favour of the great and good to ensure that justice was done. Markham could only hope that a similarly enlightened attitude would prevail this time around. On the other hand, the mere notion of a front-page splash about an Oxford don getting up to all sorts with students was guaranteed to bring Sidney out in hives . . .

'I fancy Mr Milner is well protected by his GP and Student Welfare,' Markham said, 'so we can't just charge in no matter how promising he looks.'

'There's none of 'em with a decent alibi for Colthurst an' Garrard.' Noakes continued revolving the possibilities while surreptitiously transferring the biscotti that came with their coffees from his colleagues' plates to his own.

Doyle was impatient of grey areas. 'So are we saying Garrard tried to blackmail the killer?'

Markham stirred his coffee with thoughtful deliberation.

'Yes,' he said finally. 'I think we are.'

'Apparently Garrard was virtually teetotal and very conservative,' Burton told them. 'Looks like the killer somehow lured her to the folly, got a laced drink down her and then pitched her off the tower . . . The students who were down there at roughly the same time are positive they were *two* people on the roof.'

'Why the chuff didn't she come to us?' Noakes demanded morosely, the biscotti temporarily forgotten in his indignation. 'She *must've* known it were a massive risk.'

Markham sighed. It was a perennial plaint.

'She fancied she could handle it,' Doyle concluded. 'Maybe she sympathised with the killer, felt she had a bond with them . . .'

'It didn't look like she needed the money,' Noakes put in.

'I'd say she was fairly high maintenance,' Burton countered.

Doyle considered this. 'Maybe it wasn't money she was after . . .'

'What then?' Noakes was at a loss.

'Maybe a job or a promotion, something like that, or she liked having a hold over them . . . or there was something specific she wanted and keeping quiet was the trade-off,' the young DS suggested.

'It'd have to be bloody special seeing how Colthurst died,' his mentor shot back. 'I mean, how were Garrard to know she wouldn't be next?'

'Like I say, she believed she was in the driving seat.' Doyle recalled their meeting with the museum administrator. 'She was a cool customer, able to handle herself.'

Not in the end, Markham thought sadly.

The detectives were reluctant to leave Browns, enjoying the peaceful somnolence with a pianist playing showboat songs in the background. There were fewer customers than usual in the brasserie which, despite its chi-chi interior — all mirrors, stripped back pine and chrome — had a relaxed ambience that somehow constituted the perfect antidote to the ugly realities of homicide.

'Mebbe it's all summat to do with polar exploration,' Noakes pondered, 'though for the life of me I don' see how.'

'Perhaps there's money involved in it somewhere,' Doyle commented. 'Grants and such . . . I mean, thanks to guys like Ranulph Fiennes, Antarctica's suddenly all the rage. Now you've got all these amateurs queuing up to have a go.'

'Yeah, but Garrard an' the rest of 'em weren't setting off on skis and sleds,' Noakes objected. 'They're *uni* folk, boffin types, safely tucked up at home while others end up getting frostbite.'

'True, but don't you see, sarge, all that polar stuff is suddenly *sexy* . . . People can't get enough of it, and you can bet the academics wanted a slice of the action — research awards, bursaries, and all the rest of it.'

'Snouts in the trough.' Noakes had no difficulty envisaging the venal side of academe.

'You're right, Doyle,' Markham said approvingly. 'I'll leave it to you and Kate to check out the financial angle.'

Burton was already scribbling feverishly in her little notebook.

Replete after stealthily scoffing all the biscotti, Noakes plucked at the olive-green drawstring trousers and outsized multi-coloured Hawaiian shirt that Markham could only pray he wouldn't regard as suitable attire for a press conference. His face looking more like a big red tomato than ever, the DS mopped himself vigorously with a large spotted handkerchief before proceeding to dishevel his hair till it stood up all over his head in stiff little prongs.

'What about *Colthurst's* gaff?' the DS asked Burton who had assumed responsibility for liaising with the SOCOs. 'Seeing as he had this . . . colourful lifestyle, shouldn't there be stuff down at party central?'

'It's an end-of-terrace on Rectory Road,' Burton told him. 'Bit of a tip, like his rooms in college, but no sign of anything to incriminate any of our suspects.' She frowned. 'And as for prints, well, *all* of them could have been round there at some point.'

'Why are they having Colthurst's service at Blackfriars?' Doyle asked suddenly. 'I'd have thought it'd be in Sherwin.'

'Dr Colthurst liked dropping in at the priory,' Markham replied. 'An elderly priest there was something of a polar enthusiast. They struck up a friendship, so the community got used to seeing him about the place.'

'Is this sky pilot still around?' Noakes asked.

'No, he died a few years ago, but when they heard about Colthurst the Prior suggested holding prayers in his private chapel.'

'Very convenient shifting the action away from Sherwin,' Noakes said sarcastically. 'Keeps it *respectable*.'

'There'll no doubt be an appropriate memorial service at Dr Colthurst's own college in due course, Sergeant,' Markham pointed out. 'In the meantime, this allows people to mark his passing. I imagine they'll say prayers for Ms Garrard, too.'

Noakes watched a waitress sashay past with a tray of sandwiches and scones. 'Are the priests going to do eats?' he enquired hopefully.

Doyle rolled his eyes. 'God sarge, you're such a gannet.'

'It shows respect if there's a decent spread,' the older man replied. 'As in doing the thing *properly*.' Inspiration struck him. 'Sort of honouring that ole sky pilot who snuffed it. Captain Scott an' the rest of 'em too.'

Burton looked as though she had toothache but smiled weakly.

Markham's expression was quizzical. 'I believe there will be a small collation afterwards, Sergeant, as opposed to a feeding frenzy, you understand.'

'Oh, *right*.' The essential point gained, Noakes assumed an expression of ineffable virtue.

Returning to the present and the imminent prospect of the press conference, Markham reflected that lurking round the back of St Aldate's Police Station didn't exactly suggest he intended to take this investigation by the scruff of its neck and show Charleson's lot how it was done. Squaring his shoulders, he headed for the front entrance and the dreaded Media Suite.

* * *

Three quarters of an hour later, the team emerged from the ugly 1930s building which housed the local police headquarters.

'Well, that went off okay,' was Noakes's verdict. 'We got off pretty lightly.'

Despite his unsettling resemblance to a budget under-taker, the DS had mustered a version of 'sub fusc' which didn't raise too many eyebrows, though the DCI's long-lived, wondering frown suggested that Sidney was less than impressed.

Certainly, Burton and Doyle had done justice to the Media Suite's shiny logos and press packs, though Noakes told them their trouser suits made them look like the boy band Bros.

The station press officer was a mild-mannered little man, as far removed as it was possible to imagine from oleag-inous Barry Lynch back in Bromgrove. It was clearly a relief to Burton not to have to deal with 'ole wandering hands', as Noakes called him, on top of marshalling facts and figures designed to appease the DCI and assembled 'reptiles'.

Markham had been dreading the encounter with Sidney, but in the event the DCI was distracted by a bad case of hay fever. With streaming eyes and eczema playing up, his boss cut a less than executive figure. At the team briefing that preceded the press conference, he seemed curiously diminished, as though the city of dreaming spires somehow pulled the rug out from under him. With his number one buzz cut and goatee beard, Sidney generally aimed to project a combination of toughness and cerebral acuity, but today it didn't come off and he looked more like a bad-tempered accountant than shit-hot CID supremo. Markham wryly reflected that the boss needed the accoutrements of his office in Bromgrove — the photo montage of his bald bonce bobbing alongside various 'slebs' (notably minor royalty), irreverently dubbed by the rank and file as the Wall of Fame — to project the desired image.

'Clearly you should be looking for a deranged individual,' was the DCI's opening gambit.

No shit, Sherlock. Noakes's unspoken reply filled the room.

'Grandiosity, bipolar disorder . . . possibly a patient at the Warneford.'

Needless to say, as far as Sidney was concerned Oxford's mental hospital offered a pool of suspects that was vastly preferable to any focus on distinguished academics or museum staff. Markham sighed. The DCI was nothing if not predictable.

In the end, Burton's 'bedside manner' was equal to the challenge. It helped too that she, like Sidney, had read psychology at university, so she was 'well up on all the criminal profiling bullshit,' as Noakes crudely expressed it. Somehow she managed to pacify DCI and reporters alike with carefully curated allusions to celebrity worship syndrome and borderline-pathological love fixation, distracting the press conference with so much psychological razzle dazzle that Yvonne Garrard's murder passed virtually unnoticed, or almost as a footnote to that of Timothy Colthurst.

This wasn't, however, a state of affairs that could be expected to last indefinitely.

As his parting shot had made clear, Sidney was avid for results.

'I need hardly tell you,' he'd honked stridently, 'that the reputation of Bromgrove CID is on the line . . . to say nothing of the future deployment of specialised investigative teams.'

In fairness to the DCI, Markham understood Sidney was keen that they bring laurels home to the Bromgrove backwater. And, as an alumnus of Sherwin, he felt a personal responsibility to solve the mystery of these deaths.

Now, aware of his subordinates regarding him expectantly, he came to a decision.

'Let's go back to the Reynolds,' he said. 'I want to dig deeper . . . understand Dr Colthurst better. Yvonne Garrard too, for that matter.'

He could see the thermometer element appealed to them all, it being nice and cool in the dim depths of the museum.

'Somehow the answer lies there,' he murmured, almost to himself. And then, thinking sadly of the glittering young academic with all the world before him, '*The paths of glory lead but to the grave.*'

* * *

The museum felt deliciously refreshing after the glare of the city pavements. Cool and dim like a big fish tank, as Noakes said, with no visitors due to be readmitted until the morrow.

Clive Ashworth and Jonjo Kelleher were busy organising exhibits on Norman Oxford, Brendan Potter told them, but hoped to be with the detectives shortly.

From Akhenaten to Agrippina the Younger by way of Alexander the Great, they wandered through the galleries, branching off to take in dinosaurs, species, cities, cultures, cults — essentially everything under the sun, or so it seemed to the detectives' reverential gaze.

Nothing survived death's dark extinction, Markham reflected, neither creeds nor creatures. Then he reproached himself for such negativity. In the final analysis, there was love. And for the faithful, a God who intervened. The touching words written by Birdie Bowers to his mother as his life ebbed away rose unbidden to the DI's mind:

In His keeping I leave you and am only glad that I am permitted to struggle on to the end. When man's extremity is reached, God's help may put things right. Your ever-loving son in this world and the next when we shall meet and God shall wipe all tears from our eyes.

Markham was by no means sure as to the afterlife or everlasting bliss, but confronted with such trust in the face of death he felt obscurely comforted by this glimpse of another man's culture. As far as Captain Scott's 'marvel' was concerned, the Almighty had become man for him and so there was nothing more he needed to do. Contemplating the intricacies of a double homicide, and fearful of what might follow, Markham would have given much for the certitude of such evangelical fervour. As it was, he privately commended Timothy Colthurst and Yvonne Garrard to their creator's care and vowed he would bring their killer to justice.

Predictably, Noakes took a shine to the young security guard who shambled along in their wake, and in no time at all they were deep in the subject of Captain Scott and his men.

'I'd give anything to see the wonderful lights and the solar phenomena,' the youngster confided shyly, his plain features almost luminous with enthusiasm. 'Mr Kelleher says there's two doctors planning to take on Antarctica next year. Just using skis and sledges . . . the same way Scott did.'

'Yeah, man-hauling, right?' Noakes was keen to show that he knew the correct terminology.

'It's the *British* way of doing things,' Brendan said eagerly. 'Even Amundsen had to admit there'd never been anything so heroic since Nelson at Trafalgar.' Clearly the youth didn't subscribe to Shackleton's view that a living donkey was better than a dead lion. But Noakes liked him all the better for it.

Both of them were united in dislike of Roald Amundsen.

'All very well saying that courage and willpower can work miracles and telling everyone that Scott showed men how to die, but if it hadn't been for him sneaking about and lying about his plans, our blokes would have had a free run.' The security guard's indignation found its echo in Noakes's emphatic 'They Woz Robbed alright.'

Markham listened with half an ear as the conversation turned to Shackleton's exploits, amused and impressed by the lad's rich store of knowledge and his fascination with the turn-around-or-you-die calculations that confronted travellers to the South Pole. It was wonderful how Noakes drew him out, listening with genuine interest as Brendan talked about Shackleton's loss of the *Endurance* and with her any chance of crossing Antarctica. 'But he got all his men back safely, never lost one of 'em.'

'You can't say fairer than that,' Noakes approved. 'Leadership's what counts in the end.'

'Yeah, he may not have been big on prayers or the diary-writing type like Scott, but he was a hero just the same.' Brendan grinned. 'There's a story that he was joshing with his men and told one of 'em there was a ship's tradition of eating stowaways when they ran out of food. Some cheeky young fella took a good look at Shackleton — he was a big guy, heavy build — and blurted out, "They'd get a lot more meat off *you*, sir!"'

Sucking in his paunch, Noakes's laughter at this sally was somewhat forced.

'Are you interested in training to be a curator then, Mr Potter?' Markham enquired politely, smiling at the frank open-hearted youngster.

'Dr Ashworth and Mr Kelleher gave me some brochures and stuff about it.' His face fell. 'Ms Garrard was going to get Dr Colthurst to talk to me about it too . . . She was really nice, said no reason why I couldn't do A levels at night school and then go to uni.' Suddenly he looked very young. 'Is it true she's killed herself, sir?' he asked Markham. Then, mindful of what his mother would say, 'Sorry, sir,' he mumbled. 'I shouldn't be pestering you with questions like that.'

Markham was saved from having to reply by the approach of the director and assistant curator. At the sight of them, Brendan beat a hasty retreat, melting into the depths of the gallery.

Five minutes later saw the team once more assembled in Dr Ashworth's air-conditioned office.

Both Ashworth and Kelleher looked somewhat ravaged but, with a tact for which Markham was profoundly grateful, they forbore to ask if their late colleague had been murdered.

'Did you notice any change in Ms Garrard's behaviour after Dr Colthurst's death?' Burton asked. 'Any deviation from her usual routine?'

Ashworth shook his head. 'There was nothing that I was aware of.' He turned to the younger man. 'Jonjo?'

'She seemed a bit subdued, but then we all were to be honest. Professor Hanbury was on the blower . . . something about that display in the Fellows' Common Room. Then I think Marion Peary rang up with a query about one of our artefacts. And Evie Bennett wanted us all to go out for a drink . . .'

Noakes was quick to note the curator's use of the diminutive. 'Are you an' her an item then?'

The other grinned. 'I'm working on it . . . punching above my weight, obviously.'

'Did you go for a drink then?'

'In the end, no, the idea fizzled out. It somehow it just didn't see right after . . . after what happened to Tim.'

'I hear Desmond Milner has surfaced?' Ashworth said with an enquiring expression.

'He's emotionally somewhat *fragile* right now,' Burton put in firmly before Noakes got started about 'fruit loops' or 'Brideshead types'. With a repressive glance at her colleague, she added, 'We're waiting to hear from his GP before doing any further interviews.'

'Makes sense,' Kelleher said. 'The poor guy's got to be all over the place.'

'He gets on well with Freda Carrington as I recall,' Ashworth told them. 'She lent a motherly ear when things got, er, *fraught*, with Tim.'

Doyle leaned forward. 'Would you say Dr Carrington was hostile to Timothy Colthurst . . . if she thought he treated his boyfriend badly, I mean?'

Ashworth pulled at his beard. 'I'm not sure I would go that far, but she knew what Tim could be like—'

'Hell, we *all* did,' Kelleher cut in. 'He had the charm of the devil, but if you disagreed with him, you saw the other side pretty quickly.'

'Like Maggie Rawson,' Ashworth agreed.

'Was he really such a lousy supervisor?' Doyle asked curiously.

'I think, like a lot of academics, he was far more interested in his own research than teaching,' the director replied diplomatically.

'Plus, Maggie's a strong character with a mind of her own, so there was an element of intellectual rivalry,' Kelleher added. 'On the other hand, I'd have thought *anyone* was better than Hanbury or Marion Peary.'

'*Jonjo*,' the director admonished.

'Well let's face it, neither of them ever set the Thames on fire — and Tim wasn't exactly slow to let them know it — whereas *he* was going places and Maggie had a chance to hang on to his coat-tails.'

'You said Dr Colthurst could be tricky, sir,' Markham said to the assistant curator. 'Were there fallings-out with the museum staff, with you and Dr Ashworth . . . or Ms Garrard perhaps?'

Kelleher chuckled, not at all discomfited. 'Oh, *we* knew how to handle him,' he said. 'There was the odd explosion, but they never lasted very long and frankly, what he's brought to the museum made up for it.'

'Yes, really put this place on the map,' Ashworth echoed.

There were no refreshments this time around — no Yvonne Garrard to dispense coffee and lemon curd biscuits, Noakes thought sadly — but it was nevertheless a not unfruitful visit. Certainly Dr Timothy Colthurst and the group of suspects were starting to fall into focus for him.

Back in the July sunshine, it felt hot and humid, and shirts were soon sticking to their skin.

'Let's head back to St Aldate's and regroup,' Markham said before breaking off to take a call.

It was a short conversation and then the DI was striding through the arboretum towards the exit that led towards the Cowley Road, the team panting in his wake.

'Where's the fire?' Noakes demanded.

'We've got an attempted break-in at Dr Colthurst's house,' Markham told him. 'And I believe there's a suspect in custody.'

7. DEADLY SECRETS

'What were you doing at Dr Colthurst's property, Ms Rawson?' Markham asked once they were back at the police station.

The windowless interview room with its off-white walls and Formica table, felt airless and claustrophobic, but Maggie Rawson remained composed.

'I wanted to collect some things,' she said calmly.

'What kind of things?' Noakes demanded.

'Papers . . . books . . . nothing special.'

'But it was important enough for you to go round the back and try to force the back door from Jackdaw Close,' Burton pointed out. 'Why didn't you ask us to help you collect your stuff?'

The tell-tale scar on the woman's cheek almost seemed to throb at this, but she had herself well under control.

'I didn't know for sure what was there, and anyway, I didn't want a police escort . . . as it was, I had to steel myself.'

Noakes thrust his bulldog's face across the table. 'Lemme get this right, luv. You didn't know what ole Timbo had in there, but you fancied playing Raffles an' getting yourself arrested? Give me a break!'

'It was spur of the moment, sergeant . . . Plus the crime scene tape was down and I didn't see anyone out front—'

'So you thought you were safe,' finished Doyle.

'Correct.'

'Didn't count on PC Johnson clocking you when he did his rounds of the playing fields behind the close?' Noakes jeered.

'That's about the size of it, yes.' She tucked a strand of blonde hair behind her ears, apparently unruffled. 'As I said, it was an impulse. I can see now I'd have done better to be upfront . . . but I was pretty upset.'

'Even though you hated Colthurst's guts,' Noakes baited.

This time there was a reaction, an angry flush rising up her neck.

'It doesn't mean I wanted him dead,' she flashed. 'And now Yvonne . . . The deaths are connected, aren't they?'

'We're treating Yvonne Garrard's death as suspicious, Ms Rawson, but as for any connection between the two . . .' Markham paused meaningfully, 'that remains to be established.'

After Maggie Rawson had been cautioned and sent on her way, Noakes groused, 'That one's sending us up the yin-yang. She were up to summat alright . . . an' don' tell me it had owt to do with research or poncy essays an' the like.' He thumped the custody suite front counter, startling the civilian clerk. 'The lass were sniffing around, most likely cos there were history with her an' ole Colthurst.'

Markham sighed. 'We've got nothing on her, Noakesy. And she knew it.'

'Yeah,' Doyle said. 'Practically challenged us to charge her . . . knew the CPS would let it drop once she wheeled out the "devastated friend of the deceased" bollocks.'

Burton frowned but reluctantly concurred.

'It's not enough,' she said. 'But I'd give a lot to know what she wanted to retrieve from that house.'

'I reckon her an' Colthurst had something going on,' Noakes declared, swelling up with outrage like Mr Toad. 'He's obviously not fussy, so why not Rawson . . .'

'It's not enough, Sergeant,' Markham repeated, trying not to look in Burton's direction, only too well aware of her distaste for Noakes's rampant bigotry. 'The CPS wouldn't wear it for a second . . . and there's nothing to pin her to Yvonne Garrard.'

'No alibi,' his wingman rumbled.

'Same as the rest of 'em, sarge,' Doyle ventured, earning himself a scowl from the older man.

Markham smiled at his team, showing no sign of the despondency that weighed him down.

'Enough for now,' he said. 'Let's review everything we've got on the museum staff.'

Burton brightened, though Noakes and Doyle looked thoroughly down in the mouth at this suggestion, not relishing a session with the Spreadsheet Queen.

'It's the prayer service at Blackfriars tomorrow,' Markham reminded them. 'Once we've ruled out the lower echelons, it means we can focus on the academic connection.'

The DI still had a strong feeling that this was an inside job, a university murder. As yet, however, the field lay wide open.

* * *

The church at Blackfriars Hall was early twentieth century and surprisingly large but its late-gothic design cleverly blended ancient and modern, boasting clear glazed windows, crisp black and white tiling and timber arched roof. The single aisle, set with side altars, featured simple wooden chairs with kneelers instead of pews.

''S' too bare an' *clean*,' Noakes said. 'All that white stone an' glass an' no fancy twiddles.'

Markham understood what he meant, the stark contrast with the warm Cotswold stone of the priory's frontage on St Giles was quite striking.

His wingman didn't normally go a bundle on 'fancy twiddles', the DI reflected ruefully, recalling some of

Noakes's observations on icons and statuary (especially the 'Papist' variety) in churches they had visited during previous investigations. But in this instance, the austerity and complete want of colour elicited strong disapproval.

Burton, predictably, was entranced by all the white marble and clean lines.

Cos she's like bleeding Mrs Hinch, her grizzled colleague reflected. Wants everything neat and tidy. She probably has a stopwatch out for when she and Shippers get it on . . . *Stand by your bed, two, three, trousers down* . . . then he blushed at himself for thinking mucky thoughts in church.

Doyle, like his mentor, was lukewarm and disliked the lack of furnishings. 'Yeah, too plain,' he observed. 'And too much stone. Plus all those wooden chairs lined up in rows . . .' He gestured vaguely. 'Reminds me of school assembly. Mind you, at least it's cool.'

The shade appeared small comfort to Noakes who wrenched viciously at his regimental tie, muttering under his breath at its refusal to sit straight. Seeing as this was a prayer service, he had made some sort of effort at sartorial correctness, but a light beige safari jacket entirely failed to conceal rapidly expanding semi-circles of sweat which spread out from his armpits across his off-white shirt. At least the light-coloured flannels were unobjectionable, though the way Noakes was holding himself suggested the sweaty trouser seat was an uncomfortably tight fit. The ubiquitous George boots must have pinched uncomfortably too, but that was a case of till death us do part . . .

All in all, Markham reflected, it could have been infinitely worse. He suppressed a grin at the thought of Sidney's likely reaction had his sergeant opted for shorts and billowing Aertex shirt. With the weather this steamy, he reckoned Noakes must have been sorely tempted.

The other two, of course, had hit the right note, Burton wearing a navy linen midi dress with matching jacket and two-toned court shoes while Doyle sported a slim-fit grey suit that was just the right side of trendy.

As the group waited at the rear of the church beneath the first-floor gallery, looking down its length towards the chancel stalls and altar, there was a diffident cough behind them and a tall cadaverous Dominican in the distinctive white habit offered to show them to the prior's private chapel.

There was a fleeting impression of baroque, rather fussy communal areas — double panelled doors, pilaster surrounds, pendant crystal chandeliers — and then they were in an intimate, red-carpeted room with half a dozen rows of velvet-upholstered chairs in the same rich crimson. On their guide informing them — with an air of *hey, presto* — that this was the Chapel of the Angels, the detectives slipped into the last row at the back behind the little congregation of Timothy Colthurst's colleagues and friends and waited for the service to begin.

Noakes nudged Markham to draw his attention to the remarkable gilt-framed painting directly above the simple oak table, adorned with a white cloth and two plain white candlesticks, which served as an altar and was separated from the congregation by an intricately carved mahogany altar rail.

'Thass gotta be the angels,' he whispered. '*Ackshually*,' with head on one side and the air of a connoisseur, 'I kind of like it . . . makes me think of snow an' mountains an' heavenly things.'

The DI nodded his agreement, recognising the artwork as a very fine reproduction of Gustave Moreau's symbolist *The Angels of Sodom*. He decided not to spoil his sergeant's pleasure by imparting that information, knowing that Noakes would immediately make the connection with the Old Testament story of two angelic messengers who warned Lot and his family to evacuate the city of sin and narrowly escaped being dragged into an orgy. The DS took a dim view of 'sex, drugs and rock and roll', thus the mere notion of Sodom as being considered a suitable subject for church art was likely to set him off. Much better to let him think the painting depicted angels guiding souls to some celestial kingdom.

The angels themselves were weirdly compelling, for all that they were diaphanous gold-haloed forms floating upwards into a foggy sky like cinders while the city of Sodom and surrounding hills — represented in streaks of ochre — brooded beneath them, oblivious to the coming catastrophe. The landscape held a feeling of time suspended . . . before thunder rolled in and the lightning crashed.

Markham noticed that Burton's gaze was directed towards an impressive painting on the left-hand wall. Another fine symbolist reproduction. This time *Jacob's Ladder* as imagined by William Blake, with reassuringly feminine-looking seraphs in floaty dresses, some with wings, ascending a spiral staircase against a star-spangled blue backdrop while Jacob lay sprawled out at its foot and dreaming.

Turning round to look at the narrow triple arched stained-glass window on the wall immediately behind them, Markham saw that each panel showed a different archangel in lustrous colours: Michael the Warrior in full armour thrusting his sword into a serpent coiled at his feet; Gabriel the Messenger bearing a scroll; Raphael the Healer with his staff. Neither male nor female, something about them recalled Desmond Milner . . .

As Markham returned his attention to the congregation, DCI Sidney took the last seat on the back row. Luckily, with his hay fever in full spate, he failed to notice Noakes's unconventional attire or coiffure, which — thanks to the heat of the day — was now inclining to all points of the compass. A single irritable glance in the direction of his subordinates, followed by pointed look at his watch, suggested that the DCI was willing the prior to get on with it.

As if in answer to Sidney's prayers, the prior — a rotund, cheerful looking figure with a disconcerting appearance of Friar Tuck — appeared, and everyone stood for the opening hymn, accompanied with some vigour by an unseen organist tucked away in his loft on the left-hand side of the chapel.

At funerals, Markham invariably found that mourners in their dark clothing merged into a homogenous whole. But on this more intimate occasion, it was a small congregation and he found himself able to take a discreet survey of the attendees.

Freda Carrington and Jonjo Kelleher were either side of Desmond Milner, the two men wearing immaculate lounge suits, in Milner's case accessorised with a striking paisley waistcoat. Their female companion, on the other hand, was visibly wilting in an unflattering oatmeal shirtwaister and crumpled cream jacket, rocking from one side to the other in a manner that suggested she was suffering from corns.

Clive Ashworth, also formally dressed, stood next to Brendan Potter, at one point unobtrusively passing the youngster a handkerchief when the emotion of the occasion got too much for him, though it seemed to Markham that the prior's gabbling delivery did not do justice to the sonorous prayers for the dead.

Guy Hanbury and Marion Peary appeared to be together, the latter darting the odd solicitous glance at her colleague who struck the DI as having aged rapidly in a matter of hours. Contemplating the professor's somewhat moth-eaten black suit and Peary's shapeless navy two-piece, he recalled Jonjo Kelleher's throwaway remark about neither of them ever setting the Thames on fire. Certainly, when it came to dress sense, their sense of style was on a par with Noakes's . . . though there was no danger of his sergeant ever fading into the woodwork.

Evelyn Bennett sported a sleeveless fitted pillar-box red dress which, though eminently flattering to her curves and colouring, hardly seemed appropriate to the occasion, but elicited appreciative glances from Jonjo Kelleher and a few of the museum staff.

Unsurprisingly, there was no sign of Maggie Rawson, but Markham recognised Alex Mason, the efficient scout from Sherwin, along with some other college porters and servants. Like Freda Carrington, they shifted uncomfortably, though in this instance the DI had the impression it was less a case of ill-fitting footwear and more a certain unease with the plush surroundings of the private chapel . . . as though they had suddenly wandered into a television costume drama about the Medicis.

There was no eulogy as such, though the imposing Dominican who had escorted them to the service delivered a few well-chosen words about Colthurst's visits to his fellow polar enthusiast 'Father Jimmy', winding up with a quirky tribute to their admiration for Birdie Bowers, Scott's 'fifth man'.

'What attracted them more than anything else was Birdie's modesty. After all, this was the man who said that he just wanted to do his best for "Old England" and felt privileged, as a person "without an excessive number of good points", to be a member of Captain Scott's expedition.' The speaker's lean ascetic features relaxed into an unexpectedly charming smile. 'I recall Dr Colthurst quoting these words from Birdie's last letter to his sister: *The weather is what I should find delightful at home — really Christmas-like in its aspect. Unfortunately we are unable to appreciate it.*'

There was a guffaw from Noakes who hadn't been expecting much in the way of hilarity from the death's head in a habit.

The Dominican paused impressively before continuing. 'Father Jimmy once said it was the spectacle of Antarctica, lying at the ends of the earth, that gave him a stronger sense of the Almighty's presence than anywhere else. And although Timothy Colthurst was not a regular churchgoer, I think he felt it too.'

Noakes's expression suggested some scepticism on this point, but he was magnanimously prepared to give Colthurst the benefit of the doubt.

The speaker's conspiratorial manner had the knack of making his audience feel he was addressing each of them intimately. 'Birdie said he was no party to record breakers but just wanted the polar business cleared up once and for all, declaring that if man could make for success then Scott's team had the right stuff in them and the rest was up to God.

Well, they might have not been the first to the South Pole, but they laid down a marker for achievement won through unflinching endeavour and the heroism that would not allow them to abandon their ailing companions. And so the God of love, stronger than death, at the heart of creation everywhere, saw them right in the end.' Another pause and then the friar added, 'Likewise we entrust the souls of Timothy Colthurst and Yvonne Garrard to their creator's care and pray that they may rest in peace.'

After the prior's confrere had resumed his seat, Clive Ashworth stumbled through a few words about Yvonne Garrard, though his halting delivery suffered by comparison with the other's smooth eloquence. On the other hand, the Dominicans weren't called the Order of Preachers for nothing, Markham reminded himself.

Ashworth's tribute was generous, however, and it was clear that Yvonne Garrard — for all her cool self-possession — had been anything but stand-offish when it came to mentoring junior staff and supporting her colleagues, all of whom appeared visibly overcome. Whatever mistaken impulse had led to the administrator's death, *that* was a legacy no one could take from her.

Finally, it was time for a closing hymn and the organist struck up 'For Those in Peril on the Sea', Markham's thoughts drifting to poignant funerals of explorers who had never even made it to Antarctica, consigned to the depths as lifeless parcels shrouded under the Union Jack.

Recalled to himself by the stentorian bellowing of Noakes at his elbow — the anguished expressions of his colleagues suggesting that they were less than entranced by this rendition — Markham duly prepared for a round of polite small talk over the promised 'collation' . . .

Refreshments were served in the prior's panelled library, which was suitably impressive, with Axminster carpets on parquet flooring, floor to ceiling bookshelves, richly coloured William Morris curtains, marble mantlepiece and paintings that had the dim lustre of valuable originals. Comfortable armchairs drawn up next to oak side tables easily accommodated the little gathering who stuck to their chapel groups, murmuring in a subdued fashion which suggested they fancied themselves still in church.

Sandalled friars moved unobtrusively around the room as though on castors, serving the guests. But though undoubtedly finding this rather eerie, Noakes did not let it cramp his style, tucking in with gusto once he had ascertained that DCI Sidney did not propose to join them owing to trouble with his adenoids.

Alcohol was not on offer, but the tea and coffee were good — and more to the point, piping hot, tepid drinks being Markham's particular aversion. Generously cut sandwiches on artisan bread, scones and home-made cake constituted a simple but tasty repast, though judging by the woebegone look on some faces the food had all the allure of sawdust.

Suddenly Markham felt frustrated and hemmed in, finding the room almost unbearably stuffy and oppressive for all its tasteful appointments. Looking round, he felt there was no chance in these gilded surroundings of anyone exhibiting unseemly emotion or uttering an indiscretion. It was as though the heavily polished and varnished ecclesiastical surroundings muffled and deadened everything, making him long to be outside in the fresh air.

Surreptitiously, the DI surveyed his suspects . . . Who to try next?

Catching Freda Carrington's eye as she toyed awkwardly with her roast beef and horse radish sandwich, he came to a decision.

The museum and Sherwin College had yielded nothing. Why not try Latimer?

With the languid grace that invariably made him the cynosure of every eye in any gathering, Markham crossed the room and stood in front of her.

'I wonder if we might call on you later, Dr Carrington?' he enquired. 'Provided you're not otherwise engaged, of course.'

The woman threw a distracted glance at Desmond Milner who was crumbling a scone between his long fingers, his eyes glassy and remote. The DI wondered if this was down to medication or a calculated piece of theatre. For all that he was disinclined to indulge Noakes's prejudice against affected 'Brideshead types', Markham knew better than to rule anything out.

'It's alright, Freda,' Kelleher told her with a kindly pat on the arm. 'I'll see Des gets home safely.'

Markham noticed that the curator cast a wistful glance at Evelyn Bennett as she murmured something to the prior and slipped out of the room, but if Kelleher was disappointed to miss the chance of escorting the attractive bookshop manager, he was too chivalrous to show it.

Even in the cool sanctum of the library, Freda Carrington looked hot and uncomfortable. Wary too, Markham thought, almost as though gauging how far it was safe to engage with the police. The DI made a mental note to issue a veiled warning to her and the rest of them.

Yvonne Garrard posed a threat to somebody and now she is dead. For God's sake don't decide to go it alone. Remember, Secrets Kill.

The gathering was breaking up now, people drifting out in twos and threes. Markham met Kate Burton's eyes and the signal passed between them. Nothing doing here, time to travel.

* * *

Outside in the steamy summer afternoon, it felt almost as though heat rose from the city pavements, sapping the detectives' energy so that they dawdled on the way to Latimer. Wandering down St Giles towards the Martyrs' Memorial, Markham thought of Cranmer and Ridley praying 'God is my light' and sent up his own fervent prayer for illumination.

Then it was on to Beaumont Street and the gracious academic symmetry of the Ashmolean Museum, Burton drinking in her surroundings with a look of rapture that caused

Noakes and Doyle to exchange expressive glances over her head.

Markham understood. His fellow DI had fallen in love with the city of walls, books, tall towers and deep ideas. Unlike Olivia, she bore the university no resentment for having been beyond her youthful reach, exhibiting only a touching yearning for the antiquity which stained its stones and haunted the memory.

Despite having been dragged away from Blackfriars just when a hospitable friar was pressing him to try some home-made flapjack, Noakes was in good humour, the DI guessing that his wingman preferred Oxford when it was left to the tourists. With some amusement, Markham registered the number of mobile vendors and ice cream vans feeding the visitors' insatiable appetite and demonstrating that commerce conquered everything, even the city of dreaming spires.

'All treasure disappears . . . In a couple of hundred years, or maybe less, this will all be gone,' he murmured, gesturing at the museum over whose entrance hung a banner emblazoned with details of a new exhibition on the famous Alfred Jewel.

'Yeah, I mean look at King Alfred.' Noakes was disposed to be philosophical. '*Alfred the Great*, right? But folk only remember him for burning the cakes.' Exhibit A in any indictment against the Saxon monarch as far as he was concerned.

Burton looked momentarily indignant, but in the interests of amity — and because it was too hot to argue — held her peace.

Then suddenly they were in front of Latimer College, its quirky mix of Palladian, medieval and gothic features reflecting an institution that had repeatedly reinvented itself over the centuries.

It looked very fine basking under kingfisher skies with no sign of any madcap students disturbing the cloistered tranquillity. Enquiries at the lodge elicited the information that Dr Carrington's rooms were situated first on the left at the far end of the arched walkway which linked first and second quads. Apparently, she was waiting for them, the head porter having seen her park her bicycle not five minutes earlier.

'Bet she's a bleeding menace on a bike,' Noakes muttered, recalling Freda Carrington's beanpole gawkiness and air of wool-gathering.

'Didn't have her down as the athletic type,' Doyle observed. 'No way would I want to cycle round here,' he said, thinking of his nippy little Skoda. 'All those tourists and head-in-the-cloud bookworms . . . It'd be like dicing with death every day.'

'Everyone cycles in Oxford,' Burton replied. 'But you're right, it's hard to imagine Dr Carrington freewheeling like the rest of them.'

Freda Carrington's rooms turned out to be surprisingly grand, giving the Blackfriars prior a run for his money.

Observing the Aubusson rugs, framed antique maps and vintage fittings, the DI wondered about the academic's private means, since her surroundings struck him as definitely a step up from the usual don's billet.

Noakes, of course, came straight out with it.

'Reckon your books an' stuff must be selling okay if it gets you all this, luv,' he said with an ingratiating leer at the statuette of a female nude.

Freda Carrington appeared notably more relaxed now that she was on her own territory and merely smiled self-deprecatingly. 'They're doing well enough,' she said, 'but not as well as my husband's . . . The décor's all down to him, he's got a wonderful eye whereas I'm a total vulgarian.'

Clearly that was all they were going to get.

The conversation moved on to Timothy Colthurst and Yvonne Garrard, but their interviewee's guard was up and Markham had the feeling she was fencing with them. There was one point, however, on which she proved surprisingly vehement.

'There's no harm in Maggie Rawson,' she insisted. 'She had a bit of a raw deal getting Tim as her supervisor . . .'

'The "personality clash",' Markham prompted.

'That's right. Maggie showed integrity in sticking to her guns, not easy with someone as dominant as Tim.'

'Would it surprise you to learn that Ms Rawson was caught trying to break into Dr Colthurst's house yesterday afternoon?' the DI asked. 'Do you have any idea why she would have wanted to do that?'

The woman was visibly taken aback.

'No idea at all,' she replied. Then, 'Did she tell you why?'

'She didn't, luv,' Noakes told her cheerfully. 'Went all bunny boiler on us . . . Jus' said she were looking for summat that belonged to her, wouldn't say what.'

'Will you be charging her?' Freda Carrington asked.

'*Depends*,' Noakes said gnomically. 'We're giving her time to think it over, see if she wants to *cooperate*,' he added insinuatingly.

Markham noticed that the academic's eyes kept wandering from the Chesterfield three-piece suite to the books and papers piled high on the vast mahogany desk situated in the bay window on the other side of the room.

He decided to change tack.

'I can see we're keeping you from your work,' he said before adding charmingly, 'Do you have anything particular on the go right now, some addition to polar scholarship perhaps?'

For some reason that he couldn't quite fathom, this question, designed to put her at ease, disconcerted Freda Carrington.

'Yes, a book about the relationship between Captain Scott and JM Barrie,' she replied shortly.

Burton was intrigued. 'The man who wrote *Peter Pan*?'

'That's right . . . he contributed a great deal to Scott's legend.'

'When you say *relationship*, d'you mean they were—' Noakes cast around for a suitable word before plunging in — '*at it*?'

A whimper escaped Kate Burton, but Doyle just grinned.

The don gave a thin smile. 'Scott was what they call a "ladies' man",' she pointed out. 'But he enjoyed a close friendship with Barrie. His son Peter was named after Peter Pan and a final letter to the playwright was found when the rescue party discovered the bodies of the Antarctic team. Scott refers to a falling-out that had upset him, but no one knows what the quarrel was about.' Now her voice was sad. 'They never had time to make up.'

'What's *your* angle then?' Noakes persisted. *With university boffins, there was bound to be an angle.* 'Is it this queer theory stuff?' The DS looked quite proud of himself as he brandished the term, shooting a look at Burton that said, *Two can play at that game.*

Watching Freda Carrington closely, Markham could see that this line of questioning made her uneasy for some reason though it was hard to see why.

'Obviously, I'll be looking at Victorian sexual mores and male intimacy . . . the tradition of the romantic friendship,' she said tightly, sweat beading on her upper lip.

'*Obviously*,' Noakes echoed sarcastically.

'What about Dr Colthurst?' Doyle asked curiously. 'Wasn't he pushing the boundaries with the romance angle . . . suggesting there was some kind of homosexual network? I mean, wasn't that what bothered Maggie Rawson — the fact that he seemed obsessed with a sexual connection?'

A brittle laugh. 'Well, it's not as if Tim *patented* the idea . . . But hopefully I'll be *contextualising* the Scott–Barrie correspondence, so it isn't a question of gratuitous titillation. I'm also interested in Scott's demons.' Self-deprecatingly, she bit her lip. 'That isn't quite as melodramatic as it sounds . . . Like most of us, he had insecurities which dogged him all his life, hence the jealousy of Shackleton and men like that . . . Flash Harrys who had everything handed to them on a plate.' Her eyes refused to meet theirs, roaming about the shelves crammed with books. 'The black dog was always on his shoulder . . . had to be kept in check, otherwise it spelled chaos.'

Afterwards, when they emerged into the sunny fore-court of Latimer College, Noakes said thoughtfully. 'That stuff about the paedo playwright really bugged Carrington . . . she got dead shifty all of a sudden.'

'She didn't say anything about Barrie being a paedo-phile,' Burton exclaimed indignantly. Again, it was too hot for a spat, however, and she suspected Noakes was trying to get a rise out of her so merely kicked a pebble by way of relieving her feelings.

'There's something she's not telling us,' the DI murmured. 'Something that's niggling her.'

'Well, at least no one can say you didn't warn her, guv,' Doyle said to Markham thinking of the way his boss had laid it on the line. *Secrets can kill.*

'Yes, hopefully I gave her food for thought,' Markham said soberly, feeling a sudden chill despite the muggy heat that enveloped them.

Then he roused himself. 'Right, let's call it a day.' He turned to his wingman. 'I believe Mrs Noakes is coming up for a visit tomorrow, so we can't let that pass without after-noon tea at the Randolph.'

It was comical to see how Burton and Doyle hastened to excuse themselves from the proposed revelry, but Noakes raised no objection. 'It'll be a double date with you an' your Olivia,' he beamed at the guvnor before heading off with his colleagues to the Lamb and Flag. No doubt Kate Burton would virtuously confine herself to a single drink before going off 'culture vulturing' as Doyle put it, but even she had succumbed to the mid-afternoon torpor that left the threesome feeling heavy and sluggish.

Markham decided he would walk to his hotel on the Banbury Road.

As he plodded along, he looked towards the horizon, watching how the city's lines converged to a one-point perspective.

Murder had the power to make people's paths reach their vanishing point, he reflected.

The question that pounded relentlessly through his brain was, who might be next?

Again, it struck him how bizarrely coincidental it was that these polar aficionados had all converged like this at the heart of a homicide investigation.

What had Olivia called it?

Predestined.

He could only pray they would be able to disrupt whatever sinister pattern was working itself out.

8. FALSE CALM

It might justly be observed of Muriel Noakes, as of many another matron, that she had married her husband for better or worse but not for lunch.

Which wasn't to say George wasn't a good husband, of course. And now that things were back on an even keel after . . . well, after all the *unpleasantness* of the Bluebell case, he was doing his best to make it up to her. Even wanted her to go private for the operation. On the other hand, it would help if he stopped calling it the 'Hysterical Rectomy' in imitation of his beloved Les Dawson. She had honestly wanted to drop through the floor from shame when he said that in front of Gilbert Markham, of all people. *Gilbert Markham*. It made Muriel feel hot just thinking about it . . . Naturally, Gilbert pretended he hadn't heard — always the perfect gentleman — but Olivia Mullen had this knowing little smirk that made Muriel want to slap her . . .

Of course, Olivia egged George on, and that silly infatuation meant he was always trying to impress her.

In fairness, Muriel had to admit the inspector's partner seemed less flighty these days, more settled, somehow. Her manner was definitely more respectful on those occasions when the two couples met up . . . almost *deferential*.

It wouldn't surprise her if Gilbert hadn't encouraged their friendship from a secret desire that Olivia should model herself on his sergeant's wife, since she never encountered George's handsome boss without feeling they were on the same wavelength . . . what you might call kindred spirits.

There could be no doubt that poor dear Gilbert was trapped in a mismatch and didn't know how to extricate himself. So now it was a case of making the best of it and hoping Olivia would be *guided* by an older woman who could give her a tactful nudge in the right direction. Muriel really felt if Olivia could rein in the forwardness and show-offy tendencies, there was every chance she might eventually make a passable helpmeet. Of course, English teachers were an affected bunch. Watching them wittering on at Natalie's parents' evenings over the years had convinced her that university was seriously overrated . . . If that lot at Hope had been less head-in-the-clouds (Muriel disdained any expression so crude as 'arty farty'), they would have known how to *engage* sensitive students like her daughter instead of turning them off great literature for life.

Muriel caught sight of her reflection in the long mirror adjacent to her banquette in John Lewis's first-floor restaurant where she practically had the place to herself.

Patting her newly set hair, she eyed herself complacently. No way was she going to meet Gilbert Markham at the Randolph Hotel all scarlet and sweaty from the heat. The floral tea dress with its dropped waist was both feminine and classy, she decided. No doubt Olivia would roll up in some frightful bohemian outfit that bared her midriff, but at least *she* would look the part.

That was the secret. Knowing how to age gracefully and not follow every passing fad, since true elegance was timeless.

Muriel glanced at her watch. One o'clock. There was lots of time to kill before they were due to meet at three.

She congratulated herself on having had the forethought to consult her *Pitkin City Guide to Oxford* on the train. That way, she could drop the odd reference which would suggest that she had spent the morning admiring old buildings without the necessity of getting all hot and bothered traipsing round the colleges. Olivia Mullen was sure to turn up spouting all sorts of pretentious literary gobbledygook, so she needed to keep her end up.

In the meantime, perhaps she would treat herself to a little something from the perfume counter downstairs . . . something subtle and elusive of the "barely there" variety — a classic fragrance that encapsulated the allure of the older woman. After that, she could look for something for Natalie . . . something to bring her daughter out of the doldrums.

Natalie.

Muriel frowned before recollecting *Woman and Home*'s warning that this was liable to create unbecoming tramlines.

Everything was going so well for Natalie at the Harmony Spa, her relationship with Rick Jordan, the proprietor's son, being back on track and not a cloud in the sky . . .

But now there was this chit Angie somebody or other — a jumped-up marketing executive at Harmony, who seemed to have it in for her daughter — kept accusing Nat of pinching her ideas and presenting them as hers. She even implied she was being pushed out of the company so that Rick's fiancée could jump into her shoes.

As if *Natalie* wasn't bright enough to come up with ideas of her own!

The problem being that Ms Snot-Nosed Angie, with her micro miniskirts and ratty extensions, was well in with Rick's mother Barbara who for some incomprehensible reason preferred this pushy upstart to Natalie. And her a detective's daughter, whereas by the sound of it the other's background didn't bear close inspection.

As Natalie told it, Rick had simply asked her to sit in on Harmony's staff briefings as an outside consultant and pull some ideas together for him. What was the phrase he had used . . . ? Yes, that was it, he wanted her to hold *a watching brief* given her job in the beauty industry.

A watching brief. Muriel liked that terminology, suggestive of gravitas and expertise with no hint of nepotism.

But it didn't solve the problem of bolshie *Angie* who showed no sign of retreating gracefully and leaving the field clear for Natalie.

So what if Natalie had *rebranded* the other's ideas? If all went well, Harmony would one day be her own little empire to do with as she pleased. What could be more natural than that she wished to take the business forwards by pooling knowledge?

Muriel sipped her tea, pinkie crooked gracefully after the approved fashion.

Suddenly she brightened, the clouds on Natalie's horizon dispersed as if by magic.

She could ask *Gilbert*'s advice.

Muriel pictured it . . . their low-voiced conversation away from George and Olivia, the latter wondering why Gilbert stooped down to catch every softly uttered confidence and bent to look into her face . . .

It was such a delicious scenario, that she lost herself in a reverie that lasted several minutes and left her feeling weirdly excited and strange. Like a character in romantic fiction.

Gilbert Markham decidedly resembled the heroes Muriel most admired in the novels that she regularly checked out of Bromgrove Library — hidden beneath worthier tomes of the *War and Peace* variety — but there was no conflict with her feelings for George, the unlikely suitor who had won her heart beneath the Bromsgrove Dance Club glitterball all those years ago, and who still made her laugh when all was said and done.

No, she told herself, the affinity with Gilbert Markham was a meeting of minds . . . an encounter of souls totally in sync with each other.

Sure of the moral high ground, and feeling better now that she had decided on a plan of action, Muriel smoothed her lace-trim bolero shrug which perfectly complemented the tea dress. First, she would visit the ladies and touch up her make up. Then it was down to the ground floor and the perfume counter. After that, it would be time to visit Home Furniture and browse the latest trends in interior décor. Finally, she'd treat herself to a taxi to the Randolph. That way there was no danger of having a hair out of place and she could install herself in the Drawing Room with its views of Beaumont Street and the Ashmolean. Gilbert was sure to be impressed by her being totally au fait with such manicured surroundings. Olivia Mullen no doubt favoured the nightclub scene, so all the more reason to demonstrate a discerning connoisseurship . . .

* * *

Earlier that Friday morning, while Muriel Noakes was still en route to Oxford, Markham had enjoyed a leisurely breakfast with Olivia at their hotel.

'What's your plan for this morning, sweetheart?'

'I'm going to watch a film at the Reynolds,' came the prompt response.

Markham paused, a slice of fried bread halfway to his mouth.

'I didn't know the museum had a cinema,' he said.

'It's in the basement, only opens over the summer . . . They're showing *Shackleton's Antarctic Adventure*, shot on location apparently.' She scooped up the last of her scrambled egg and washed it down with coffee before adding, 'Felt I should give it a try after taking in the polar display yesterday.' She gave a mischievous grin. 'Besides, I can fantasise about using crampons and pickaxes on dear Muriel.'

'What did you think of the exhibition then?' Markham enquired, ignoring the latter observation.

'Very impressive. Old Shacks was an amazing character even if he was at daggers drawn with the saintly Captain Scott.'

'Hmm.' Markham considered this. 'Were they really such great enemies as people have made out?' he asked.

'I mean, Scott gave Shackleton a pivotal role on his first Antarctic expedition.'

'Yes, but he sent him back early on a relief ship and Shackleton never forgave him for it.'

'Wasn't that on health grounds?'

'That's how it was spun, but there were all kinds of stories going round, that Scott was furious and accused him of being a wuss. The museum director said the fur really flew later when Shackleton broke his promise not to encroach on Scott's territory and Scott called him out for it . . . told everyone he was nothing but a plausible rogue. Things got so bad that when he learned about Scott's death, Shackleton gloated over the fact that *he* had never lost one of his men whereas Scott lost as many in one season as all the Antarctic expeditions for the previous fifteen years put together . . .'

'Sounds quite mild to me,' Markham demurred.

'Oh, it was pretty strong stuff for those days . . . plus Scott said the way Shackleton pumped sensational stories into the press gave him the creeps.' Olivia clearly relished the notion of the two explorers falling out over 'Pole bagging'.

'I take it Dr Ashworth didn't mention any romantic angle,' Markham said drily.

Olivia looked nonplussed.

'It's just that Dr Colthurst was apparently making the case for there being romantic relationships between the men, underpinning it all,' he explained. 'Not everyone liked that line of thought.'

'Really? Like who?'

'Maggie Rawson — the postgrad student we caught breaking into his house — thought it was tacky and sensationalist.' Recalling Freda Carrington's comment about needing to avoid 'gratuitous titillation', he added, 'and the more conservative element in the university might find it hard to stomach.'

'Hmm. Dr Ashworth didn't mention anything about the explorers getting it on. And anyway, his assistant said Shackleton was a real skirt-chaser.' Olivia giggled. 'I take it

George doesn't subscribe to the theory of amorous antics under the Aurora Australis . . . that's the Southern Lights to the uninitiated,' she added with a wink.

'God no . . . Actually, Noakesy looked very black when Ashworth and his sidekick were talking about the theatricals Scott and Shackleton used to organise, didn't like it one bit.'

'Well, it was a whole different mindset wasn't it? They were romantic dreamers as well as adventurers. The South Pole represented their escape from boring reality . . . There's this letter in the exhibition which quotes Shackleton saying he wanted to die away on one of his expeditions. "I shall go on going, old man, till one day I shall not come back."' Her grey-green eyes sparkled. 'Seriously, he had more adventures in one week than most of us have in a lifetime!'

'Romantic dreamers, eh?'

'Absolutely. Cultured and literary with it. Remember, I told you Shackleton's nickname was Browning because he was so obsessed with the poet . . . And guess what he was reading on his first tramp south with Scott?'

'Enlighten me, Liv.'

'*On the Origin of Species.*' Her delicate features contorted with concentration. '*No animal performs any action for the exclusive good of another species,*' she declaimed, '*each tries to take advantage of the instincts of others.*'

'Sounds about right,' Markham retorted, the policeman in him responding to the cynicism.

'Even those who hated Shackleton came round to him in the end,' Olivia pointed out. 'Captain Scott's wife, for one.'

'According to Clive Ashworth, she'd said she would happily assist at Shackleton's assassination.'

'She was singing a different tune by the end . . . told everyone he'd pulled off a magnificent achievement.'

'Well, Liv.' Markham hastily swallowed the last of his coffee. 'Sounds like you're turning into a regular polar devotee.'

Liv shrugged in reply. 'They've done a great job with that exhibition,' she told him. 'All the wonderful letters and journals and little details . . . like the men using soot and snow for toothpaste, Shackleton stopping his men shooting an albatross because he remembered the curse from *The Ancient Mariner*, or the whalers who rescued Shackleton and his crew being scared out of their wits because they all looked like Ben Gunn.' Markham's voice was soft.

'Admit it, you've been seduced by these polar buccaneers.'

'They were all so extraordinary and eccentric, Gil. Jonjo Kelleher showed me some of the original journals they've got on loan. Incredibly touching . . . There's this passage where one of Shackleton's crew writes about riding a bicycle out on the pack ice, says no one could imagine what it meant to him to have a bike and a place to ride it no matter how heavy the going.' She paused. 'And then all those incredible pictures . . . You can practically hear the water-squelch and the creak of ship's timbers.'

Markham doubted that Ashworth and Kelleher had ever been graced with a more appreciative audience.

'Sounds like you got the guided tour,' he said with an ironic inflexion, recalling Kelleher's appreciation of a pretty face.

Olivia shrugged. 'I expected the place to be packed out given everything that's happened. But there weren't that many visitors through the turnstiles when I visited, although,' she matched his ironic tone, 'it may have picked up later on account of *two* deaths being connected with the place.'

'Did you tell Ashworth and Kelleher about us?'

'*Honestly* Gil, give me credit for *some* subtlety! I didn't want them going cold on me . . . If they knew we were a couple, I wouldn't have seen them for dust. As it was, I had a high old time, totally spellbinding. Apparently much of the credit goes to Timothy Colthurst. Kelleher said Dr C literally had to beg, steal and borrow to make the exhibition a success — him and that administrator who fell from the tower.'

'We think Yvonne Garrard was pushed, Liv.'

Her eyes widened. 'Another murder then?'

'Looks very much like it.' He hated to quench her enthusiasm, but she'd have to know sooner or later so it might as well be now.

'But *why*?' Her voice fell to a whisper.

'We're working on the theory that she tried to blackmail the killer, though we're not sure about the bargaining chips.' Markham ran a hand through his thick dark hair that curled over the back of his collar — 'like some sort of matinee idol' as Sidney was wont to carp. 'It's the age-old story, Liv. That poor woman overplayed her hand.'

Normally Olivia would have made short work of the remaining croissants, but now she looked as though her appetite had deserted her.

'D'you reckon there'll be another murder, Gil?'

'Sad to say, but that's our best hope of catching them,' came the grim reply. 'C'mon, Liv, I don't want you fretting about it.' He grinned. 'Forget murderers and go back to your fantasies about clubbing Muriel with a crampon.'

She groaned theatrically.

'Oh God, Gil, I'm not sure I can stand a session with Muriel doing her gracious lady number, looking at me like I'm something the cat dragged in while fluttering her eyelashes at you!'

He grinned. 'You and the missus are "bezzie mates" now according to Noakesy.'

Another groan. 'That's only because I spend the whole time biting my lip . . . when in my mind I'm flicking V signs at her.'

Her partner adopted a tone of mock pleading. '*For me*, Liv.'

'For you and George,' she retorted. Then, 'He's so terribly proud of her,' she said more gently. 'And protective . . . like she's a piece of fine bone china that might crack.' Olivia's tone suggested an analogy with tungsten might be more apt. 'A legacy of the Bluebell affair, I guess,' she concluded.

'Something like that,' he agreed. 'Other people's marriages are a mystery, but his "missus" and Natalie are the sun, moon and stars to Noakesy . . . I suspect behind all the social-climbing bombast, Muriel's a lonely soul—'

'With a fixation about her husband's boss,' Olivia interrupted tartly. 'Comes over all Heloise and Abelard whenever *you* appear on the horizon.' She mimed throwing up. 'Twin souls with but one beating heart and all that. In the meantime, she lives for the day when the scales fall from your eyes and you give me the old heave-ho.'

Conscious of the reproach in his gaze, Olivia relented.

'Alright, alright, I'll try not to brain her over the petits fours . . . I'll even wear a frock and pretend to listen while she bangs on about *Inspector Morse* and *Endeavour*.'

'That's my girl.'

They sat companionably, enjoying the peaceful interlude. But Markham's reference to another murder being the team's best hope of catching the killer preyed on Olivia's mind.

'Are you really nowhere nearer to figuring whodunnit?' she asked.

'Well, at the minute all we've really got is the fact that Dr Colthurst was a bit of a prima donna . . . That's what Ashworth and Kelleher implied at any rate, though it seems they liked him, and they both agreed what he brought to the table was worth any number of tantrums.'

'What about the housebreaker woman? She insisted it was spur of the moment, and Dr Freda Carrington — that's the don at Latimer who supervised her after the bust-up with Colthurst — was adamant Rawson isn't a killer.'

Olivia noticed that he looked troubled.

'Is Dr Carrington in the frame as well?' she asked.

'It looked like *something* was bugging her, but all we got out of her was this mini-lecture on J.M. Barrie.'

She was intrigued. 'Mister Peter Pan?'

'The very same . . . apparently there was some sort of "bromance" with Captain Scott.'

'Oh lord, what did George make of that?'

'Just scowled a lot, and called Barrie a paedo once we were safely out of there.'

Olivia chuckled. 'What about Colthurst's toy boy — that student who had a fit of the vapours?'

Markham sighed. 'Desmond Milner's sheltering behind his GP and Student Services. We can't get at him for the time being . . . certainly seemed out of it during the prayer service at Blackfriars. It looked like Professor Hanbury and Dr Peary were propping him up.'

'They're the two from Sherwin?'

'That's right. The story goes that Colthurst left Hanbury in the lurch over a student suicide. But we went through the college's paperwork on it. Colthurst didn't get involved in the disciplinary hearing at all — stayed well clear — whereas Marion Peary provided a witness statement and glowing character testimony.'

'Loyal to a fault then?'

'Well, as Doyle said, you look at her and think *Boringville*, but I reckon there's fire underneath. Noakes is convinced she had a crush on Colthurst, but one of the scouts said he saw her cut Colthurst dead at a formal dinner in Hall . . .'

Olivia was gripped. 'Curiouser and curiouser.'

'There's a comely ex-girlfriend of Colthurst's who's another contender in the broken heart stakes,' Markham continued. 'Noakes calls her the Disney princess.'

'Ah . . . Are we talking Elsa from *Frozen*?'

'Yes, but with black hair.' Markham frowned. 'She gave a very convincing impression of being well and truly over Colthurst.'

'Hmm. And what's the latest on Sidney? Is he breathing down your necks?' she asked sympathetically.

'Not as much as you'd expect. Distracted by his hay fever.'

'Not chafing for instant results . . . That doesn't sound like Judas Iscariot!'

'Kate played a blinder at the press conference, kept us nicely on the fence and distracted all the hacks by implying Colthurst's death had something to do with an obsessive love disorder.'

'A *fixated stalker*?' Olivia tried to keep from sounding querulous but felt a little flash of irrational resentment at Markham's evident warm admiration for Kate Burton. *Beat it down*, she told herself, *beat it down*. She hated the idea of Gil knowing she was prey to such jealous fears.

'Well, Colthurst was by way of becoming a quasi-celebrity . . . in academic circles at any rate.'

Olivia pondered this. 'Could Professor Hanbury have resented him for being the up-and-coming expert on Antarctica?'

'Hanbury didn't seem rattled, said there was room for everyone . . . But it's possible he's a very good actor. The same goes for Marion Peary and Freda Carrington. The talkative scout at Sherwin said Dr Peary's bagged herself a British Council grant for a book on the history of Antarctica . . . so essentially they're all at it.'

'Oh my, Gil. It sounds like you've got your work cut out.'

Markham pushed his chair back from the table. 'We're going to review all the statements again this morning and hopefully have another crack at Sherwin's scouts later on,' he grinned, 'once we've done our duty at the Randolph.'

She blew him a kiss. 'See you at three, on my best behaviour.'

There was plenty of time before she had to set out for the museum. Soon Olivia was lost in her glossy exhibition catalogue, chuckling over *Captain Scott's Ponies*.

'His comrades felt that the way Oates handled the poor creatures might have proved a model to any governor of a lunatic asylum,' she read.

Something she would be sure to remember when dealing with Mrs Muriel Noakes!

* * *

To Muriel's intense gratification, afternoon tea at the Randolph Hotel was all that her heart could desire.

True to her word, Olivia was attentive and respectful even though the arch trilling and desperate coquetry affected her like fingernails being scraped down a blackboard. Noakes, starched and buffed to within an inch of his life, didn't commit his usual depredations on the sandwiches and scones, a sure sign that he too was minding his Ps and Qs. There was something so touching about his transparent pride at Muriel's masterclass in gentility, that Olivia refrained from any unseemly raillery, feeling in consequence that her light was pretty much under a bushel.

At the end of the meal, Muriel secured the desired tête-à-tête with Markham by the simple expedient of drawing him over to a sofa in the spacious hotel lobby and leaving the other two to fend for themselves.

Like a scene out of *Bridgerton*, Olivia thought crossly.

But all irritation was dispelled when Doyle came rushing through the Randolph's entrance, rudely disturbing the idyll.

'Sir, you've got to come at once,' he said urgently to the DI. 'There's been a development over at Sherwin.'

Mrs Noakes looked avid on hearing this, but Markham's eyes flashed a warning at the young detective.

'Muriel, it's been a pleasure,' he said, with a courtly bow which, with anyone else, might have suggested burlesque but seemed perfectly natural from him. 'Police business calls, I'm afraid.'

With a fluttering self-consciousness which suggested that she was enjoying the effect of this byplay upon bystanders, the lady graciously released him.

Only pausing to say goodbye to Olivia and collect Noakes, they headed into Beaumont Street.

'What's happened?' Noakes puffed as he tried to match Doyle's long stride, tearing off his second-best blazer as if it was a straitjacket and snorting away like a steam engine.

'It's that porter — Alex Mason. They've found him with his throat cut!'

9. TURNING THE SCREW

Kate Burton was waiting for them in Sherwin's long narrow Third Quad by the entrance to the Hatton Library. A gaggle of onlookers clustered at the bottom of an adjoining staircase, watching with frightened faces.

'Who found him?' Markham asked.

'The assistant librarian when she went up to the first floor to check a reference for one of the fellows.' Burton moistened dry lips and ran a hand through her damp fringe, clearly shaken by this latest discovery. 'There are these little carrels on each floor, and he was in one of them, so at first she thought it was a postgrad catching up on some research but something about the way he was sitting, slumped over, caught her attention. Then she noticed the bloodstains.'

Markham had always loved the Hatton — a cosy affair dating from the 1860s which was dominated by the reassuring presence of glowing hardwood, with leather chairs, brass lamps, wrought iron spiral staircases and wraparound rectangular balconies over four floors. Named after an Elizabethan courtier, it had more the feel of a gentlemen's club than a centre for study. That its quiet precincts should have been polluted by murder struck him as a desecration.

Her colleagues ducked under the police tape and followed Burton up to the second floor, the filigree of the little staircase shaking as though to protest against such an invasion.

'You can access each level from Staircase Thirteen next door,' Burton explained. 'And there are lifts too. But the librarian came up this way.'

Dr Merrick was already at the carrel, with Alex Mason's slight form tilted backwards as he gently probed with gloved hands.

At the detectives' approach, he signalled to a paper-suited SOCO to help him turn the chair around so that they could see the body.

'No point worrying about contaminating the crime scene,' he said quietly. 'When the librarian began screaming, half a dozen people came running. Your lot got rid of them, but not before everyone and their mother came trooping through.'

Markham wasn't surprised to learn of the librarian's reaction, since the young porter presented a ghastly sight, eyes wide open and staring and his throat laid open by a savage gash so that the upper airway was clearly visible, glistening like red corral.

Noakes leaned against a bookcase for support, the exposed trachea reminding him horribly of tinned salmon with the white curd-like bits that looked like bone fragments. Observing the wound, he felt the sandwiches from his afternoon tea repeating on him and gulped convulsively.

'Jesus, Mary and Joseph,' he breathed. 'What did the poor lad do to deserve *this*?'

'There would have been a moment of intense pain,' the pathologist told them, 'but mercifully brief and no time for him to even realise what was happening.'

'Presumably the killer arranged to meet him up here,' Doyle said faintly.

'Nice an' quiet an' tucked out of the way,' Noakes speculated. 'No one around to hear anything.'

Dr Merrick nodded. 'I'd put time of death somewhere close to midnight last night. Apparently there's very little traffic in here this time of year and there was no sign of anyone around when they set the alarm.'

'Alex Mason would have had access to a set of keys what with him being a porter,' Burton said.

Noakes looked around at the mahogany bookcases with gilt-tooled volumes and turned to the pathologist. 'I thought you said the place was alarmed'

'Presumably he knew how to disable it,' Doyle volunteered.

Two more SOCOs appeared with a collapsible gurney, and the gruesome business of removing the body got underway.

'Can't you shut his eyes?' Noakes muttered to Jigsaw Man as the little cortege passed by.

'They won't close,' the other replied levelly. 'But I promise I'll make sure he's presentable for viewing after the autopsy.'

'What about next of kin, Kate?' Markham asked as the stretcher party headed for the lift.

'Parents and a sister in Cowley,' she replied. 'I've got the address here.'

'Right, I need to get down there before the vultures descend on them,' he said. 'You can come with me, Kate. In the meantime, Noakes, I want you and Doyle to round up the other porters and housekeeping staff. Find out what Mr Mason was up to yesterday, alterations to his usual routine, anything unusual that they noticed about him.'

'You don' reckon *Mason* were up to blackmail too?' his wingman demanded incredulously.

'We can't even be sure this is connected to Colthurst and Garrard,' Doyle observed.

'It's *gotta* be connected,' Noakes retorted fiercely. 'Too much of a coincidence him turning up dead straight after the two of 'em snuffed it.'

'I agree,' Markham said slowly, 'though it's hard to see where such a junior college employee fits in.'

With that, he left them to it, phoning St Aldate's to arrange transportation to Cowley.

The weather had turned since they were in the library, a stiff breeze whipping up and sending the trailing wisteria of First Quad into a frenzy. As he and Burton got into the squad car, the DI braced himself for the condolence visit, praying that he would be able to find appropriate words of comfort.

When they arrived at the little terraced house in Long Lane, they were greeted by Brendan Potter, an old schoolfriend of Alex who'd been alerted by a text message from one of the porters. Ashen faced, he told the detectives he wanted to go in with them and Markham saw no reason to deny the request.

Mr and Mrs Mason were a diminutive white-haired couple — 'like something out of *The Borrowers*', as Burton put it afterwards — who, at first, seemed unable to process the news of their son's death. It was easier when Alex's sister Irene arrived, having got a taxi from Headington where she was visiting a friend. The stocky forthright blonde took the news calmly, assuring Markham that she would take care of her parents and dismissing Brendan's clumsy sympathy.

'I always knew it'd catch up with Alex in the end,' she said with a meaningful glance before firmly closing the door in their faces.

'What did she mean by that?' Markham asked as they walked back to the squad car.

'It's not really my place to say,' Brendan replied.

'This is a murder investigation,' Burton reminded him. 'If you know anything that could be relevant, we need to hear it. Plus you owe it to his family.'

'Get into the car, Mr Potter,' Markham said gently. 'We'll give you a lift home if you like.'

'My shift at the museum starts in half an hour,' the youth said.

'Fine, let's head to the Reynolds then,' Markham instructed the driver.

At the museum, they led the security guard into a trellised gazebo.

123

It was still breezy and overcast, but there was a bench and the secluded spot was dry with no risk of them being overheard.

Burton promptly returned to the attack.

'So, what did his sister mean by saying that about something catching up with Alex?' she demanded.

Looking deeply uncomfortable, Brendan gazed sightlessly into the middle distance.

'Alex was gay,' he said finally.

'Yes?' Burton rapped impatiently.

'His mum and dad didn't know cos that's the way Alex wanted it . . . He was dead protective of them, especially his mum.'

She cut to the chase. 'Was he promiscuous?'

'I wouldn't know anything about that,' Brendan mumbled. 'He belonged to some group called the Titus Oates Society.'

'Was this a gay club, Mr Potter?' Markham asked gently.

'Yeah, kind of *underground*, though, nothing official to do with the university.'

'Where'd they get the name from?' Burton was confused. 'I mean, if they named it after Captain Oates that's a bit weird seeing as he wasn't gay . . . *Uh-oh*,' in a tone of sudden comprehension, 'did it have something to do with Dr Colthurst?'

'Yes.' Brendan gnawed his lip. 'Alex told me Dr Colthurst founded it . . . But *hey*,' he suddenly flushed up to the roots of his hair, 'they weren't doing anything wrong and besides, it wasn't my business. All I know is that they were into Antarctica like me, had evenings where they talked about all kinds of stuff, no holds barred . . .'

'What do you mean by "no holds barred"?' Markham pressed.

Brendan shifted uncomfortably. 'Well, some of it was quite far out . . . like the idea that Scott might've been in love with Oates and kind of engineered his death by way of revenge . . .'

Burton appeared profoundly sceptical. 'You mean *because Oates rejected him*?'

But Markham recalled Olivia talking about Oates's mother blaming Scott for her son's death.

'Do you know who came up with this theory about Scott and Oates?' he asked.

'Alex never said — only mentioned it the once — and I didn't want to pry. But I think that's how they came up with the name . . . more jokey than anything else.'

'Hilarious,' Burton said trenchantly. Then, 'Did women have anything to do with this secret society or was it just men?'

'I seem to remember Alex saying women sometimes came along. They were quite relaxed about that . . . just so long as people were discreet, and everything stayed under the radar.'

Markham eyed him closely. 'And you were never tempted to get involved, Mr Potter, despite your enthusiasm for Antarctica and polar exploration?'

The security guard's expression was guileless.

'It wasn't my scene,' Brendan mumbled before blurting out, 'and besides, my mum'd kill me if I got mixed up in anything dodgy.' He flushed. 'Not that *I* think it's dodgy, but she and my dad are set in their ways.'

To Markham, it had the ring of truth.

Burton was at her most terrier-like. 'Was there anything else to make you think it was *dodgy*?'

'Oh, I dunno, just the fact of it being secret, I s'pose . . .'

'Presumably Irene thought Alex was putting it about?' Burton pressed.

'Yeah, something like that,' he conceded with obvious reluctance.

'Do you know if he had a regular boyfriend?' Markham enquired.

'Honestly, Mr Markham, he didn't talk to me about stuff like that.' Brendan's expression eloquently conveyed that he preferred to steer clear of such personal topics. Not unlike himself and Noakes, the DI thought wryly.

Watching the security guard, miserably hunched over and darting anxious glances towards the museum, Markham took pity on him.

'Thanks for your help, Mr Potter.'

Brendan Potter was what Olivia would have called 'a big lummox', but there was a curious dignity about him as he took his leave.

'Alex had so much life in him, Mr Markham . . . When push came to shove, he'd always stand in your corner. See you get whoever did this.'

Markham locked eyes with the security guard and nodded gravely.

Whatever he saw in the DI's face seemed to reassure Brendan.

'Right,' Markham said attempting to sound purposeful, after Brendan had departed, 'I'd better get back to Mr Kelleher. We're doing a mock-up of the cairn they erected over the tent with Captain Scott's body, with the cross made from skis on top . . . sort of a replacement for the art installation, and a description alongside saying how him, Wilson and Bowers looked when the rescue party found them — someone broke Scott's arm when they were checking his clothes for diaries, and the bodies were all yellow and frostbitten. There's a map as well, charting where they are now.'

Seeing that Burton looked mystified, he added, 'As in how far out to sea they've floated.'

'God, that's a bit morbid,' she exclaimed watching his retreating back. 'Recreating *the grave* and working out where the corpses are likely to wash up!'

'Kids will love it,' Markham smiled. 'Mummies under the ice . . . They'll lap it up.'

She shuddered. 'D'you reckon the killer's involved with this Titus Oates Society, sir?'

'Well, looks like it's the only real lead we've got for Alex Mason.' With measured deliberation, Markham added, 'I believe we need to see if Desmond Milner can shed some light.'

'Think we'll be able to get near him, guv? I mean, seeing as he's having a nervous breakdown or whatever it is.'

'Oh, I'd say so, Kate, now there's been a *third* murder.' He got to his feet, gazing thoughtfully at the museum with its uncompromising planes and angles, the crisp modernism in such sharp contrast to the twining roses of the old-fashioned gazebo. 'Come on, the squad car can take us back to HQ and then we'll work out a strategy for getting to the bottom of this secret society business.'

'Did *you* ever belong to anything like that, guv?' she asked wistfully once they were back in the car heading to St Aldate's. 'I mean private clubs . . . the kind people like David Cameron and Hugh Grant belonged to.' Burton's expression was pensive. 'I suppose it's very exclusive, invitation-only,' she added.

Markham recalled their last investigation in Oxford, when she had confessed to inventing stories of a riotous social life for the parents who were so proud of her going to university, lest they should imagine she was 'Billy No Mates' and a complete failure. It was a curiously intimate conversation which had made him warm to Kate Burton as never before. It would doubtless have surprised her to learn that behind the veneer of an Oxbridge education and stellar career, his own background had been one of emotional privation dating from the arrival of an abusive stepfather.

'I'm flattered you imagine I had that kind of clout, Kate,' he said lightly. 'I believe the clubs you mean are the Bullingdon and Piers Gaveston . . . Come to think of it, the Piers Gaveston Society was named after a male lover of Edward the Second who ended up being executed by jealous barons.'

'Is it a gay club then?'

'No, I don't think so. It's just that Gaveston was this flamboyant character with great charisma who died tragically young.'

'That's how Dr Ashworth described Tim Colthurst,' Burton observed thoughtfully. 'Called him *flamboyant* on account of his having a colourful private life.'

'Well, it sounds as if Colthurst was the driving force behind this Titus Oates set-up.'

'What did you make of all that stuff about Oates being gay, sir?'

'I think it's speculation, to be honest, Kate.' Catching the eye of the stolid young constable driving them, it occurred to Markham that their conversation must sound surreally weird, but their chauffeur's inscrutability never cracked. 'We will obviously never know and it was obvious Brendan didn't take it seriously, though it sounds like there was *someone* emotionally invested in the idea.'

'Colthurst?'

'Possibly.' Markham thought hard. 'Olivia's gone into it a bit . . . Apparently there was this anti-Scott mythology propagated by people like George Bernard Shaw, a theory that Scott abandoned Taff Evans and later sat staring at Oates until he walked out of the tent into that blizzard then, as the *pièce de résistance*, he talked Wilson and Bowers into lying down with him and waiting for the end.'

His fellow DI boggled. '*Seriously?*'

'Oh yes. And Oates's mother got in on the act too . . . slept in his bedroom for the rest of her life and covered everything including herself in black. She wouldn't even go to Buckingham Palace to collect his posthumous Polar medal. Spent the rest of her days obsessively grilling anyone who'd travelled with Scott in an attempt to paint him as this cold-hearted villain who was little better than a murderer.'

'I've heard of mother love, but she must've had a screw loose.'

'Agreed . . . As for Scott, well when you've got this hero on a pedestal, there's bound to be a posse of critics panting to knock him off it . . . According to Olivia, he could be short-tempered and there's no doubt he was a bit of a martinet, but some of the stories are just plain scurrilous. One commentator even claimed he contracted syphilis which triggered a personality change.'

'*Blimey* . . . To be honest, sir, *I'd* always seen Captain Scott in the light of a national hero. Where on earth did all this stuff come from?'

'Innuendo and rumour. And Oates did a fair bit of carping about Scott in his letters home — they were always falling out over how to manage the ponies — which didn't help. Even though he wrote to his mother later and told her not to take the badmouthing too seriously because he was having a bad time, the damage was done. Just after he walked out into that blizzard, Wilson wrote a letter to his mother saying that Oates told him she was the only woman he had ever loved, so it was a short step from there to deciding he was homosexual.'

Burton's eyebrows shot up. 'Bit of a push, sir.'

'Yes, but Olivia said when it comes to queer theory anything can be re-evaluated.'

For once Burton was oblivious to the Oxford panorama. 'So what's going on here, guv?' she asked in bafflement. 'Is it a vendetta against this Titus Oates Society? Has the killer got a thing about people taking pot-shots at Scott? Or are we talking some kind of sexual feud?'

'Hmm . . . Don't forget, Brendan said the society welcomed women, so we're not necessarily looking for a gay man.'

'The love angle seems more likely than someone going on a killing spree over a difference of opinion,' she ventured.

'Don't count on it, Kate.' Markham gestured to the Martyrs Memorial as they passed along St Giles. 'History teaches us that people are prepared to kill for their beliefs.'

'I guess so, guv,' she conceded reluctantly. 'But you'd have to be a real nutjob to kill just because someone made up stories about Captain Scott. I mean, that's seriously paranoid.'

'Maybe that's the key to the mystery . . . some deep-seated paranoia or kink—'

'Connected with polar exploration?' Her tone was doubtful.

'Yes, I think so, Kate, though I still don't see how it all fits together.'

They were coming into St Aldate's.

'So we're going to interview Desmond Milner then?' she enquired.

'Correct. But let's get the FME to check him over first. That way we won't face any flak about undue pressure or him being unfit for questioning.'

'D'you want me to sit in on the interview, boss?' she asked eagerly.

'Absolutely.' He smiled conspiratorially at her. 'The other two will be busy at Sherwin for a while. We might be called out for cruel and unusual punishment if we inflict Noakesy on Milner.'

The normally solemn brown eyes sparkled with genuine mirth.

'God no. That'd just about finish him off!' Shyly, she added. 'Sarge is quite struck on these polar types, guv. Admires them no end.'

'Don't I know it . . . right down to the xenophobia and racism.' The conspiratorial note was back. 'Olivia tells me Oates and Bowers were pretty bad when it came to that. As far as they were concerned, the rest of the world was just waiting for a pretext to throw themselves on England and destroy it. Now *there's* paranoia for you.'

She smiled impishly. 'But Oates was "King and Country" all the way wasn't he, guv? Right up sarge's street.'

Markham returned the smile. 'Well, he was ex-army and picked up a shattered leg fighting in South Africa, so some of his comrades christened him "No Surrender Oates". I guess you're right about Noakes reckoning him to be a kindred spirit.'

They drew into the station car park and the moment of them being in cahoots had passed. Markham shot his cuffs. 'Right, let's see if Mr Milner can shed some light on this underground network. Something tells me it's the key to these murders.'

'Do we tell him about Alex Mason?' Burton asked.

'If he's our killer, he already knows,' was the sombre reply. 'Let's keep our powder dry until after we've interviewed him.'

* * *

'Do I need a solicitor, Inspector?'

It was hardly a propitious opening, but Markham was calm.

'You're free to leave at any time, Mr Milner, but in light of Alex Mason's murder we wondered if you might be able to enlighten us about a club to which we understand he belonged.'

'The Titus Oates Society,' Milner said.

The undergraduate was less glassy-eyed than he had appeared at Blackfriars, but he looked dishevelled, and Markham caught a whiff of alcohol overlaid with extra strong mints. Added to which, the student was enunciating with unusual distinctness as though to cover up a lapse. All in all, it gave credence to his assertion that he had 'got blotto' at home the previous night, albeit there were no witnesses to corroborate this alibi.

The interview room was stale and muggy. Burton felt sweat pooling in the small of her back under the linen jacket of her trouser suit, but she followed Markham's lead and showed no sign of impatience. The boss in his superbly tailored Savile Row lounge suit looked as cool and collected as if he had stepped out of the shower, a slight tightening of the jaw the only sign of tension.

'And you're asking me about the society because I'm gay,' Milner continued, his voice flat.

'Correct,' Markham replied simply. 'Were you a member?'

'I went to some of their meetings if that's what you mean . . . There wasn't an initiation ritual or anything daft like that.' His lip curled. 'Not like those entitled swaggering

131

idiots who end up plastered all over the tabloids in their penguin suits . . . David Cameron and that pig's head!' he scoffed, referring to the notorious story of the former prime minister.

Markham was aware of Burton squirming slightly at this.

'But the club's proceedings were clandestine, is that right?' he asked.

'It was "friend of a friend" stuff . . . word of mouth, very discreet.'

'Why all the secrecy?' Burton asked mildly.

And now Milner was fully awake, something kindling at the back of the intelligent grey eyes.

'Look, it was mainly gay men with a common interest, nothing to do with drugs or jumping on tables and abusing the plebs . . . We didn't want to be tagged with the same label as those posh boy clubs where it's all about posing and sneering at ordinary folk.'

Hearing this, Burton found herself warming to the man opposite them.

'There were dons who belonged . . . Dr Colthurst, for example?' she prompted.

'Yeah, Tim was a leading light, him and Professor Hanbury.'

Burton was startled. 'Professor Hanbury? But wasn't he married?'

Milner shot her a pitying look that seemed to deplore her naivete. 'Everyone knew he was in the closet . . . once his wife died, it was easier for him.'

Markham took over. 'You said people who went along had a common interest. Presumably that was polar scholarship?'

'That's right.' His tone suddenly fierce, he said, 'Most of us would sacrifice a kidney rather than walk to the South Pole or face anything like the hardship those men did . . . Scott and Shackleton and the rest of them, they're a breed apart.'

It was exactly how Noakes might have put it, Markham thought, recalling his wingman's respect for the men who mounted such a huge endeavour into the unknown.

'I gather you didn't shy away from potentially controversial subjects,' he said.

Milner looked wary. 'What do you mean by *controversial*?'

'Theories about gay intrigue amongst the explorers,' Markham said baldly.

The other gave a short sharp bark that was strangely at odds with his delicate physique.

'You mean Scott-bashing? Well, we weren't sycophants. Hagiography's boring . . . Tim liked to get inside their heads and figure out what made them tick, the good, the bad and the ugly. And anyway,' the student's voice was sibilant now, almost caressing, 'they're still there, Scott and his men . . . frozen in the ice on their way out to the ocean. They're the only ones who know the whole truth.'

There was a silence after this, but then Burton broke the spell.

'And women were allowed along?'

A wry smile. 'They weren't actively encouraged, but yeah they made up the numbers now and again. We didn't want to be precious about it.'

'Where did you meet?' Markham asked.

'Tim's rooms mostly. Dr Ashworth let us have the café at the Reynolds now and again. There was also the Lamb and Flag and a few local pubs.'

A headache was building behind Markham's eyes in the oxygen-less room. Burton too was visibly wilting.

He pushed paper and a pen across the table.

'Before you leave, Mr Milner, I'd be grateful if you would write a list of people who attended the club's meetings, to the best of your recollection.'

'Gladly.' The student looked surprised, as though he'd anticipated further interrogation. 'Is that all?'

'For now, yes.'

They left him to it and stood in the corridor outside.

'Looked like Milner felt he was getting off lightly, guv,' Burton remarked.

'Hmm. He's at least given us food for thought, Kate.'

'Yeah, like Professor Hanbury being involved with this society . . . Wonder what else Hanbury's kept schtum about.'

'Indeed.'

Markham gazed thoughtfully through the glass panel of the door to the interview room, watching the student's head bent over his task and wondering what other secrets remained for his team to drag into the light of day.

10. HIGH STAKES

The afternoon of Saturday 31 July found Markham and Olivia strolling through the War Memorial Garden on their way to Christ Church Meadow.

It was a perfect summer day, and the garden was looking its best, the velvety grass so lush that it almost invited visitors to ignore the ostentatious little fence separating the lawn and gravelled pathway. Raised flower beds and borders jostled with myriad colours in a dizzying perspective, and all was still but for the faint echo of music coming from the meadow where summer picnickers caroused down by the river.

'Some of the men who travelled to Antarctica with Scott ended up dying in the First World War,' Olivia murmured. 'I wonder if they remembered scenes like this when they were crouched in the trenches. *There's some corner of a foreign field that is forever England . . .*'

'I'm sure they did,' he replied. 'But after Antarctica, they'd have been better prepared than most to look death in the eye.'

They lingered by a lavender border inhaling the heady scent.

'I guess that's part of the fascination,' Olivia said at last. 'Scott and Bowers and the rest of them always underplayed the danger, talked about getting into a tight corner or legging it across the ice, like it was some schoolboy lark . . . The pictures of those huts with the gramophone and pianola in pride of place are something else — if it weren't for all their scientific research, you'd think they were throwing some tea party at the ends of the earth. Scott even left a notice telling future visitors to leave the dishes clean.'

'Hmm. You have to remember, they were men of their time.'

'You can say that again, Gil.' Olivia grinned. 'The women were just as bad.' Adopting an affected upper-class accent, she lisped, '"You *shall* go to the Pole. Oh, dear me, what's the use of having energy and enterprise if a little thing like that can't be done!"'

Markham chuckled. 'Which of them came up with that pearl of wisdom?'

'Kathleen Scott. But they were *all* the same, especially the mothers. Weird how Scott, Oates and Bowers were all what you'd call mummy's boys.'

'Presumably they weren't all as neurotic as Oates's mother,' Markham observed.

'God no, she was in a class of her own. *Birdie's* mum was this sweet little widow who said she was proud he didn't abandon his skipper. Lots of his friends kept in touch with her and she was thrilled to bits about going to Buck House and collecting a medal from King George. Scott's mother was tricky and a terrible snob. But he was wonderful to her after the family fell on hard times and his brother Archie died of typhoid . . . agonising about whether he'd been a good enough son to her right at the end.' She paused thoughtfully. 'I suppose it was a blessing that nothing was left unsaid between them.'

Markham felt a sharp pang at this. Estranged from his own mother for many years, the veil was only lifted at her deathbed when the past came rushing back with an intensity which obliterated old hurts.

Olivia saw the shadow cross his face. She had enjoyed a happy upbringing but knew Markham had never ceased to mourn the mother who was only truly restored to him at the end. Inwardly, she cursed herself for her thoughtlessness and turned the conversation into safer channels.

'From what you were telling me, this secret society doesn't sound like it was too reverential towards Scott and the rest of them,' she observed.

Her tactic worked. Markham was recalled to the current investigation, a topic they had postponed discussing until their 'down time' at the weekend.

'Well, maybe it's a bit like your lot at Hope,' he said. 'A reaction against all the triumphalist nationalism that surrounded Scott's expeditions.'

'*Play up! Play up! And play the game!*' she quoted sardonically.

'Something like that,' he agreed. Gesturing at the garden, he added, 'I reckon two world wars took the gloss off notions of pointless heroism and gentlemanly service to the empire.'

'*You* don't believe it was pointless do you, Gil?' she asked softly.

'No, I think what Scott and Co did was extraordinary, but I'm not surprised at the trend for viewing them as types of English emotional inadequacy.'

'That's the snowflake generation for you,' she snorted. 'Totally blind to the way those men tossed off great achievements as nonchalantly as they changed their socks. *That's* what clinches it for me,' she added, grey-green eyes alight with enthusiasm. 'How *casually* they took it . . . all that about being in a "nasty hole" or "queer street", or Shackleton saying he never expected it to be a feather bed, when they were conquering a bloody *continent*!'

Markham laughed at her passion.

'By the by,' she said archly, '*was* there some sort of lover's quarrel behind all of this?'

'Well, jilted exes are a bit of a running theme. It seems Dr Colthurst got up a debate about Scott and Oates having a relationship that turned sour. But he could just have been putting maverick ideas out there—'

'By way of rehearsal for his next book or lecture tour?'

'I wouldn't be at all surprised.' Markham frowned. 'And now with the murder of Alex Mason at Sherwin . . .'

Olivia reached for his hand.

'Appalling,' she whispered. 'Was *he* involved with Dr Colthurst?'

'We told Desmond Milner about Mason before he left St Aldate's . . . he seemed genuinely shocked, but who knows? Milner's prominent in OUDS, so it could just have been a polished performance. He told us Mason was between boyfriends and gave us their names. Both have solid alibis for the night of the murder, but there may be another partner we don't know about.'

They turned their steps towards the New Walk, savouring the shade of the poplars.

'Of course, the whole jealous lover theory could be a complete blind alley,' Markham said as they sauntered down to the river. 'Mind you, it reared its head again when we got on to JM Barrie's entanglement with Scott. Freda Carrington seemed decidedly twitchy about it for some reason.'

Olivia thought of the child named after Barrie's most famous work.

'Sad isn't it that Scott's son never knew him,' she mused. 'The story goes that when he was a toddler he told his mother, "Daddy won't come back". Like he had a premonition or something . . .' Abruptly she jerked herself back to the subject under discussion. 'Why was the Carrington woman uncomfortable talking about it?'

'No idea, but there were *Keep Out* signs all over the shop.'

Olivia pondered this. 'Didn't you say she took up the cudgels on behalf of the girl who fell out with Colthurst, the one who broke into his house?'

'That's right,' Markham agreed. 'Maggie Rawson . . . she seemed protective of her.'

'Well maybe *that* was what upset her? She didn't want you feeling Maggie's collar.'

'Possibly. Dr Carrington's a motherly kind of woman, I noticed it when she took charge of Desmond Milner after the prayer service at Blackfriars.'

'I should have gone with you to that instead of mooching around the colleges,' Olivia said guiltily.

'You were well out of it, sweetheart,' Markham replied kindly. 'There was an interesting tribute from one of the Dominicans, but only Noakesy did justice to the edibles. 'Evelyn Bennet — that's Colthurst's ex-girlfriend — couldn't get out of there fast enough, and Jonjo Kelleher looked as though he'd like to have gone with her. As for Clive Ashworth, he just seemed plain miserable.'

'What about the Dreary Twins?'

'The *what?* Markham broke into a laugh. 'Oh, you mean Professor Hanbury and Marion Peary. Actually,' he added with grave deliberation, 'maybe not so colourless after all . . . Hanbury was a leading light of the Titus Oates Society — "in the closet" forever, if we're to believe Milner. He seemed very thick with Dr Peary, so maybe she's a dark horse too.'

Ambling by the river, the horror of murder seemed a million miles away.

And yet an image rose up before Markham eyes as he watched a lone oarsman cutting through the sparkling water . . . a shrouded shape wrapped in tarpaulin half in and half out of the water, like some giant seabird or the fabled albatross which brought bad luck . . .

He shook his head to banish the ghosts of that earlier investigation, though it seemed to him that if he listened carefully, he would hear them breathing down his neck, along with all the other victims whose sad faces hovered just beyond reach, like a flicker in the corner of his eye.

Olivia was watching him anxiously. 'Penny for them?' she asked lightly.

Markham forced the image down, reluctant to conjure memories of that watery exhumation.

'Just letting my thoughts drift . . . thinking what a special place this is.'

'Hmm, willows and woods and water . . . idyllic.'

They found a bench and sat watching as more boats came into view, sculling lazily upstream with no sense of urgency now the training season was over.

A voice jolted Markham out of this agreeable reverie.

'Good afternoon, Inspector.'

Startled, he recognised Freda Carrington. Wearing close-fitting spandex shorts, T shirt and trainers, with the flyaway hair tightly braided, she cut an athletic figure far removed from the lackadaisical don of his recollection.

'Good afternoon, Dr Carrington.' Politely he introduced Olivia, realising as he did so that the woman had only greeted him because she thought he had clocked her. In fact, his thoughts had been far away, and he barely registered her except as one of the 'Lycra brigade' out pushing a bicycle and making the most of the sunshine.

'Are you a rower?' he asked courteously.

'I try to get out most days when work allows — just for my own pleasure, though I was in Latimer's first eight back in the day. I'm on my way to the boathouse now.'

It felt as though the admission had been dragged out of her and, seeing that she was clearly loath to linger, Markham said charmingly, 'Nothing half so much worth doing as simply messing about in boats. Please don't let us detain you.'

She smiled at the allusion, but her expression was tight.

'A bit of a sportswoman then,' Olivia observed as Freda Carrington continued along the towpath without looking back.

'Well, she certainly looks a different person in her rowing kit.' He sighed. 'Another dark horse.'

With an effort, he consigned the riddle of Freda Carrington to the back of his mind, to be taken out and puzzled over later.

'How did you enjoy that film you went to see at the Reynolds . . . *Shackleton's Antarctic Adventure*, wasn't it?'

'It was amazing seeing it on a giant screen, Gil. The photographs were incredible . . . His ship was like *The Flying Dutchman*, only spookier.' She gave an involuntary shiver.

'And the crew in their balaclavas and layers and huge gloves looked sinister . . . like medieval warriors in chain mail.'

Sinister. The word hung in the air.

'Well, they were bashing seals and penguins over the head, weren't they?' Markham quipped, struck by the analogy. 'I suppose it was a question of survival.'

She shook herself as though to dispel a bad dream. 'On the one hand, Shackleton's crew clung to civilised rituals . . . their concerts and singalongs and toasts, playing football out on the ice pack—'

'Like the soldiers on Christmas Day in No Man's Land.'

'Yes, or some Edwardian fantasy, but at the same time, they're these expressionless creatures muffled up to the eyeballs like a regiment of statues or Abominable Snowmen, so you can't tell one from another.'

'That's Antarctica for you — an inhuman landscape,' Markham observed.

'Too right. The icebergs made me think of giant molars waiting to gobble them up.' Shamefaced, she added, 'I'm letting my imagination run away with me.'

'Not at all. Seems to me it's beautiful but deadly out there at the ends of the earth.'

'Like Narnia, all bleached and pure but one false step and you die. There's something deceitful and twofaced about the way it beckons people to their deaths.'

Hearing this, Markham had the uneasy sense that he had missed something. Something which eluded him, its snake tail sliding back beneath the surface . . .

But it was gone, and Olivia was speaking again.

'Dr Ashworth's invited me to a private view at the museum this evening. You could come too?' she added diffidently.

'A private view . . . Hmm, sounds rather exclusive,' he remarked, raising his eyebrows.

'Some of the exhibits are only on loan for a limited time,' she told him. 'And there are others that didn't even end up getting put on display. Dr Colthurst's murder threw everything up in the air and they had to cancel some events.

It was hard on the museum staff, too. I think Dr Ashworth wants to salvage what he can.'

'I've no objection, sweetheart, but in the circumstances, I'd best make it official and bring the team along . . . D'you think Ashworth could cope with that?'

'Well, with George being such an enthusiast, perhaps he won't mind.'

'Doyle and Burton too . . .' Markham smiled. 'Shouldn't wonder if Kate isn't in Blackwell's scouring the Natural Sciences shelves as we speak.'

Olivia felt a pinch in her chest. Markham was quite unaware that his voice softened whenever he mentioned his earnest colleague, but his girlfriend's jealous ear registered every nuance. Even though Kate Burton was now officially 'spoken for', there was still that indefinable *something* between herself and 'the guvnor' — an affinity that nibbled at the edge of Olivia's consciousness and troubled her. However, she hated the idea of anyone intuiting her discomfiture, least of all Markham, and so turned a bright face towards him.

'The more the merrier,' she said.

Markham, as oblivious to Olivia's unease as she had intended, smiled back at her, his mind already on the opportunities the evening might give him to speak to more people in relation to the murders. He imagined Professor Hanbury would be in attendance at the museum, which also offered a useful opportunity to probe his affiliation to the Titus Oates Society.

'Jonjo Kelleher suggested a meal afterwards,' Olivia said, breaking into his thoughts.

'I'll leave you to do the honours,' he replied. 'Me and the team need to divvy up the tasks for tomorrow.'

'Working on a *Sunday*, Gil?' she lamented.

''Fraid so, Liv. We need to follow up what Milner's given us on the Titus Oates membership as well as that suicide in Sherwin.'

'I thought you said there was nothing doing on the suicide.'

'The college's records dot the i's and cross the t's, but Doyle's had his ear close to the ground and reckons there was a great deal of bad feeling swirling around, so there may be something . . .' Markham hoped he didn't sound as if he was clutching at straws.

'When's your next love-in with Judas Iscariot?' Olivia grinned. 'Too bad those pesky adenoids prevent him giving you his full attention.'

'Sidney's coming up on Monday, so we need traction on Alex Mason's murder.'

'We're only booked in at The Parsonage till Tuesday, Gil.'

'I may have to extend our reservation . . . If push comes to shove, we can always get in at the Randolph.'

Her eyes gleamed mischievously. 'Muriel was up to high doh at afternoon tea. Even George sawing away at the scones didn't bother her.'

He shot her a satirical glance. 'You behaved very well, Liv. I think all in all, Muriel had a good day.'

'And got first-hand news of a murder.' She chuckled. 'She was in such a flutter of self-importance, I had a job decanting her into a taxi.'

'They say virtue is its own reward, sweetheart.'

'Humph. Where Muriel's concerned, I need more than that.' She wrinkled her brow. 'She had a bit of excitement in John Lewis as well.'

'Oh?' He was only half-listening now, lulled by the summer haze and the distant cries from an impromptu game of cricket further along the bank.

'Yes, it was a bit odd. Apparently she spotted a dress that she liked in Women's Fashion, probably one of those godawful Queen Mother numbers she favours. The store was fairly quiet, so she popped into a changing room to try it on. Everyone has their own curtained cubicle . . . so there's no risk of anyone seeing a beached whale moment.'

'*Liv.*' But, despite his obvious efforts, the reproof was mixed with amusement.

143

'Anyway, the changing rooms were empty and she found it a bit spooky. She'd just wrestled herself out of the old corsets or whatever, when suddenly there was a noise and this bloke's face appeared round the corner of the curtain. Gave her quite a turn.'

'A member of staff presumably?'

'*God*, Gil, you're behind the times . . . They don't allow men into the ladies' changing rooms.'

'I'm sure I've seen waiting areas with gents lolling about in armchairs.' He grinned. 'Desperate to get out of there . . . like they're trapped in that *Father Ted* sketch about men lost in the lingerie department.'

'Priests,' she amended. 'That's what made it so funny.'

'Indeed. Well, to get back to your story, what did Muriel do?'

'Nothing. She just gaped at him . . . couldn't find her voice, which makes a first. He stared back and then disappeared.'

Markham yawned drowsily. There was something hypnotic about the flowing water and the desultory slap of oars. 'So, all's well that ends well,' he concluded.

'I guess so. But she seemed pretty freaked out . Reported it to the staff but didn't get the feeling they took her seriously.'

'I wonder she didn't mention it to me,' he said then smiled. 'Too delicate a subject perhaps.'

'You mean the notion of Muriel in the altogether might have aroused unseemly passion?'

'Liv, you're incorrigible.' But the hawklike features were tender. 'Muriel was too full of Natalie's woes to get sidetracked by her adventures in John Lewis.'

'How come?'

'Tensions at work . . . some artful minx who's accused Natalie of pinching her ideas.' He rolled his eyes. 'We were interrupted by the news of Alex Mason's murder, so I got off lightly.'

'She'll corner you again, Gil, just wait and see.'

'Well, for now I've got a reprieve.' Reluctantly, he got to his feet and extended an arm. 'Come on, I'm in danger of dropping off if we stay here much longer. We can walk back via the Botanic Gardens and look at the roses.'

'*Sweet rose, Thy root is ever in its grave, And thou must die*,' she sang, and jumped up to join him.

'That's what I get for having an English teacher in my life,' he joked, wrapping his arm around her. 'Poetry on tap.'

But later, as they arrived back at the Old Parsonage, he found that somehow the words had lodged themselves in his brain and would not be dispelled.

Thou must die.

It felt almost like a prophecy.

* * *

The private view turned out to be thoroughly enjoyable.

If Ashworth and Kelleher were uncomfortable at learning that Olivia was Markham's partner, they gave no sign. Proceedings commenced with a short talk followed by a tour of the exhibits, Noakes in particular drinking everything in with a wide-eyed wonder which was eminently gratifying to their hosts.

'*Imagine it*,' he breathed. 'All that time out on the ice an' at sea. Then marching nonstop across South Georgia to get help for the blokes left behind on the island, poor sods must've been terrified Shackles wouldn't make it an' then they'd be stuck there forever like Robinson Crusoe . . . sinking in all that penguin shit, like drowning in fish paste or summat.'

The director smiled indulgently at this. 'One of the crew actually refused to eat penguin because he believed the souls of dead fishermen lived inside them.'

Like his boss, Jonjo Kelleher clearly enjoyed Noakes, regaling him with anecdotes about sailors whose cutlery froze to their lips and tongue, though some of the snootier visitors looked askance at the loudly guffawing policeman.

'It says here the surgeon handed out cocaine to keep 'em going, "Forced March" tablets . . . Must've been high as kites when they got to that whaling station.'

Olivia, lissom in a turquoise wrap dress and sandals, red hair coiled in a simple bun, linked her arm through his. 'Come over here, George . . . There's a sailor said he put his friend's feet between his stomach and jersey to warm them up — just like a hot water bottle!'

Markham smiled as he watched his wingman and partner oohing and aahing over the exhibits. Burton and Doyle were no less fascinated, though less exuberant about it, the latter poring over the account of an improvised amputation on Elephant Island and gleefully reciting the gory details to his colleague.

Burton was unnerved by images of the polar explorers, commenting on their strange homogeneity. 'Like blank eyed zombies,' she said.

'So would *you* be after fifteen months stuck on the ice,' Noakes retorted, overhearing this remark.

'It's just that it's strange seeing the photographs of them in best bib and tucker at dinner on the ship and then wrapped up in their reindeer pelts or whatever in the snow . . . like creepy golems or ice men,' she qualified defensively. And Markham was reminded of Olivia's earlier fearfulness when discussing the realm she called Narnia.

The team's unfeigned interest in everything that was on offer allowed the DI to step back and take the measure of the other guests.

Apart from Desmond Milner, his suspects were all there. Professor Hanbury and Dr Peary arrived together, the latter's expression distinctly sour — as though she considered it bad taste to proceed with the evening after Alex Mason's murder. The director had already apologised to Markham for that.

'It's by way of a thank you to some of our sponsors,' he had murmured, gesturing to two well-heeled elderly dowagers. 'Arranged some time ago.'

This didn't appear to cut much ice with Marion Peary, however, while Professor Hanbury had the reluctant demeanour of one who felt obliged to show his face but had little expectation of enjoying himself; added to which, his bad leg appeared to be troubling him.

Maggie Rawson and Evelyn Bennett were also together. Markham felt there was something almost febrile about Rawson whose eyes glittered with a strangely malicious expression, as though the emphasis on the heroic age of exploration stood for a repudiation of Timothy Colthurst and all his works. He noticed that Bennett was getting heavily stuck into the free drink without this having any noticeable effect on her poise or pleasing appearance. Strikingly attired in a peach Arabella dress that skimmed her curves, she easily outshone her companion who wore palazzo pants and a loose top.

'Didn't know those two were mates,' Doyle murmured at his elbow.

'Oxford's a small world,' the DI replied in an undertone. 'They also both had reason to resent Colthurst, maybe even hate him.'

Freda Carrington arrived after the talk in a flurry of apologies which were brushed aside by the director. Like Marion Peary, her outfit was what Olivia would call 'thrown together': a nondescript blouse and skirt. Despite appearing to pay close attention to the exhibits, she appeared ill at ease, never settling in one place and almost seeming to shun the rest of the company.

Markham wasn't sure what he had expected, but felt increasingly deflated as the evening wore on.

It was absurd to imagine the killer would let their guard slip, he told himself. And yet, as he surveyed the gathering from under lowered eyelids, he felt a sensation of something rising ominously to a crescendo, even as the stormy Arctic seas had swilled and surged about Shackleton and his bunch of desperadoes. There was *evil* here in the Shackleton Rooms, but he couldn't seem to locate it though it raised pinpricks all along his neck, his wrists, his arms . . .

The evening gradually wound to a close until only the museum staff were left.

'Sure you won't change your mind about coming for a curry, Gil? We're going to Aziz.' With a mischievous glance at Noakes, Olivia added, 'Jonjo says their poppadoms are the best.'

Markham ignored the expression of naked longing on his wingman's face.

'We've got work to do,' he said firmly, leading his team towards the exit.

Outside it was a lovely balmy evening, the sky still streaked with remnants of a glorious sunset.

Noakes shrugged off the suede fringed jacket which made him look like an overweight Wyatt Earp.

'What about our tea?' he rumbled. 'Them poxy cheese straws and peanuts don' count.'

'We'll pick up fish and chips from that takeaway down from the station,' Markham told him inexorably. 'Then I want to hear what you've got for us on that student suicide, Doyle. Plus,' he gave a thin smile, 'we need a plan for Monday's meeting with the DCI.'

'The draft of a paper Colthurst gave to the Titus Oates Society turned up in the stuff from his house, guv,' Burton told him. 'It was bizarre — full of strange psychological weirdness.'

Noakes looked decidedly down in the mouth on hearing this.

Listening to Burton bang on about Freudian crip-crap was guaranteed to put him off his chips. It was bound to be Oedipus or one of that lot.

But Markham's expression was remote and veiled. What was it Olivia had said about explorers and mothers? Maybe Timothy Colthurst's words held the elusive clue to three murders . . .

This was a race against time as urgent as any Ernest Shackleton had faced.

And the stakes were the same. Life and death.

11. ADRIFT

As Markham sat in his minuscule incident room at St Aldate's Police Station early on Monday 2 August, he felt his perplexity deepening.

For one thing, he wasn't sure what to make of the paper Timothy Colthurst had read to the Titus Oates Society, concluding that Noakes was not unjustified in calling it 'a load of old cobblers'.

Undoubtedly ingenious, it recast the story of Scott's first expedition to the South Pole — when Shackleton had to be towed back to base on a sledge — as a tale of sublimated sexual desire, twisting the accounts of competitive man-hauling into something far darker; assigning Sir Clements Markham a role as the evil genius who had 'turned' both men. Even Shackleton's breach of his promise to Scott not to winter in McMurdo Sound, the 'grave sin' that Scott never forgave, was rewritten as a romantic rather than a professional rupture.

Olivia had scoffed at the very idea. 'Sir Clements was a nice old cove,' she said. 'A real schemer but good fun with it. When the prime minister, Arthur Balfour started boasting about being the "father" of Scott's first expedition, Sir Clements more or less told him to put a sock in it. Told everyone Balfour had a damn cheek. Dr Ashworth said he wrote this letter which said the PM "deliberately announced his intention of allowing them to perish on two occasions: a nice sort of father!!!"'

Markham wished he could summon up the same gung-ho spirit in dealing with DCI Sidney, who he felt was unlikely to be impressed by theories of homosexual intrigue however artfully framed by Kate Burton.

Colthurst's essay had pursued the same tack with Scott and Oates, spinning the love from their mothers, emotional constipation and professional differences into an unarticulated mutual passion and dance of death that was somehow written in the stars.

Although hugely entertaining, it struck Markham that the whole stack of cards was liable to topple over with one good shove. He wondered if Guy Hanbury, Marion Peary or Freda Carrington had been tempted to pinch the life out of Colthurst's fizzing pyrotechnics . . . But a desire to clip the provocative academic's wings was a long way from murder.

Again, Olivia had poured scorn on the whole 'caboodle'.

'Jonjo wasn't at that meeting, only heard about it on the grapevine, thought it was a scream but a million miles from the truth . . . Oates wasn't Scott's type, see. He was well-off and not bad looking — a positive Adonis next to Birdie Bowers — but not the sharpest tool in the drawer. Wilson was quite cruel about it. Let me see if I've got this right, yes, he told Oates, "The way thoughts flash through your mind, Titus, reminds me of a snail's climbing a cabbage stalk." Pretty withering. So, actually, Dr Ashworth said if there was any unconsummated love affair going on, it was the one between Scott and *Wilson*. In the letters and journals, they just *rave* about each other. When the rescue party found the bodies, Scott had his arm flung out across Wilson . . . bedfellows at the last. And Scott's marriage was downright odd. Kathleen was obsessed with the idea of passing on a set of his "heroic" genes, but she messed around with other men. So I'm not sure what kind of physical relationship she can have had with her husband . . .'

In the end, Markham decided he was in Kelleher's camp on this, deciding that Colthurst's theory was merely a clever fiction designed to stir up controversy and publicity. As for Clive Ashworth's speculation about Dr Edward Wilson, he didn't buy that either. With men like Scott and Wilson, what mattered was *the sameness of the goal*. And besides, they had enough to do to keep body and soul together out there in the frozen wastes without expending energy on carnal dalliance.

Colthurst had cleverly parlayed speculation into some eye-catching PR, but it didn't explain how Alex Mason wound up in the Hatton Library with his throat cut.

Maybe Colthurst's theories had nothing to do with it at all.

Maybe his polar obsessions weren't relevant either.

Maybe there was another coefficient they were missing. *But what?*

In the meantime, how to handle Sidney?

He switched on the dilapidated desk fan which appeared on the point of giving up the ghost. Slowly and splutteringly, it began to turn, eventually settling into a rhythmical hum as it stirred the tepid air and fluttered the papers in front of him.

There was barely room to swing the proverbial cat, but no doubt Superintendent Charleson would vacate his own office in the interests of accommodating Sidney. Or 'smarming' as Noakes put it.

Markham's thoughts turned to his wingman, who had startled him on Saturday night after the team meeting by tentatively broaching the subject of leaving the force and life after CID. 'Not yet, guv. Not while you need me, but my face don' fit any more an' I can't dodge the bullets forever . . . Slimy Sid'll get me out one way or another.'

Looking at the battered pugilist's face, Markham felt — like Captain Scott about Wilson or Birdie Bowers — that he could do without *anyone* except this man.

Aloud, all he said was, 'I can't see you being content going down the allotment, Noakesy.'

'Well, the missus won't want me under her feet, that's for sure. An' there's lots out there for ex-job, guv — security in retail for starters . . . one of them big department stores.' Markham could almost hear Olivia's mocking tones: 'And staff discounts to keep Muriel in posh clobber.'

'Or mebbe,' he continued, with elaborate sangfroid, 'I could set up on my own . . . private detective, like.'

The piggy eyes searched Markham's while he rubbed one foot against the back of the other.

'You've got the common touch alright, Noakesy.' *Though quite possibly not tact, diplomacy or a gift for paperwork.* 'And no one can touch you for determination.' *Or sheer bloody mindedness.* 'I reckon you'd be a natural.' He was likely to regret the next bit. 'And you know you can always count on me.'

The DS shuffled his size twelves and stroked his face down hard, making his bulbous nose more mottled in the process. Clearly much gratified, he grasped the guvnor's hand and wrung it hard. 'Mind, I'm not ready to jog on yet, boss. Reckon there's life in the old dog yet.'

'I don't doubt it.'

When Markham reported this exchange to Olivia, she was tickled pink by the notion of Noakes as a gumshoe. 'I think it's *brilliant*. Perry Mason eat your heart out, and one in the eye to Judas Iscariot!' she added gleefully.

Temporarily parking the conundrum of Noakes, he turned back to the current investigation and the frustrating lack of progress.

There was no way Sidney would wear any overly speculative psychoanalysis informed by twenty-first century hindsight, though he had no doubt Kate Burton would do her best.

At the moment, all they had was the undoubted acrimony generated by that student suicide which appeared to have stirred up various partisan factions.

He thought back to their discussion on the subject . . .

Doyle told them Desmond Milner had been a close friend of the youth who killed himself by jumping from Sherwin's clock tower. 'Word has it that Milner and Colthurst fought

. . . Milner was angry cos lover boy wouldn't go on record about Hanbury being a bully.'

Burton pursed her lips. 'Hanbury doesn't look the bullying type,' she said dubiously.

'The prof's gone downhill in the last few months according to the porters,' her colleague said. 'He wasn't always a decrepit old saddo.'

'Could Hanbury have been sexually involved with his student?' Markham enquired.

'If he *was*, nobody's prepared to stick their neck out about it,' Doyle replied gloomily. 'By all accounts, Maggie Rawson, Marion Peary and Freda Carrington were right behind him and thought Colthurst was a fink for the way he behaved. That lot at the museum didn't like it either . . . in their eyes Hanbury's a decent bloke, whereas Colthurst was always throwing his toys out of the pram.'

'Any connection that we know of between Hanbury and Alex Mason?' Markham pressed.

Doyle shook his head. '*Nada*, boss. Nothing more than what he had with all the porters at any rate — you know, just the odd friendly word here and there, nothing out of the ordinary.'

So that left him with precisely *zilch* for Sidney.

Markham pushed his chair away from the rickety desk and walked over to the window.

There was little traffic outside at this hour, but it already felt oppressively warm, and he thought wistfully of Olivia who would shortly be on her way to Blenheim Palace. 'Got to pay my respects to Winston Churchill's birthplace,' she had announced the previous evening. 'By way of reinforcing my capitalist credentials at Hopeless, you understand,' she added with a wink. Sensing his dejection at the prospect of briefing the DCI, she had told him, 'Why don't you take a tip from Churchill, sweetheart.'

'Let's hear it.'

'Some toff or other challenged Winston to a game of backgammon, warning him that he played well. "That's alright," replied the great man. "I play low." So you see, that's the best way to tackle His Sliminess, Gil. Remember, *play low*.'

Excellent advice, if only he could pull it off . . .

In the event, Markham wasn't obliged to resort to such tactics because Sidney appeared almost *sympathetic* to his dilemma, which practically caused Noakes to fall off his chair.

'Christ, has he had a personality transplant or what?' the DS demanded afterwards. 'I mean, he were almost *reasonable*.'

'It's his hay fever,' Doyle interjected cynically. 'He just wants to lie down in a darkened room and not have to bother about pervy dons and secret societies.'

Burton was thoughtful. 'He didn't dismiss the psychology angle out of hand.'

'Thass cos he wants to look trendy an' *with it*,' Noakes said scornfully. 'Plus, getting a criminal profiler in makes it look as if things are moving . . . when they bleeding well *ain't*.'

'I think he appreciates we have to tread carefully,' Markham countered. 'Remember, it's only been a week.'

'An' *three* sodding murders.'

The DI reflected that his wingman was a walking incarnation of the famed Churchillian 'capacity for being utterly unreasonable'.

'The DCI seemed to think a press conference about the psychological consultation might be in order,' he said.

'As in ole Shippers,' Noakes said with a confidential nod in Burton's direction. 'Though Sidney looked a bit creeped out when you got on to them LGBT crime statistics an' interpersonal whatchamacallits, luv.'

'Transgressions,' she said resignedly.

'Yeah, them.' Her colleague was totally unabashed. ''Course, you prob'ly get a higher class of hack with it being Oxford, so if you wheel out the Bamber Gascoigne bollocks they'll most likely go gaga.'

Burton looked pained but didn't dispute the value of this modus operandi.

'A nexus of inchoate correlates,' Sidney had brayed at the conclusion of her recital, plundering the latest whizzy lexicon.

'In other words, a better class of criminal,' Doyle translated afterwards. 'Though preferably a drone not a don.'

Whatever the reason for his reprieve, Markham was devoutly thankful.

'Let's follow the example of Shackleton,' he said wryly, 'and take our stand in Patience Camp.'

'*Eh*?'

'That's what Shackleton called the tents and boats they pitched out on the floe after the *Endurance* went down,' he explained to his baffled number two.

'Oh, I'm with you, boss.'

Noakes plucked irritably at the soup bowl sized hemispheres of sweat already creeping across his chest from the armpits of his ill-fitting blazer. '*Phew*, that fan's chuffing useless an' it's too hot to *think*. Why don' we get outa here an' crack on . . . in the field,' he added, for all the world like he imagined this was *CSI* Markham thought ruefully as he contemplated his paunchy subordinate's ill-concealed eagerness to escape from the station.

There was a knock and a young woman's head appeared round the door.

'There's a gent at the front desk asking for you, Inspector . . . something about a disappearance.'

Markham nodded to Noakes.

'Out *in the field* you said, Sergeant. Looks like your wish is about to be granted.'

* * *

The man in question was a mild-featured middle-aged character, with thinning sandy hair and a stoop, who appeared tired and strained.

Without preamble, he told them, 'My name is Frank Carrington and I want to report a missing person, Inspector . . . my wife, Dr Freda Carrington. She told me you visited her in college the other day, so I remembered your name.'

Quietly and without fuss, Markham had a civilian clerk sort a room (*not* a soulless interview room but one with a window) and well-sugared tea. He tried to give no hint of alarm, but something deep inside warned him this new development was unlikely to end well.

With the sure instinct he rarely displayed in dealing with his superiors but that never failed him in dealing with victims or anyone 'in a jam', Noakes said, 'The doc's gaff in college was dead impressive . . . She said it were all down to you. *My* missus'd *never* trust me to do a place up.'

The tired face relaxed.

'Freda has very good taste,' he smiled, 'but she always left that side to me. Oxford Brookes is all plate glass and steel, so it was a treat to be let loose in Latimer.'

Gently, Markham brought him round to the circumstances of his wife's disappearance.

It turned out that Freda Carrington had headed down to Christ Church on Sunday afternoon for 'a bit of a workout'.

'Was that her usual routine?' Burton enquired.

'Yes.' Another weary smile. 'She loves the river and keeps herself fit. Didn't want the dreaded rounded shoulders from being hunched over her books all the time. As you can see, it's too late for me, but she was a decent oarswoman and tried to keep her hand in.'

'When would you have expected her back?' Markham prompted.

'Well, she left around two . . . I was surprised when she wasn't back by six, but I had a meeting in Headington, so my mind was on that.' He pulled a face. 'I wouldn't normally go in on a Sunday, but we're pitching for a grant and there's a deadline looming. We unwound afterwards with wine.' Sheepishly he added, 'Quite a lot of wine.'

Noakes was full of sympathy. 'Know the feeling, mate. I feel the same way after one of our freaking inclusion workshops.'

A frown puckered Kate Burton's brow, but Noakes's irreverent aside seemed to reassure their visitor who resumed his story.

'I was late getting home . . . didn't realise she hadn't come back.'

'You don't share a bedroom then?' Doyle asked bluntly, colouring at the look Burton shot him. She looked even more disapproving when Noakes helpfully explained, 'Posh folk always have separate rooms.'

But Frank Carrington was untroubled, smiling at the uncouth policeman's gloss.

'I use my dressing room if I'm back late and don't want to disturb Freda. She's a poor sleeper, you see.'

Markham was struck by that. Recalling the woman's distracted body language at the private view, he wondered if there was something particular preying on her mind.

Doyle was anxious to redeem himself. 'When did you realise something was wrong?'

'This morning when I went in with a cup of tea at six. The bed hadn't been slept in and there wasn't any message.' Anticipating their next question, he continued, 'We were happy . . . everything was going well. There was no reason for her to go off like that. It would be totally out of character.'

'Could she have gone to see a friend . . . spur of the moment?' Burton pressed.

'No, I don't think so. She kept office hours even during the holidays and would never do something like that "on a school night", certainly not without telling me. She's considerate . . . knew I'd be worried.'

'So as far as you know, the last place she went was the river?' Despite the easy tone, Markham saw that Noakes's left leg was jiggling under the table. Like his boss, the conviction was creeping over him that Freda Carrington had come to harm.

At the hands of a killer who had already taken three other lives.

Burton and Doyle looked tense, the former carefully smoothing the lapels of her Zara jacket in a gesture that Markham recognised as her displacement mechanism.

'Inspector . . .' Frank Carrington had got there too. 'Could this be linked to the museum murders?' He placed one lean hand on top of the other as though to stop it shaking. 'Freda was terribly upset when she heard about that porter at Sherwin . . . kept saying it made her feel like she had blood on her hands—'

'*Blood on her hands?*' Markham interjected swiftly. 'But why would she think his death was *her* fault.'

Frank Carrington raised his hands palm upwards in a helpless gesture then let them drop.

'It didn't make sense . . . Now I curse myself for not really paying attention. I answered something like, how was she to know? What could she have done? and she clammed up . . . said maybe she should have been more upfront about Tim Colthurst, academic rivalries . . . that sort of thing.'

'You're sure she said academic rivalries?' Burton asked intently.

'Not totally,' he replied wretchedly. 'I could see she didn't want me to go on about it, so I backed off and talked about something else. My wife's very high-minded . . . takes things to heart. So I decided she was blowing things out of proportion and taking everything on her own shoulders.' He laced his fingers tightly so that the knuckles showed white. 'Now I wonder if maybe she wasn't trying to tell me something, but I was just too selfish to listen.'

'Don' beat yourself up.' Noakes leaned over and gave him a clumsy pat on the arm. 'Happen she were jus' trying to work things out . . . didn't want to talk about it till she'd thrashed it out in her own mind.'

Carrington looked at him gratefully. 'Yes, that was probably what she planned to do at Christ Church Meadow while she was sculling.' A faint laugh. 'She used to say she made some of her best decisions out on the water.'

With a cold feeling at his heart, Markham suspected Freda Carrington had been steeling herself to come to the police.

Only, someone intercepted her.

He looked at Burton.

An unspoken signal.

Keep him here while we get down to the river.

She cleared her throat. 'Sir, Sergeant Doyle and I are going to go through the background with you while Inspector Markham makes some enquiries.'

Carrington looked dazed.

'Shouldn't I come with you, Inspector? I know she's not at the boathouse. I checked on the way here. It was unlocked. I called through the door, but no one answered.'

Again, Noakes's meaty paw rested on his arm.

'Me an' the boss are jus' going to have a word with the college folk in case—' Inspiration struck him, '—some spotty student nerk had a breakdown an' your missus had to look after 'em.'

'*All night?*'

'Mebbe it were a big crisis . . . hospital job even.' Noakes clearly had no trouble imagining some bolshie undergraduate going doolally.

'Or she could've had a big idea . . . for a book or summat, an' decided to go into the office. Y'know, *burn the midnight oil* . . . Ain't that what you brainy types call it?'

The pale strained look subsided into a smile of genuine amusement.

'I'm not sure about an essay crisis, Sergeant, but it's possible something came up at Latimer that I don't know about.'

It sounded almost like a plea.

'DI Burton'll look after you,' Noakes said kindly. 'She an' the lad here are *graduates*.' For once he didn't make it sound like a term of abuse. 'Know all about "isms" an' whatnot . . . right up your street.'

Burton gave Doyle, who was catching flies, a sharp nudge. The young detective got to his feet, his tone smooth and untroubled.

'If you'll follow me, sir. We can just pop into the . . . inspector's office. It's tedious going over things like this, but the more we know the better.'

He had been going to say, 'incident room', but stopped himself in the face of Frank Carrington's stricken expression.

'I'll be along in a minute,' Burton said, springing up to open the door.

Once they were safely out of the room, she turned to Markham.

'Not looking good is it, guv?'

'I'm afraid not.'

The DI raked his thick black hair with an unusually savage gesture.

'She didn't trust us enough,' he said.

Noakes heard the undertone of raw anguish.

'You *warned* her, guv. Sounds like she were gearing herself up to tell us but . . .'

'She ran out of time,' Burton finished bleakly.

Markham straightened up. 'Whatever trouble she ran into, I reckon it was there down by the river. Either someone lured her to the boathouse, or she made an arrangement to meet them—'

'Or they knew her routine and followed her,' Noakes chipped in.

'Correct. So we'll scope out Christ Church Meadow while Kate and Doyle get as much as they can from that poor bastard back there.'

It was rare for Markham to lapse into the vernacular, and Noakes's expression comically suggested he couldn't have been more surprised if the guvnor had embarked on a striptease. Burton, meanwhile, concentrated on looking inscrutable.

'C'mon, Noakesy,' his boss said grimly. 'Time to walk.'

* * *

As they made their way to the meadow — Markham striding impatiently ahead while his wingman puffed along behind like a superannuated tugboat — the DI reflected on Kate Burton's generosity of spirit in allowing herself to be relegated to the subordinate job of statement-taking. Instinctively, she had understood that something in him baulked at subjecting her to a rerun of their last horrible riverside salvage operation and, while her feminist hackles might have bristled at his misplaced chivalry, she surrendered the honours to Noakes who was as comfortable to his boss as an old pair of slippers.

They reached Latimer's boathouse in double quick time.

It was a trim old-fashioned building, rather like a barn conversion, with black timber cladding and a quaint weathervane topped with an owl, its steel wings outspread. A little wooden jetty led down to the river.

'I seem to remember they built an extension for new changing rooms and showers,' Markham muttered, leading the way round the back.

The ladies' showers were what Noakes considered manky.

'Don' think much of the grouting,' he said. 'An' as for them scratty ole curtains . . . *Oh no* . . .'

His grumbling tailed off abruptly as he came to the final shower stall.

Amongst the flowering pansies of the fabric were ugly crusty brown stains that they recognised immediately as dried blood. A trail of similar splotches led from the cubicle along the nonslip quartz flooring to the emergency exit which swung wide open.

'So it *wasn't* pre-arranged,' Markham breathed. 'The killer was stalking her . . . caught up with her as she was about to get in the shower—'

'But she escaped somehow an' ran out to the riverbank.'

The two men, now moving as one, headed through the side door and back round to the front of the building. Looking up at the boathouse, it now seemed to Markham that the previously harmless-seeming owl was transformed into a predatory harbinger of disaster.

They followed the blots along the sandy gravel of the boathouse forecourt and down to the water's edge.

'Nowt there,' Noakes said hoarsely, sagging with relief. Then he jackknifed as though someone had punched him in the solar plexus. 'Oh *fuck*.'

Markham followed his wingman's gaze to a narrow spit of silt on the far side.

It took a moment for the DI to register that he wasn't looking at a sandbank.

Radiating out from the dark shape that he had taken to be sludge were long strings of moving spawn.

And *still* his stubborn brain struggled to process it.

Not pondlife.

Hair.

Despite the heat of the day, Markham felt suddenly ice-cold, suddenly back in that nightmare where Timothy Colthurst's waterlogged corpse rose up from the depths and would not stay down.

He forced himself to breathe deeply through his mouth, steadily in and out, until he was able to speak.

'We need a recovery team and Dr Merrick down here right away.'

To the DI's surprise, his own voice sounded perfectly normal, though Noakes's putty-coloured face looked as though it could never recover its usual apoplectic hue.

Afterwards Markham would remember that his last thought before turning away was thankfulness that Kate Burton never saw the long strands undulating like eels in the stagnant water.

12. DEATH SPIRAL

The Old Parsonage Hotel reserved its library exclusively for the team's use that night.

It was a quirky space whose uneven, creaking floor-boards reminded Markham of the Grapes, their favourite pub in Bromgrove where there was also that feeling of listing gently in some nautical floating home.

On the other hand, the black and white photographs of 1960s Oxford gave the room a slickly modern feel, though there was a wraith-like and poignant dimension to the students intent on their punts and croquet.

Once sorted with drinks, they drifted out onto the little courtyard terrace, Doyle carefully closing the sliding glass doors for greater privacy. The evening air was sweet-scented and balmy, with the voices of late-night promenaders borne on the summer air.

'I'm not buying it,' Noakes growled after his first gulp of Ruddles. '*No bleeding way.*'

'Bleeding' being the operative word, Markham reflected as he savoured his restorative Châteauneuf-du-Pape.

'Let's think about what Dr Merrick told us,' he said carefully. 'As things stand, it appears Dr Carrington became

163

disorientated and somehow managed to knock herself out or slip in the ladies' showers at the boathouse.'

'*Phsaw.*' Noakes was disgusted, the stubbly face seamed and grubby with the exertions of the day, having crumpled his blazer into a ball with the carelessness of an old seadog.

Burton and Doyle, still smart and immaculate, had attracted no untoward notice when they arrived at the hotel, though the duty manager's expression as he eyed Markham's wingman strongly suggested he was longing to recommend that 'sir might care to freshen up'. In the end, the wary concierge decided discretion was the better part of valour.

The DI tried again. 'Something or someone disturbed Dr Carrington at the boathouse. According to Dr Merrick, there were no signs that she had suffered a stroke or seizure or anything of that nature, so his best guess is that she was startled and initially banged her head in the shower after stumbling . . . then she came out of the changing rooms and lost her bearings due to concussion.'

'*Gimme a break.*' The Ruddles was no antidote to Noakes's rage. 'We *know* what happened. *Chummy came for her.*'

Now Doyle stepped up to the plate. 'Merrick said her body didn't show any signs of a struggle . . . no defensive injuries or signs of her being forced to take anything.'

Noakes scowled. 'That's cos the killer didn't *need* to chuck owt down her throat or have a wrestling match. Once she'd injured herself, it were a walk in the park chasing her into the river.'

'What about those reports of a Peeping Tom hanging round the boathouses?' Burton put in. 'Superintendent Charleson seemed to think what happened to Dr Carrington might relate to that . . . nothing to do with the museum murders.'

'Charleson couldn't find his way out of a paper bag,' Noakes said scornfully. ''Sides, him an' the colleges are freaking *desperate* to play down stuff about pervy dons, sex games an' secret societies.'

'True,' Markham observed quietly. 'But the fact remains, what happened could have been a tragic accident.' He suddenly remembered Muriel Noakes's close encounter with a voyeur in the changing rooms at John Lewis. 'Dr Carrington slipped and fell — blood inside the shower stall is consistent with that — and then staggered outside. Whether or not she was surprised by an intruder is a matter of conjecture. As things stand, forensics can't make it stand up.'

'Useless gits.' Was Noakes's scathing verdict. Then his prize-fighter's features softened. 'I thought poor ole Frank were going to keel over on us. Like it were somehow *his* fault she couldn't swim. An' then rambling on about her having Celtic blood an' the Irish being afraid of water . . . poor ole sod.'

'Not being able to swim wouldn't have made any difference if she was dazed and groggy,' Burton pointed out. 'Though,' with a frown, 'you'd have thought it'd be compulsory for rowers.'

'Infringement of their human rights,' Noakes jeered. Then, 'Jigsaw Man knows as well as we do . . . That maniac came for Carrington . . . knew her routine, so it were easy to corner her.'

'Proving it is another matter, Noakesy,' Markham said mildly. 'At least with things as they are, we don't risk banner headlines about victim number four.' He nodded approvingly at Burton. 'You did a good job damping things down when the *Oxford Mail* got on to it.'

His fellow DI smiled thinly, reflecting that she had earned her spurs over the years deflecting various persistent newshounds back in Bromgrove.

'Carrington died some time Sunday afternoon,' Noakes ruminated. 'Which means practically any of 'em could have done it.' He polished off his beer, looking wistfully towards the bar inside. 'Disney Girl an' the crosspatch lass had the best opportunity of all. I mean, they admitted being out there *jogging*.'

'Evelyn Bennett and Maggie Rawson,' Burton amended punctiliously, having never accustomed herself to Noakes's chronic habit of rechristening suspects. 'Mind you, Professor Hanbury and Dr Peary were at the Head of the River having that pub lunch . . . They're each other's alibi, which means that either or both of them could have slipped away from the beer garden and nipped down to the boathouses.'

'Can't see Hanbury "nipping" anywhere with that gammy leg,' Noakes objected.

'Ashworth and Kelleher were working at home, doing their notes for that Norman catalogue thingy,' Doyle mused. 'Which just leaves Milner propping up the bar in the Lamb and Flag . . . only no one has a clear recollection of him being around for the whole afternoon.' He gave a gargantuan yawn. 'Like you said, sarge, any of 'em could have done it.'

Noakes clearly found the endorsement cold comfort.

'So what are we gonna do?' he demanded.

'Get our heads down for now,' Markham said firmly. 'With a good night's sleep, maybe things will seem clearer in the morning.' His gaze beady, he added, 'That means straight back to Malmaison, Noakesy, and no pit stops en route.'

'We need summat to mop up the booze,' his wingman said craftily.

'Room service. *Within reason*, mind, or Sidney'll create a stink about officers living high on the hog.'

Point won, the DS led his colleagues away, Burton flashing Markham a resigned smile as they headed through the terrace doors.

After they had gone, Markham sat for a long time staring into the inky blackness of the night.

In his innermost being, he felt that what had happened to Freda Carrington was no accident. Closing his eyes, he recalled the sodden bundle fished out of the ooze and scum, its eyes staring upwards. Freda Carrington was still in her rower's kit, but the flyaway hair had been loosened from its braid, an elastic toggle round her wrist suggesting she had been interrupted just as she was preparing to rinse herself off, a deep gash on her forehead the only sign of injury. He had felt *himself* to be the voyeur as the dead woman's flesh slapped wetly beneath Dr Merrick's gloved hands, the pathologist intent on his task like some demonic fishmonger, gulls swooping overhead in a bid to stake out potential carrion. Involuntarily, the DI recalled the museum's photographs of skuas and petrels which picked their way through the remains of dead seal pups in Antarctica and shuddered.

Finally, slowly, he roused himself, drained the last dregs of his red wine and headed for bed.

* * *

Markham had hoped not to wake Olivia, but she wasn't asleep, curled up in an armchair that she had pulled onto their little balcony.

She already knew about Freda Carrington courtesy of a text earlier, but now listened attentively as Markham got changed and made tea, heaping the cushions on their double bed round her as he swiftly glossed over the riverside horrors in favour of the team's theories as to why the don had ended up in the water.

'Something's bothering you,' he said eventually, recognising the signs. 'So go on, what's wrong?'

'It only came to me this afternoon while I was wandering round Blenheim,' she said.

'What did?'

'I was looking at this painting of gun dogs when I remembered.'

He waited patiently.

'That about the black dog,' she said.

'Sorry, Liv, my brain's turned to mush what with everything that's happened today . . . You'll have to rewind for me. What black dog are you talking about?'

'When we were pottering round the grounds here yesterday, you told me how Freda Carrington said Captain Scott suffered from demons. "The black dog was always on his

167

shoulder, and it had to be kept in check or there'd be chaos", something like that.'

'Yes, that's right.' Markham was still mystified as to where this was leading. 'Dr Carrington was interested in the whole man, not just the heroics . . . What of it?'

'Jonjo Kelleher used that exact phrase when we went for our curry after the private view,' she said slowly. 'He was talking about Scott and used the very same words . . . black dog and chaos . . .'

'Maybe he remembered it from a conversation with her.' Suddenly watchful and alert, he added, 'But that's not all, is it?'

'There was something odd about the way he said it, Gil . . . almost a snarl, and then his expression changed back so quickly I couldn't be sure I hadn't imagined it.' She hugged a brocaded cushion as though in self-defence. 'But it wasn't just that . . . Dr Ashworth got on to Scott and J.M. Barrie . . . said something about it being a shame Jonjo hadn't staked a claim to the Barrie stuff for his PhD—'

'But Kelleher never completed a doctorate,' Markham put in. 'Joked about getting distracted and not sticking at it.'

'I think there may have been more to it than that, Gil. You see, Jonjo shot Dr Ashworth this dirty look . . . It was obvious Dr A was embarrassed, as though he'd dropped a clanger . . . he got off the subject in double quick time.' Afterwards, when we'd dropped Jonjo back home, I asked about it and he said it was a bit of a sore point—'

'What was?'

'How Tim Colthurst had muscled in and pinched Jonjo's proposal when they were both at Manchester and passed it off as his own.'

There was a loaded pause before Markham asked quietly, 'How did Colthurst do that?'

'Tim championed queer theory and the idea of looking at the polar explorers from a sociological point of view . . . It's pretty much old hat these days, but back then it was new and buzzy. Apparently, Tim took Scott's involvement with Barrie as his starting point after he got wind of what Jonjo was planning . . . plagiarised a bunch of stuff by the sound of it.'

'So you think Jonjo Kelleher may have hated Colthurst for stealing the glittering future that by rights should have been his?'

'Dr Ashworth played it down . . . said it was ancient history.' Olivia plucked uneasily at the embroidered cushion she was hugging to her. 'But then I thought back to Manchester and remembered hearing something about a massive row between Tim and another student—'

'And you think it may have been Kelleher?'

'Again, there was just *something* about Jonjo's face. For a second, he looked like he wanted to *bite* Dr Ashworth . . . I almost didn't recognise him . . . And then his face went back to its usual calm expression.' Olivia raised troubled eyes to Markham's. 'Plus, there was something he said when we were going round the exhibits at the private view. There was this letter one of Scott's friends had written about Shackleton, condemning him for using McMurdo Sound as the route for his own attempt at the Pole even though he had promised Scott he wouldn't. Jonjo was almost gloating over the letter and kept saying, "Shackleton was in a death spiral after that." Like he thought Shackleton dying young was a *punishment* or retribution for what he had done to Scott.' She pulled a face. 'There was something so cold about the way he said it. Implacable.'

Her uneasiness was rapidly infecting Markham.

A deadly rivalry.

He thought of the Titus Oates Society . . . of Desmond Milner and Alex Mason.

'Is Kelleher gay? I thought he fancied Evelyn Bennett.'

'I wondered about that on account of Jonjo tapping into queer theory for his PhD,' Olivia replied. 'I asked Dr Ashworth about it and he just chuckled . . . said he believed Jonjo is pansexual but as celibate as a monk these days, like himself.'

But what if that wasn't true?

169

Suddenly Markham's mind was racing at warp speed.

What if the long-ago student rivalry with Tim Colthurst had never really gone away?

What if it had just gone into hibernation?

What if the kraken had now awoken . . . ?

So many 'what ifs'.

In that instant, Markham's thoughts travelled to Blackfriars and Desmond Milner sitting between Kelleher and Freda Carrington, with the curator offering to see that the undergraduate got home safely. Could it be that Kelleher's display of interest in 'Evie' Bennett was really a feint to distract attention from a sexual attraction to *Milner*?

Had Kelleher borne Colthurst a grudge not just for stealing his intellectual property but for taking the youngster for whom he nursed a secret passion?

Easy, easy, Markham told himself, the tea going cold as his mind teemed with possibilities.

Olivia's eyes were huge in her pale face.

'Is it *him*?' she whispered. 'Is it *Jonjo*?'

'I think it might be Kelleher, yes,' he told her. He took a sip of the stewed tea and pulled a face.

It broke the tension. Olivia laughed and padded over to the mini fridge.

Deftly, she poured him some red wine.

'It's nothing special and hasn't had time to breathe,' she said. 'But here's some Green and Black chocolate to go with it at least . . . you look as though you could do with an energy boost.'

Markham laughed shakily.

'Is that what Jonjo is now, Gil . . . your *prime suspect*?'

'It's a weird coincidence him coming out with the exact same phraseology as Freda Carrington,' Olivia said slowly. 'And I don't like coincidences.'

Olivia broke off a chunk of chocolate and watched him intently.

'Taken with how you said Kelleher looked,' he continued, 'I wonder if Freda Carrington had confronted him about Tim Colthurst, quoting those words . . . and they triggered something in him . . . then later he followed her to the boathouse . . .' Markham took an urgent swill of wine, now so adrenalized that he knew there was no risk of it having any soporific effect. 'Plus there's the fact that Dr Carrington talked about J.M. Barrie the last time we saw her—'

'So you think she somehow found out what happened at Manchester?' Olivia interrupted eagerly. 'And that made her wonder about him . . . wonder if he had killed Tim?'

'She could have found out about it from someone at the university,' Markham said. 'But if she was doing research on Scott and Barrie, then maybe she came across something by Kelleher.'

'*Of course.*' Olivia was fired up. 'Jonjo would have been doing an MPhil thesis with the idea of upgrading to a PhD later.'

'Didn't he do an MA?' Markham asked. 'I remember Clive Ashworth saying he wrote about the role of the Royal Geographical Society.'

'That's right.' Olivia rolled her eyes. 'But a thesis about some stuffy old institution wouldn't exactly have set the world alight.' Cross-legged, with her hair in bunches, she looked almost too young to be addressing the subject of postgraduate studies with such authority. 'The thing about a PhD proposal is that it has to be *original*. You take a small subject, Gil, and then polish and polish your idea to get it past the university research committee.' She frowned. 'It's quite stressful . . . There are people who just can't be bothered with the pettiness of the whole thing and drop out or have their thesis turned down.'

Markham was temporarily distracted. 'Were *you* ever tempted to do a PhD, Liv?'

'Well, ideally you need an Oxbridge background or to have got a first and—' she shrugged — 'I never managed either . . . And there's the risk you could end up with a lazy supervisor or hostile examiners.'

He suspected Olivia's iconoclastic tendencies might also have proved to be an obstacle, but her feisty independence

171

of mind was one of the qualities that had drawn him to her in the first place.

'You give a copy of the MPhil to the university in partial fulfilment of the PhD, and they make it available online for research. So even if the MPhil doesn't get turned into a book, there's nothing to stop other people citing it as an unpublished thesis . . .' Her voice rang with conviction. 'Tim Colthurst wouldn't have cited Jonjo in his own PhD and subsequent publications — not if he was stealing ideas from him — but maybe someone else credited his theory about J.M. Barrie and Freda Carrington came across it.'

'She would have realised there was this rivalry between Colthurst and Kelleher dating back years,' Markham surmised. 'But how come Colthurst got away with appropriating Kelleher's ideas in the first place? I mean, if you're right about a PhD needing to be original, how was he able to swipe stuff about J.M. Barrie? Wouldn't the university get wise to it?'

'I imagine Tim was clever about it, Gil. He didn't do anything so crude as just copying out chunks of Jonjo's notes . . . maybe just got him talking and sharing ideas—'

'Then plundered them wholesale for his own research?'

'Something like that . . . He most likely went for a niche option like examining parallels between Victorian culture and the Antarctic mythology and then wove JM Barrie into it.'

'Sounds pretty obscure,' Markham observed doubtfully.

'That's the beauty of it. The more abstruse and unusual the better . . . And anyway, Captain Scott's gang were a well-educated lot. Dr Ashworth said you can pretty much tell, from day to day, what they were reading just from looking at the journals and letters . . . It was the same with Shackleton.'

He raised his eyebrows. 'Ah yes, crazy about Robert Browning as I recall.'

'Correct.'

'What about queer theory?' Markham's tone was quizzical. 'Did Colthurst nick that idea too?'

'Jonjo could've planted the seed when they were both postgrads and then later Tim ran with it . . . used it as a springboard to success.'

'I follow your logic, but I think this might be a hard sell.'

She chuckled. 'You mean George.' Her voice tart, she added, '*Kate* is *bound* to like it. Sure to come up with something highbrow about homosexual semiotics.'

He groaned. 'Don't go there, Liv . . . We need to stick to the facts.' Markham contemplated his wine glass as though surprised to find it empty, got up from the bed and began pacing the room. 'Freda Carrington was uncomfortable when talking about her research into the connection between Scott and J.M. Barrie. So much so, that I warned her it was dangerous to keep anything back.'

'Then Dr Ashworth let something slip about Jonjo having researched that very topic when he was a student at Manchester University,' Olivia said. 'And Jonjo didn't like it one bit . . . It was pure Dr Jekyll and Mr Hyde the way he looked.'

'It's possible that Freda Carrington discovered Kelleher had undertaken research on Scott and Barrie at Manchester University when working towards his PhD,' Markham continued, 'maybe via some mention of his unpublished MPhil thesis in a footnote or index . . . at any rate, there was an allusion or citation that led her to wonder about some buried rivalry with Dr Colthurst.'

'Only it wasn't buried,' Olivia said, half-rising from her cushions.

'That's right . . . and something fanned the embers into life.' Markham leaned his forehead against the built-in wardrobes before resuming his pacing. 'It could have been Colthurst's involvement with Desmond Milner for whom he nursed a secret infatuation . . . Or it might have been resentment of Colthurst's increasing fame that he believed came on the back of *his* ideas . . . Or a fatal combination of both.'

'Where does Yvonne Garrard fit in?' Olivia asked.

'Somehow she worked out Kelleher was the killer and tried blackmail,' he said sadly. 'Though we can't be sure of the dynamics between them.'

'Maybe she fancied him,' Olivia suggested. 'Jonjo's like that actor Stephen Mangan . . . lean and rumpled and boyish . . . sexy but appeals to the maternal instincts.'

'I'll take your word for it,' he said, amused. 'Though Ms Garrard didn't exactly strike me as the motherly type.'

'Straightforward lust then,' she grinned. 'Or maybe she wanted to extend her power base at the museum and wanted his support.'

He considered this. 'A coup to replace Dr Ashworth?'

'Yep, with the two of them in the driving seat.'

'You make her sound like Lady Macbeth but yes,' he said slowly, 'I can envisage such a scenario.'

Olivia was pleased with the effect of her arguments. 'She may have sympathised with him as well . . . having to play second fiddle to Tim who behaved appallingly at times.'

'And if he told her about what had happened in Manchester, she'd have been even more on his side . . . more inclined to drop her guard.'

'Exactly.' Jiggling with excitement, Olivia was on a roll. Then she stopped abruptly. 'But where does the murder of poor Alex Mason come into it, Gil? Did *he* go down the blackmail route too? Was he involved with Jonjo and somehow twigged he was a killer . . . ?'

'I don't see Kelleher having a relationship with one of the porters,' Markham replied.

She wrinkled her nose. 'Why, because it was infra dig?'

He thought of the handsome raconteur taking them through the treasures at the Reynolds Museum. 'Something tells me he's a man who places a value on himself. Added to which, I reckon he might be sensitive on the issue of status.'

'Because he's just an assistant curator and not a don?'

'Possibly.'

'Maybe it was connected to that secret club,' she hypothesised. 'The Titus Oates Society.'

'Kelleher was on Desmond Milner's list of people who'd attended meetings,' he shrugged, 'but so were the rest of our suspects along with half of Oxford.'

'Perhaps there's an inner circle Milner, Jonjo and Alex belonged to . . . Alex could've cottoned on to Jonjo being in love with Milner and figured it was a crime of passion.'

'That seems the most likely scenario,' Markham agreed. 'And in terms of blackmail, if Alex had ambitions to get on at Oxford, then Kelleher could have been very useful.'

'There's something terribly cold-blooded about it, Gil,' she said with a shiver. 'If he believed Jonjo had killed Tim Colthurst and Yvonne Garrard, how could he square it with his conscience to stay silent?'

'Self-interest is a powerful motivator, sweetheart. And then, he may not have wanted to turn Kelleher in . . . The man's charismatic and engaging. I imagine he could bring anyone over to his side.' Even at the risk of their life.

'True,' she admitted. 'He was just the same at university . . . don't know how I escaped falling under his spell, but I was somehow immune.'

'Maybe you sensed the trouble he might cause.'

Olivia burst out laughing. 'No, I was waiting for my prince to come,' she told him with a twinkle.

Markham sank down on the pillows next to her.

'We need to blitz Freda Carrington's rooms,' he said. 'See if we can make the connection between Kelleher and JM Barrie.'

'That won't be enough on its own though, will it?' she asked anxiously.

'No, but if we can get something from Manchester University too — something about Kelleher's abortive PhD — it could confirm he's our man.'

'Then what?'

'We set a trap . . . You see, there's no point leaning on Milner or any of the others, because we're not sure of them and don't want to alert Kelleher. Somehow we have to provoke him into a confession.'

'Why don't you use *me*?'

Markham stared at her.

'There's our connection from uni, so he'd be lulled into a false sense of security . . . wouldn't think it was a set-up. Plus, I made a point of telling him and Dr Ashworth that you kept me well clear of your investigations, otherwise they'd have been on edge all the way through supper. I basically said you were paranoid about my safety yada yada . . . So you see, he'll figure you'd never let me disappear somewhere on my own with him if you had any grounds to suspect he was the murderer.'

'Damn right, Liv,' Markham said fiercely.

'*Think about it*, Gil,' she continued earnestly. 'If I were able to lead him on so he agreed to a romantic tryst some-where nice and private — Isis Lock or Folly Bridge, say — you could stake the place out and be waiting for him.'

He shook his head. 'You've got it all worked out, haven't you!'

'You know it makes sense,' she said sweetly. 'All you have to do is shine the spotlight on Milner, so Jonjo thinks he's in the clear because you're going with the idea that Tim's death was a crime of passion . . . He'll assume there's nothing to worry about.'

His expression half admiring, half alarmed, Markham asked, 'What the hell would you say to him?'

'Well, once I'd hooked him — got him believing I was on his side — I'd lead the conversation round to that story about Tim Colthurst blowing up at someone when we were at university. I'd ask if it was him . . . ask if there was some-thing between him and Tim that went sour. I could pretend Freda Carrington had said something to me at the private view which implicated him . . .'

'But Liv, you're *my partner*, remember? Wouldn't Kelleher expect you to go straight to the police if you sus-pected him of murder?'

'Freda Carrington didn't go to the police, did she?' Olivia declared triumphantly. 'He was a friend and she cared about him. Maybe she hoped he would do the right thing and turn himself in? Maybe she wasn't even sure he had killed anyone in the first place and wanted him to prove her wrong . . . It's what people do all the time, right? Take matters into their own hands?'

'Dr Carrington *died* because she decided to go it alone, Liv,' he pointed out gravely. 'If we're right about Kelleher being the murderer, then she must've confronted him with her suspicions — maybe given him an ultimatum — which led to that ambush at the Latimer boathouse.'

'Yes, but it'd be different this time round . . . You'd have staked out our meeting place, so no risk to me.'

'There's *always* a risk.'

But Olivia could tell he was weakening.

'Sidney won't wear it,' Markham said, his brow corrugated at the recollection of his boss's salvoes on previous occasions when Olivia became embroiled in an investigation. 'And besides, it could be dangerous if Kelleher doesn't buy the idea of you being infatuated with him and decides you're better off dead.'

'Oh, I reckon Judas Iscariot would have no problem with me being pushed off a bridge,' she said drily. 'RIP your busybody "lady friend".' Her imitation of the DCI's hectoring bray was uncanny. 'But if the stunt nets a serial killer who (joy of joys) isn't a don or the vice-chancellor, you can bet he'll take full credit . . . spin it as some cunning honeytrap, I shouldn't wonder.'

'You're not going to end up under *any* bridge,' Markham said passionately, twirling a strand of her red hair round his fingers. 'Let's hit the hay and maybe things will be clearer in the morning.' He suddenly felt dog-tired, fatigue hitting him like a sledgehammer. 'I forgot to ask about your excursion to Blenheim,' he murmured drowsily.

She smiled. 'I bought a present for George in the gift shop.'

'Oh yes?'

'A cushion embroidered with some words of wisdom from Churchill.' The gleam in her eyes suggested this was a double-edged souvenir.

'Let's hear it.'

'*I get my exercise as a pallbearer to my many friends who have exercised all their lives.*'

He winced. 'I'm not sure that'll go down too well with Muriel.'

'That's the whole point, you duffer. Subversive or what . . . And the best bit is, Muriel professes to love Winston and all his works, so she won't be able to chuck it without looking unpatriotic.'

'Such guile!'

'Well, Winston and George have a huge amount in common.'

'As in a bottomless appetite and infinite expanse of backside?'

Her soft gurgle seemed to come from far away.

'The guide told me Winston hated food faddists, said nut eaters were destined to die young after a long period of senile decay . . . Which means Kate Burton had better look out!'

* * *

Markham's colleagues were as flabbergasted as he had expected.

'*Kelleher*! Nah, you've got it wrong, guv. That one's sound.'

Noakes contemplated his newly acquired Skechers trainers with satisfaction, glad that Doyle had talked him into the purchase with the crowning argument that he'd be better able to give chase when suspects had it away on their toes. He wasn't sure the Day-Glo orange went well with his striped polo shirt and chinos, but it was good to be at the cutting edge of fashion . . . show those snotty DCs at St Aldate's he wasn't some country bumpkin.

'Hear me out, folks,' Markham said before telling them about his conversation with Olivia the previous night.

His wingman wasn't convinced.

Even his partiality for Olivia didn't sway him.

'It don' add up to diddly-squat,' he insisted stubbornly. 'So what if he used the same phrase as Carrington? Mebbe he just picked it up from some boffin chat about Captain Scott. An' the fact that Colthurst got all the glory for this queer theory stuff don' mean Kelleher killed him for it.'

'Olivia said Kelleher's face changed so dramatically that he almost looked like a different man. And the way he carried on about Shackleton's "death spiral" spooked her . . . For some reason Kelleher seemed heavily invested in the idea of Shackleton being punished for his betrayal of Scott. He was *unnaturally* hung up on it.'

'It's like Scott and Oates,' Burton said unexpectedly. 'Going down together . . . kind of locked into a death-struggle.'

'Only Kelleher ain't going down.' Noakes took great satisfaction in pointing out the obvious.

'He will if we can extract a confession,' Markham said quietly.

The DI explained Olivia's offer to rendezvous with Jonjo Kelleher.

'Are you *nuts*, guv?' Noakes demanded. 'This ain't some bleeding honeytrap scenario like the Rachel Nickell case . . . an' anyway, look how *that* turned out.'

Burton looked equally concerned, marshalling her thoughts as she flicked some invisible fluff off her immaculate taupe trouser suit.

'It's expecting a lot of Olivia,' she said finally. 'And there's no saying how Kelleher will react. He might slash her . . . like Alex Mason. No matter how close we get on the stake-out, all it takes is one mistake, one ill-judged word and then,' she mimed throat-cutting, '*finito*.'

'We haven't got anyone else in the frame,' Doyle mused. 'Nothing to lose really.'

''Cept for looking total prats when we don' get a result and Kelleher sues cos it's one big fat cock-up,' Noakes growled. 'You can bet Sidney an' Charleson an' the rest of 'em won't hold their hands up, guv. It'll be *you* left holding the parcel when the music stops.' He turned away. '*Jesus*.'

'As Doyle has pointed out, we don't appear to have another viable suspect,' came the chilly rejoinder.

Noakes looked at his boss long and hard.

'Where does your Olivia fancy having this little conflab with Kelleher?'

Hearing this, Markham knew the battle was won.

'She suggested Isis Lock or Folly Bridge . . . somewhere off the beaten track.'

'What about Revenger's Folly,' Doyle said suddenly. 'Seeing as he killed Yvonne Garrard there, it must have some special significance for him, 'specially if he gets off on all that stuff about the place being haunted . . . the geologist murdered by his jealous rival and all that jazz.'

'That's not a bad idea,' Burton nodded approvingly. 'Just being back there might flip a switch.'

Markham turned to Noakes. 'Let's you and I do a recce, Sergeant.' To Burton he said, 'Kate, I want you to go through the contents of Dr Carrington's rooms at Latimer. See if you can find any reference to Kelleher in her J.M. Barrie research. Real needle in a haystack, I know,' he added apologetically.

'I'll get her PC checked, and I can see if there was anything she'd had from out the Bodleian.'

Markham suppressed a smile. There was nothing Kate Burton enjoyed so much as trawling libraries, and the Bodleian was arguably the finest bookstore on the planet, having been four hundred years in the making.

'At the private view, I heard Dr Carrington talking about the Map Room,' Burton continued eagerly. 'She was interested in a book Shackleton published in Antarctica—'

'A *book*!' burst from her colleagues simultaneously.

'Him and Scott took their own printing presses,' she said shyly. 'Something to keep the men occupied during the winter.'

Noakes and Doyle exchanged a long look. Trust Burton to ferret out the schoolmasterish stuff.

'Anyway,' she said hastily, aware that football on ice was more to their taste, 'the librarian in there might have an idea what Dr Carrington was looking at, specific reference books or periodicals, that kind of thing.'

'Good idea, Kate. We'll also need a script if we're going to pull this off . . . something to push Kelleher's buttons.'

'I'll get Nathan to help, sir.'

For once, Noakes refrained from any sly digs at 'ole Shippers'. If Olivia Mullen was to be used as bait, then he wanted the whole thing watertight. And words were Kate Burton's forte.

'Doyle.' The youngster snapped to attention. 'I want you to visit the museum. Give Ashworth and Kelleher the idea that we're following up the Titus Oates membership from that list Milner gave us.'

'Chasing our tails, sir?'

'Precisely.' Markham gave a grim smile. 'Have them think we're distracted by the secret society stuff and that I—'

'Can't tell your arse from your elbow,' Noakes grunted.

'You took the words right out of my mouth, Sergeant.'

'What should I say about Dr Carrington, sir?' Doyle asked eagerly, clearly sold on the idea of being a decoy.

'Tell them we're treating her death as unrelated to the other murders . . . potentially down to a Peeping Tom or local lowlife. Arrange for discreet surveillance of Kelleher as well. I want eyes on him at all times.'

'Got it, boss.'

There was an air of suppressed excitement about Burton and Doyle as they hurried off to their respective assignments. Markham could only hope that Olivia's hunch was correct, and they were close to snaring their quarry.

'I know it's a gamble, Noakesy,' he said, 'but if this is a death spiral, we need to stop Kelleher before he takes anyone else down.'

* * *

'I don' like this place.'

Noakes shivered as they moved through the stone interior of Revenger's Folly. 'It feels damp an' dank . . . like you'd get rheumatism living out here.'

'It's just a shell now, Noakes, but once upon a time it was the principal's private retreat.'

'Yeah, *thass* what I don' like about it — the once upon a time bit . . . like we're buried away in the woods in some creepy fairy-tale castle.'

Markham laughed at this.

'We're in the grounds of Ridley College, for heaven's sake . . . just minutes from civilisation.'

'It's got bad vibes, like someone's behind us . . . running their hands along the walls. Yeah, like that extra person Shackleton fancied was following 'em around . . .'

'Get a grip, Sergeant. It's just because you know this place has a history of violence.' Markham touched the chord which was bound to concentrate his wingman's mind. 'If Olivia arranges to meet Kelleher here, then we need to figure out the logistics.'

The strategy worked. Suddenly Noakes was all business.

'There's nowhere to hide,' he said. 'Like you said, the place is a shell.'

Markham thought hard. 'There's the roof.'

'He'd be sure to check it out, wouldn't he?'

'The only way up to the terrace is via the staircase on the right-hand side . . . If we put in some kind of wicket gate and fence the stairs off at the first floor, he won't be able to get up there but we can come down. Olivia can meet him on the ground floor wearing a wire. We'll be on the roof terrace listening in, with access to the stairs so we can get down to them in minutes.'

'Won't he smell a rat?' Noakes asked doubtfully.

'Why should he? Provided we make it look like Ridley got contractors in after the SOCOs moved out, there's no reason why he should query it. I'll get Kate to liaise with the facilities people so it looks authentic . . . this time of year, there's always building work of one kind or another in progress.'

Noakes ran a stubby finger nervously round the collar of his polo shirt, as if he felt some ghostly watcher breathing down his neck.

'Won't he wonder why your Olivia wants to meet *here* of all places? I mean, if she thinks someone's a triple killer — *four* if you count Freda Carrington — wouldn't she want somewhere with folk around? Plus, Garrard got shoved off the roof, so it'd be downright screwy to choose this ole ruin.'

'But that's just it, Noakes. Olivia has to come across as thoroughly disillusioned with her policeman partner and looking for diversion elsewhere . . . moonstruck over Captain Scott and Shackleton and the whole Antarctic shebang.'

'Yeah, but turning a blind eye to *murder* is a whole different ball game . . . And what'll she say put her on to Kelleher in the first place? The connection with the Peter Pan bloke?'

'Yes. And that happens to be the truth, because it was when Dr Ashworth mentioned Kelleher losing out to Tim Colthurst over JM Barrie that alarm bells began to ring.' Markham leaned his forehead against the wall as though willing the stones to speak. Wheeling round on Noakes, he continued, 'She could say she was in touch with a mate from Manchester who mentioned some bust-up with Colthurst . . . We can make up a story that Freda Carrington noticed her warmth towards Kelleher and warned her to steer clear of him. Essentially whatever sounds credible.'

'Okay, but how's she gonna make him cough?' The DS scowled. 'We need a confession, remember, an' he's a crafty sod.'

'She drowns him in sympathy, so he thinks she's making a play for him, looking to ditch the stolid cop boyfriend for something more intellectually satisfying . . . more *romantic*.'

Noakes's piggy eyes opened wide at this.

'She hints at wanting to leave teaching and move into the museum sector,' Markham elaborated.

'No more scabby teenagers . . . Hello Captain Scott an' all them heroic types.'

'Something like that,' the DI agreed, 'but it's got to ring true.'

'Think she can do moonstruck, guv?' Noakes asked anxiously.

'Well, it helps that she and Kelleher were on each other's radar at Manchester. Then they got pretty cosy at the private view and that outing to Aziz.'

'An' she's genuinely nuts about Scott an' Shackles,' the DS pointed out. 'Got the Antarctic bug bad . . . even worse than Burton.'

'It'll be the thespian challenge of a lifetime, but she's up for it.' Markham's voice was proud. 'Actually, she's been reading up on Scott's wife Kathleen—'

'Oh aye, bit of a weirdo weren't she?' Noakes said, remembering what Clive Ashworth had said about her wanting to assassinate Shackleton.

'Yes, decidedly strange, if not unbalanced. Had this bizarre obsession about producing the perfect "boy baby" and picked Scott as the man for the job.'

'For stud, you mean.'

'In a manner of speaking, yes. She saw him as this decent and rock-solid naval officer who would rescue her from the rackety kind of life she'd been living as a girl about town.'

Noakes wasn't impressed. 'A bit cynical if you ask me.'

'Scott's mother would agree with you there. She wasn't at all keen on this cuckoo in the nest.'

'But the lass got a sprog out of it, right?'

'Yes, Peter . . . Kathleen hit the bullseye with Scott, because her son became a distinguished conservationist, painter and naval officer. Hell, he even won a medal at the Olympics.'

Noakes frowned. 'Bit of a miracle seeing as his mum were a crackpot.'

Markham smiled his rare, charming smile. 'She was rude about everyone apparently, even Winston Churchill — said that he might be a genius, but he disguised it very well.'

Noakes's frown deepened at the disparagement of the great man. 'At the private view, Dr Ashworth said Mrs Scott were a real piece of work. One bloke ended up in an asylum cos of her an' she had a fling with some Norskie explorer while Scott were away . . . yeah, fella called Nansen.' The

DS had his witchfinder general's face on as he pronounced judgement. 'Scott were way too good for her, only he jus' couldn't see it. Ashworth showed us some pukey letters he wrote . . . dead soppy.' He sniggered. 'In one of 'em he kept apologising for not fitting in his round hole.'

Trust Noakes, thought Markham wryly. King of the single entendre.

When his sergeant's mirth had subsided, he said, 'Olivia's going to "do a Kathleen".'

'How d'you mean, guv?'

'Give Kelleher the idea she's flighty and volatile . . . fed up with me and ripe for a fling on the side with someone who shares her passion for Antarctica.'

Noakes pondered this.

'You need to build up to it,' he said. 'Let him see the two of you arguing or summat . . . otherwise with it coming out of the blue, he might be suspicious.'

Markham saw the sense in this. 'What would you suggest?'

'Well, while we've got eyes on Kelleher, he can't top anyone else . . . Mebbe you an' Olivia could visit the exhibition together — pretend she wants to show you a bunch of stuff you didn't get round to seeing last time. You come over all lovey-dovey an' she keeps slapping you down like it's a drag.'

'Hmm, sounds like a plan.'

Noakes warmed to his theme. 'She does the Kathleen bit an' makes out like she's got the hots for her very own Arctic Prince. She speaks his language, arty-farty university lingo . . . so he gets the idea she wants summat *intelleckhsal*.'

Markham presumed there was a compliment to Olivia in there somewhere, if you looked hard enough.

'Look boss, if we're going to set up in this dump,' Noakes gestured dismissively at the folly, 'that'll take twenty-four hours. There's the college an' Charleson's lot to be squared an' Olivia needs to be word perfect. In the meantime, you can fit in a side-show to soften Kelleher up — make him think Olivia's interested in him. That way, it's not such a stretch to think she wouldn't grass him up for the murders.'

'I wonder . . . I wonder . . .'

'Sidney'll have you directing traffic if it goes tits up,' Noakes warned.

'Correction. Sidney'll have us *all* back in uniform if we screw up, so let's make sure we *don't*.'

It wasn't a prospect either of them cared to contemplate for very long.

A shaft of sunlight struck through the diamond-paned windows, casting crisscross shadows on the stone floor.

'What if Kelleher don' bite?' the DS asked suddenly, playing devil's advocate.

'I think he *will*, Noakesy.' Markham's clear-cut profile had the concentrated intensity of a bird of prey. 'I think by now the man's under considerable strain with his double life. The need to unburden himself is probably overwhelming . . . and along comes Olivia: the perfect listener.'

Noakes's fists clenched and unclenched. 'If Kelleher tells her what he did, he might decide to kill her instead of doing the dirty on you.'

'Yes,' Markham said simply. 'Once he's established that she hasn't told anyone about meeting him — least of all *me* — then he'll feel safe from discovery.' The DI was as cool as though discussing the weather, but this alternative scenario made his blood run cold.

'How would he . . . you know . . . ?' The other's voice was hoarse.

'Most likely it would be strangulation. No comeback for him to worry about — no connection with the museum. She was in the wrong place at the wrong time. Stranger homicide. Some copycat killer. Case closed.' Markham gave a mirthless laugh. 'Hell, Kelleher might get a kick from imagining *I* could end up in the frame . . . a lovers' tiff that turned nasty. You know the kind of thing. Workaholic detective, mercurial girlfriend, incompatible lifestyles, a fight that got physical. The *Oxford Mail*'d have a field day.'

Noakes's expression said louder than words: *Over My Dead Body.*

Markham grinned. 'Sidney'd have a stroke.'

'Every cloud an' all that.'

The DI suddenly relaxed. Captain Scott had Birdie Bowers and *he* had George Noakes. They *would* make this work.

'My money's on Olivia to draw him in so that he ends up confiding in her by way of romantic foreplay,' he told the DS. 'And then we swoop.'

Noakes nodded slowly.

'Do you remember when we investigated that cult?' he asked unexpectedly, referring to their most recent investigation in London which had centred on a Catholic saint who died tragically young and subsequently achieved worldwide fame.

Markham was intrigued. 'How could I forget!'

'Well, the Captain Scott business is jus' the same. Someone dying young an' folk making it out to be dead glamorous. Even though Scott screwed up big style — making mistakes an' getting beaten by the Norskies — he kind of came out on top an' people thought he were a hero. That Brendan from the museum said the fuss about Princess Di were nothing to it. According to him, it were a bigger story than the *Titanic* going down.'

'It helped that Scott and his men died,' Markham said with an ironic curl of his lip. 'From a PR point of view that's always useful.'

'Only the good die young,' his wingman observed philosophically. 'Bren said the government used the story as war propaganda . . . You know, get the soldiers to think about Scott an' Oates so they wouldn't mind going over the top.'

'A shrewd strategy given that the British army was described as lions being led by donkeys.'

'It's like Scott an' the rest of 'em were saints,' Noakes mused.

'The shock of a million dead soon changed that,' Markham observed. '*Then* it was time to pull Scott down from his pedestal.'

'Yeah, that's when all the conspiracy theories started up . . . stuff about Oates's feet dropping off an' Taff Evans going insane . . . There were even this bonkers argument about which of 'em was last to die an' what happened in that tent at the end.' Noakes's chin jutted out belligerently in a way that Markham knew well. 'But *I* reckon they were proper English gentlemen who stuck it out an' never whinged even though they could've topped thesselves.'

'Olivia would agree with you there,' Markham said gently. 'Scott's death might have been a catastrophe, but there was something glorious about it too . . . It's not surprising his story made others feel they could triumph over disaster, even death.'

Mollified, Noakes remarked with some compunction, 'I may have been too hard on Scott's missus. I mean, *imagine* how she must've felt . . . Out at sea getting this message he'd reached the South Pole when it were all a mistake cos they'd got him mixed up with Amundsen . . . all keyed up to welcome him back not knowing he'd already been dead nearly a year.'

'She certainly got a mixed press.'

'Didn't stop 'em making her *Lady Scott*, though it were really on *his* account.'

'He was a remarkable man.' With a gleam of mischief, Markham added, 'And Olivia says he wrote the most beautiful English to boot.'

'Yeah, scribbling away till he only had that crummy little stub of a pencil an' saying he wanted his family looked after . . . even if his missus *did* get up to all sorts.'

'We need Olivia to give the impression she's somewhat fixated on Kathleen . . . *obsessed* almost—'

'You mean on account of Kelleher being the same an' having a thing about Scott?'

'Exactly.' Markham deliberated for a moment. 'I believe the psychiatric term is *folie à deux*.'

Noakes was interested. 'Like Fred an' Rose West . . . or the Moors Murderers?'

'Yes, only we're not dealing with pathological sadism here . . . more a warped self-identification with Scott and his circle.'

188

Time to extract maximum advantage from the extraordinary concatenation of coincidence surrounding this case, the DI thought.

The DS clearly appreciated the possibilities. 'D'you reckon Kelleher thought him an' Colthurst were rivals like Scott an' Shackleton, or Scott an' Oates, kind of a fight to the death?'

He looked somewhat embarrassed at this flight of fancy, but Markham nodded.

'Yes. There was a sexual struggle too, centring on Desmond Milner.'

Noakes blinked as he absorbed this.

'So Colthurst had to be punished for betraying Kelleher by pinching his stuff an' nabbing his boyfriend . . . same as Shackles an' Oates got *their* comeuppance for falling out with Scott.' The DS whistled. '*Blimey.*' Then, 'What's the idea with your Olivia then. Is *she* going to act like a barmpot?'

'We want Kelleher to think *here's* someone who can understand him . . . who can enter into his fantasy world . . . Someone who's prepared to wink at murder.'

'If he's hyped up like you said an' she comes over all flaky, it could work,' Noakes conceded.

'It's *got* to work,' his boss said tensely. 'Right, let's get a move on . . . we need to liaise with the facilities people at Ridley and see how quickly they can improvise some temporary scaffolding.'

'D'you remember all that about relics when we cracked the Saint Therese case?' Noakes asked as they took their leave of the gatehouse, descending from the upper storey via the spiral staircase.

'Indeed I do.' It had been one of the most gruesome aspects of the cult they had investigated.

'Well, folk treat Scott like a saint . . . apparently his last biscuit sold for four thousand pounds.'

'*His last biscuit*? Wasn't he supposed to have starved to death?'

'His missus pretended they found it in his tent an' it passed down through the family. But it was all a big con. It most prob'ly came from his belongings, not the death tent.'

The death tent.

Markham looked back at the sinister little building, repressing a shudder.

Revenger's Folly had proved a house of death for others. But not, he vowed, for Olivia.

The legend of Captain Robert Falcon Scott lay behind the murders of four people.

Time to break the curse.

13. TERMINUS

It was late afternoon on Tuesday 3 August as Markham and Olivia approached the Reynolds Museum, pausing for a minute to contemplate the sun whose rays struck the tinted plate glass windows like so many golden arrows and steeped the arboreta in a rosy glow that brought trees and sky together in one glorious irradiation.

Markham's colleagues were already inside, ostensibly going over statements with the museum staff while in reality they were observing Jonjo Kelleher.

Olivia paused next to an abstract sculptural installation of a big white arch in two overlapping sections that resembled angel's wings.

'My hands are clammy, Gil,' she said nervously. 'I hope I can bring this off.'

'We're right behind you, sweetheart. And thanks to the Bodleian tipping us off, I'm even more sure that Jonjo Kelleher is our man.'

'Is it *really* enough . . . someone quoting him in an obscure reference book?'

'*That's* the book Freda Carrington consulted, according to the Map Room librarian. We figure she came across the footnote which referred to Kelleher's unpublished MPhil.

191

Then she apparently accessed Manchester University's online catalogue, and there it was . . . Kelleher's MPhil thesis entitled *Robert Falcon Scott, JM Barrie and a Polar-Literary Relationship* . . . I think Dr Carrington recognised the germs of Tim Colthurst's PhD and post-doctoral publications. She must have realised that Colthurst had somehow annexed the queer theory angle for himself, effectively squeezing Kelleher out and demoralising him so badly that he never upgraded his MPhil to a PhD and ditched it all for a boring MA on the Royal Geographical Society. To use a polar analogy, Colthurst planted his flag squarely in Kelleher's territory.'

'In other words, Tim got in first,' Olivia said.

'Yes, it was a case of sharp elbows and unscrupulousness.'

'And just like Scott with Shackleton, Jonjo never forgave him,' Olivia mused, looking apprehensively up at the modernist building, as though fearful of being watched. 'He followed Tim here to Oxford and history repeated itself — only this time it was sex.'

'Correct. Colthurst beat him again, embarking on a relationship with the young man for whom Kelleher nursed an infatuation.'

'You said it looked like Jonjo was carrying a torch for Tim's ex-girlfriend,' Olivia told him tentatively.

'That's right, Evelyn Bennett.'

'So maybe that was *another* conquest he resented,' she suggested.

'It could well have rankled, along with Colthurst's meteoric rise to the top while he languished in relative obscurity as a humble assistant curator.'

Olivia shivered despite the sunshine. 'Horrible to think he waited all that time, watching Tim go from strength to strength . . . determined to end it all . . . extinguish all that promise out of jealousy.'

'He probably rationalised it as Karma. Pay-back for having been thwarted in his career.' Markham's face was sombre. 'That first murder must have been hugely cathartic, liberating . . . whereas I think the rest were a question of expediency.'

'Yes, posing Tim in that creepy ice cube thing. God, that was *ruthless*. Like he was sticking two fingers up to all Tim's achievements.'

She shivered again.

'What made me think I could do this, Gil? Just standing next to him is going to make my flesh crawl.'

'Follow Nathan's cues. Remember, you're a fellow-obsessive . . . hooked on Scott, Kathleen and the rest of them and fed up with the boring policeman who invariably spoils your fun.' He grimaced. 'Don't go overboard. Too much Sarah Bernhardt and he'll be suspicious. I'll do some moody glowering on the sidelines, so he gets the idea that we're thoroughly disenchanted with each other.'

'I'll try to pace it right,' she said. 'If I send out signals of availability and sympathy as per Nathan's script, then hopefully he'll suggest we meet up privately . . . though I've got to make it look like the idea comes from him.'

'Good.' Markham nodded approvingly. 'The team will have sown the idea that we're interested in Milner, so he'll be feeling quite smug and pleased with himself—'

'Ready to cock a snook at the police by stealing your partner.'

'Exactly . . . If he sees you as this kindred spirit trapped in a mismatch, so much the better. The notion of himself as a white knight rescuing you from my clutches will flatter his ego and make him lower his defences—'

'— so he won't be surprised when I condone murder,' she finished grimly.

'That's right. Apart from straightforward animal attraction,' Olivia winced at this, 'you give the impression you're totally on his side because you see him as the victim in all of this — cruelly wronged by Colthurst's machinations—'

'Just like Scott when Shackleton broke that promise not to usurp his "rights" over McMurdo Sound.'

Markham regarded her admiringly.

'You certainly know your stuff, Liv.' He didn't add that her life might depend on it.

'It's strange, Gil,' she replied. 'Somehow Scott and Shackleton and the rest of them have become very real, so that I can almost sense them there beside me . . .'

'Good. That's the vibe Kelleher needs to feel, that you're plugged into the whole polar thing as intensely as him . . . totally on his wavelength.'

'So, how do we play this from here?' she asked.

'We go in together and you zero in on Kelleher straight-away. Ask him about the exhibits, act flirtatious, lean in and create a feeling of intimacy . . . like it's just you and him and no one else exists. We need him to suggest that you get together *privately*. That's the goal, remember.'

'What if he doesn't suggest Revenger's Folly, Gil?'

'He will if you act coy and give him the idea you've got a morbid fascination with the place on account of the ghost stories and Yvonne Garrard having died there . . . Lead him up to it by talking about the supernatural and Shackleton's superstition—'

'That there was always one more person than could actually be counted.'

'Precisely. Nathan reckons Kelleher will find it irresistible to go back there and reinterpret that second murder to a sympathetic audience . . . integrate it into some sort of romantic narrative that enables him to recover his self-esteem.' Markham wanted to caress her but checked himself. Who knew if Kelleher might be watching? 'You arrange to meet him at the folly tomorrow evening, by which time we'll have organised a stake-out on the roof with you wired up.'

'He's lost touch with reality, hasn't he?' she said sadly.

'Yes. His personality's been grossly disfigured by jealousy and the need for self-preservation.' Markham told her. 'Which makes him extremely dangerous.'

'What'll happen to him?'

'A hospital order if he's lucky.' No need to add that Markham thought Jonjo Kelleher was most probably looking at a life sentence in prison. He didn't want Olivia dwelling on likely outcomes in case that somehow affected her projection of an equally disturbed personality.

'Okay,' she said. 'I'm ready. Let's go.'

* * *

Inside the Reynolds, Markham had a bizarre sense of being outside his own body, the feeling of unreality heightened by the aquarium-like atmosphere of dimly lit corridors and galleries.

Olivia lost no time in seeking out Jonjo Kelleher on the third floor. Cleverly, she focused initially on the exhibits, drawing him into conversation about Captain Scott and his expedition colleagues as she moved along the rows of cabinets and display cases.

Snatches of their dialogue reached Markham as he loitered a short distance away.

'No wonder Scott was worried about getting hitched to Kathleen if *that* was his marriage budget. It says here it worked out at about £15,450 in today's money and he had to find them a house on top of that, as well as supporting his mother and sister . . . all out of his naval pay!'

'He suffered from the want of funds all his life,' Kelleher told her with a wry smile. 'Shackleton too. Added to which, Shackles had a disreputable brother who went to prison for fraud.'

'*Really!*' Olivia's wide-eyed impersonation was hitting its mark, Markham decided as Kelleher joined her at a display case.

'Oh yes, fifteen months hard labour. At one time, he was even a suspect in the theft of the Irish crown jewels.' Kelleher's tone was insinuating as he added, 'Frank Shackleton was a rogue, but he held a lethal fascination for the ladies.'

Two heads, one dark and the other red-haired, bent over the exhibits, Olivia ensuring that she stood closer to the assistant curator than was strictly necessary.

After some thirty minutes, with Markham ostensibly brooding on the sidelines as he watched the animated pair, Noakes appeared and lumbered over to his boss.

'You've got a face like a smacked arse, guv,' the DS said.

'That's the general idea, Sergeant,' Markham replied out of the corner of his mouth. 'I'm meant to be channelling the green-eyed monster, remember. That's why Olivia stalked away from me when we came up here.'

'Oh aye, well it's dead convincing.'

'Where are Burton and Doyle?' the DI asked.

Noakes waved vaguely towards the end of the gallery.

'They've taken over a storeroom to go through statements,' with a wink at the guvnor. 'My turn to keep tabs on his nibs.'

'Who else have we got?'

'Two undercovers from St Aldate's pretending to be punters.'

'They haven't been rumbled?' Markham enquired tensely.

'Relax, guv. They're almost as geeky as Burton . . . One of 'em even pretended to Ashworth that his kid's school is doing a project on the South Pole. Got the full VIP treatment an' kept Ashworth out of our hair.'

'Where's Ashworth now?'

'Well, now him an' Dad of the Year have finished their love-in, he's jus' floating around doing his big cheese bit.'

Noakes followed Markham's gaze which was trained intently on Olivia and Jonjo Kelleher as they passed to and fro along the gallery.

'She's doing great, boss. Got Kelleher jawing away about the Norskies naming summat after their king . . . Noggin the Nog—'

'Or Haakon,' Markham corrected him drily.

His wingman grinned back at him, not the least abashed.

'That's the fella. Any road, there were some palaver about them calling this plateau after him when Shackleton had named it after King Edward VII.' Noakes yawned eloquently. 'Kelleher's boring away about it an' your Olivia's standing there all starry-eyed like she can't get enough . . . He looks like the cat that got the cream.'

Some of the tension left Markham's body.

So far so good.

'Who's on the ground floor?'

'The undercovers are down there now, drifting round the gift shop an' the stuff on Roman Britain . . . Got a good view of the front entrance. An' we've got two more plain clothes outside.'

Markham could still see the two heads leaning towards each other at the far end of the gallery next to the lifts and the model of Captain Scott's final resting place, an unsettlingly realistic mock-up of a cairn with exposed cross-section using mannequins and props to show the position of the bodies and their pitiful belongings.

Suddenly there was a minor commotion with museum staff running from all directions towards a party of schoolchildren halfway along the gallery.

Markham and Noakes moved quickly towards the disturbance which, it transpired, had been caused by a child passing out. A quarter of an hour later, the ambulance was organised and order restored, but when the DI returned to his vantage point in front of the *Cape Evans Hut* display, Olivia and Kelleher had disappeared. He and Noakes checked and rechecked the third-floor exhibits, but there was no sign of them.

'See if you can find Dr Ashworth while I try the other floors,' Markham instructed Noakes urgently. 'Get Burton and Doyle on it too. And round up the undercovers *discreetly*, in case Kelleher's watching and susses that the game's up. Then come and find me in the storeroom.'

Heart pounding, he traversed dim corridors, recesses, walkways and passages, trying not to attract attention by his haste, but there was no sign of the two he sought. Almost as though a breeze block in one of the museum's massive concrete walls had slid back, drawn them in and closed behind them — like they were actors in some B movie horror film, Markham thought, trying to quell his rising alarm.

Arriving back at the third-floor storeroom, he found Noakes, puce in the face and looking as though he was about to have a coronary, haranguing two men, one lanky and bespectacled, the other stocky and well-built with weight-lifter's shoulders. Both were casually dressed in jeans, T shirts and trainers. The dismayed faces of Burton and Doyle immediately alerted Markham to the fact that something had gone very wrong.

'This is Dad of the Year.' Noakes jabbed a finger at the stocky one. 'Go on, then. Tell the inspector what you told me.'

'We nipped into the café next to the gift shop. Just for a breather after listening to all that stuff about ancient civilisations.'

Normally Noakes would have sympathised, but not this time.

'*Go on*,' he said menacingly.

'The coast was clear, so we compared notes and checked the map you gave us . . . Wanted to be sure we knew where all the exits were.'

'*And*?' the DS prompted.

Markham had a sickening feeling he knew what was coming.

'We didn't notice anyone come in. There's a kind of partition between where we were sitting and the counter. He must have been on the other side and heard . . .'

'*Who*?' Markham's jaw was clenched.

'The director bloke . . . with the funny little goatee . . . Dr Ashworth, right?' Dad of the Year licked his lips nervously. 'He must've been stood there while we were chatting . . .'

The lanky one took up the story. 'We heard a noise on the other side like someone putting their tray down. When I looked over the top, there was Ashworth walking towards the foyer.'

His companion put in, 'Look, we didn't figure he'd worked it out. He wasn't hurrying . . . looked the same as usual . . . Like he'd remembered something, changed his mind about getting a cup of tea.'

'You chuffing *idiots*.' Noakes's Yorkshire vowels had never sounded so ominous. 'Ashworth hasn't been seen since. Plus there's no sign of Kelleher an' the guvnor's missus.'

'Ashworth must've tipped Kelleher the wink,' Doyle concluded.

The tall undercover said, 'They didn't go out the front door. I checked with reception, and the girl on the desk hadn't seen them.'

'What about the basement?' Burton asked.

Four pairs of eyes were fixed on her.

'That's where they have the cinema and interactive stuff . . . It's closed right now, but Brendan Potter's just told me it goes through to the underground staff car park.'

'CCTV?' Noakes rapped.

'They never got round to doing the basement. The car park's permit holders only with electric barriers,' she told them, 'so they didn't see any need.'

Noakes was furious. 'It's not marked on the chuffing map.'

'It's staff only.' Burton was equally frustrated.

'Kelleher and Olivia were standing next to the lifts when I last saw them,' Markham said. 'It's a blind spot, but I'm willing to bet Ashworth came up to the third floor and somehow persuaded them to go with him—'

'Down to the basement and out through the car park,' Burton put in. She twitched the lapels of her jacket. 'Assuming Dr Ashworth warned Kelleher we were on to him, does that mean he's been helping Kelleher all along?'

'*Two of 'em* . . .' Noakes's face was the picture of dismay as the concept of *folie à deux* took on a whole new meaning.

'We can't be sure of anything until we catch up with them,' Markham said.

He turned to the wretchedly squirming undercovers. 'Don't blame yourselves. I took my eye off the ball as well. That commotion with the schoolchildren distracted me. I should have left that to Noakes and made sure of keeping Kelleher in sight.'

Burton cleared her throat. 'If you hadn't responded to an emergency and Kelleher noticed, he might've asked himself why not,' she said. 'He might've twigged you were following him, sir.'

Seeing the concern in the big brown eyes, magnified to twice their normal size by the spectacles she had forgotten to take off, Noakes took note. *Shippers had better look lively and get a ring on her finger before she changes her mind and goes back to mooning over the skipper.*

Almost as though she intuited what the DS was thinking, Burton suddenly became briskly efficient. 'What now, sir?' she asked.

'If I'm right, Kelleher knows the game's up,' Markham said slowly. 'But I reckon Olivia will be able to convince him she had no idea he was our prime suspect.'

Noakes whirled round on the undercovers.

'When you were shooting your mouths off, did either of you two numpties say owt about Revenger's Folly?'

'No,' the tall one said firmly. 'We were focused on Kelleher . . . knew he'd be up on the third floor till at least seven, what with it being late-night opening till eight thirty. I'd told Ashworth I wanted to do a recce of the polar stuff and asked what time would be best for that. He said to wait till the school groups were gone and join the last guided tour with his assistant at six . . . that's Kelleher, right?'

His stocky colleague chimed in defensively. 'Look, there's two plain clothes outside. We knew DS Noakes was patrolling the third floor, then we saw you come in and head up there, sir. So—'

'You thought you were safe to slope off to the caff,' Noakes finished.

'Needed a cuppa after all that crap about artefacts from bleeding Pompeii,' the undercover shot back. 'Ashworth was like the frigging Duracell Bunny . . . went on and on.' The colour rising up his beefy neck he added, 'At least outside they get to eat ice cream.'

'Never mind the pigging cornettos,' Noakes hissed. 'The inspector's missus is in danger thanks to you.'

'Enough, Noakesy.' Markham's voice was firm. 'Recriminations won't help Olivia.'

'Yes, the post-mortem can wait till later,' Burton said, then blushed at the unfortunate choice of words, glancing swiftly at Markham. But he appeared oblivious, as though conducting some internal colloquy.

'I reckon they'll head for Revenger's Folly,' he said finally. 'Olivia will have told Kelleher it's the one place no one will look because the police have finished with it and the gatehouse is closed to the public.'

'Won't he think it smells a bit iffy, sir?' Doyle put in. 'If Kelleher knows you've rumbled him,' with a scornful look at the cringing undercovers, 'won't he assume Olivia's in on it?'

'It's a fair point,' Markham said quietly. 'But my money's still on Olivia making Kelleher think I don't talk shop with her . . . and her resenting being outside the charmed circle.'

It occurred to him with a jolt that this might well be a factor in his partner's occasional flashes of bitterness about Kate Burton.

'Olivia's a good actress,' Markham continued. 'She once said to me it's part and parcel of a teacher's bag of tricks — the ability to assume a particular persona . . . project characteristics that aren't your own.'

'Yeah, like Cruella de Vil,' Noakes agreed. 'Cos it's the law of the sodding jungle in schools these days.'

'The thing is, sarge, she needs to be the *opposite* with Kelleher,' Doyle volunteered. 'Kind of neurotic and clingy.' The young detective looked doubtful that Olivia Mullen could successfully impersonate a maladjusted basket case.

Surprisingly, Burton shared Markham's belief that Olivia could bring it off.

'Kelleher's knowledge of Olivia dates to when they were at university,' she said. 'That means he has no real insight into who she is or what makes her tick. He'll see what he *wants* to see. That's why Nathan's told her to display neediness, emotional insecurity and a fixation with Scott and Shackleton. The idea is that she's been setting them up in her mind as a heroic contrast to her current circle.'

'She means you an' me, mate,' Noakes said dourly to Doyle.

'I mean *all* of us, sarge,' Burton said earnestly. 'The polar explorers are Olivia's pinups . . . almost like a fetish verging on erotomania.'

Noakes and Doyle looked at each other.

Shoot me now.

'It's not the same as erotomania,' she hastened to assure them. 'More like an obsessive-compulsive addiction.'

'Thank chuff for that,' was Noakes's sarcastic rejoinder. 'So, what are the symptoms then?'

'Sensation-seeking, depression, anxiety . . . poor sense of identity,' Burton replied.

Doyle was dismayed. 'How's she meant to have shown that lot in under an hour?'

'Yeah, she weren't with him long enough,' Noakes objected.

'Nathan thought of that,' Burton told them, not without a certain complacency. 'He told her to get it in as early as possible that she was a thrill-seeker . . . wanted the inside track on murder and gory stuff . . . only,' she carefully avoided looking at Markham, 'her partner never spilled the beans because he was boring as hell.'

She watched as they digested this.

'He told her to get Kelleher on to the subject of the supernatural — as in the ghost Shackleton believed marched alongside them when they were trekking across South Georgia.'

Comprehension dawned in Noakes's eyes.

'Work up to the idea of him taking her to Revenger's Folly, you mean?'

'That's right, sarge. If she planted the seed early enough, then even if they got interrupted or something else happened, Kelleher would feel he had a handle on her emotions . . . And the urge to confide in her would be irresistible.'

Noakes had no trouble believing in the irresistible allure of Olivia Mullen, but like Doyle he demurred. 'If he's got his back to the wall, why bother with that ole ruin . . . There's gotta be better places.'

'But don't you see, sarge, thanks to Olivia his mind will be running on the folly. If he's as detached from reality as we think he is, then it'll fit with his grandiose idea of himself . . . Nathan thinks it's highly probable he identifies with the geologist killer who murdered his rival in the folly, which makes it even more suitable for the final act of the drama.'

Noakes didn't like the sound of that.

'Final act . . . as in we take him in,' he scowled.

'Absolutely,' Burton agreed, belatedly aware how Markham, fearful for his partner, might interpret those words.

'Where does Ashworth fit in to all of this?' Doyle asked.

Burton shrugged. 'God knows.'

'He may've tipped Kelleher off, but I somehow don' see lover boy taking him along for the ride.' Noakes stopped and gave the DI an alarmed look. '*Hey*, you alright boss?'

Markham's face was the colour of putty, but his next words were calm.

'I want the museum evacuated quickly and quietly. Use the fire alarm or whatever it takes to empty the place. Then we fan out and check that Ashworth's not around somewhere.'

'He'll be long gone,' Noakes protested.

'I reckon he'll have followed Kelleher and Olivia,' Markham replied. 'Olivia would be sure to tell him where they were headed, even if Kelleher was in a world of his own.'

'We need to notify Ridley College so they can make sure everyone stays well clear of the folly,' Burton said, moving towards the door mobile in hand. 'I'm on it, boss.'

'Kelleher's a grade A nutter, guv,' Noakes told Markham. 'Most likely he jus' wants your Olivia as an audience for some crackpot speechifying about Scott an' the rest of 'em before he blows his brains out or ends it all.'

Markham devoutly hoped such was the case but couldn't suppress the idea that Kelleher might decide to take Olivia with him, seeing it as a victory over the authorities if nothing else.

His colour returned as he gave the order. 'Let's get to it. I want the museum cleared with as little fuss as possible. No one comes back inside, and we sweep the building for Ashworth. After that, we head to Revenger's Folly. No blues and twos, just the team.' He raised a hand, forestalling any objections. 'Alert St Aldate's and we'll have Charleson down on top of us in full hostage negotiation mode. I take it nobody wants that.'

His colleagues nodded wordlessly.

Kate Burton slipped back into the room.

'All clear at Ridley,' she announced. 'The contractors weren't due in till tomorrow, but there's a notice outside saying the site is closed due to ongoing building works.'

'Good.' Markham began to feel a return of confidence. 'Olivia's not wearing a wire, but I think she can stall Kelleher till we get there.'

'Yeah, she's got the gift of the gab,' Noakes said admiringly. 'An' she's so well up on the polar mob, she can keep him gassing about 'em till kingdom come.'

'What about Ashworth?' Doyle demanded. 'Could he throw a spanner in the works?'

'Little weedy bloke like him ain't going to take on Kelleher single-handed,' Noakes observed scornfully. 'I reckon he'll try an' talk him round . . . tell him to do the decent thing, release the damsel in distress blah blah.' He scratched his chin meditatively. 'Jus' might work an' all,' he concluded ruefully. Then, jerking a finger towards the under-covers, 'Right, Tweedledum an' Tweedledumber, you can help me clear the building.'

* * *

As Noakes drove them to Ridley College, Kate Burton thought that Oxford had never looked more beautiful, its ancient buildings gilded by the setting sun so that they seemed tipped with fire.

There was an air of unreality to what was happening, the evacuation of the Reynolds Museum and search for Clive Ashworth now a blurred memory as they approached the red-brick facade which seemed to glow, holding the warmth of the day as in a crucible.

Two figures in academic gowns were waiting, which caused Markham to curse softly under his breath.

'It's alright, sir, you wait here and I'll deal with it.'

Kate Burton was out of the car in a trice, smoothing her suit and tucking her pageboy behind her ears, the better to convey an impression of understated competence.

'Whatcha tell Batman an' Robin?' Noakes asked on her return, impressed despite himself by the speed with which she had dispatched the reception party.

'That there was nothing to worry about and we had everything in hand — ongoing investigation, so I couldn't give any details.' She blushed slightly. 'When I got in touch with them before, about getting contractors in, I gave the impression it was something to do with a crackdown on student misbehaviour, drug dealing and parties getting out of hand over the summer — I didn't let on it was anything to do the museum murders.'

'You're a devious little beggar coming up with whoppers like that on the spot,' Noakes said. 'S'pose you need to be up to everything with that lot at Southampton Row.' There was a note of paternalistic pride as he offered this tribute, almost as if he took some credit for her acquisition of these skills.

Burton looked as though she was about to make a caustic retort, but something in Markham's bleak expression stopped her. Fleetingly it crossed her mind that there was a time when she would have given anything for him to feel for her the way he did about Olivia Mullen.

Was, she told herself. *As in Past Tense. He belonged to someone else and anyway, she had Nathan who was a decent bloke, even if he didn't make the breath catch in her throat. They had something good, and she wasn't going to spoil it by hankering after what she could never have.*

Suddenly she became aware of Noakes's sly grin, as though he saw something that amused him very much. Ignoring him, she marched ahead through the arched passageway they had used before.

'Slow down, luv,' Noakes puffed. 'We ain't even decided what we're going to say to the mad bastard — assuming he's there in the first place.'

This brought Burton up short and she turned back, looking anxiously at Markham who hadn't uttered a single word since they left the museum save for his impatient expletives when he saw the welcoming committee.

'How do you want to play this, sir?' she asked simply. 'Go in all guns blazing and say we've got armed backup on the way, or try softly softly . . . tell him we know why he did it, but if he kills himself, he won't be able to tell his story and nobody'll know the whole truth of how Tim Colthurst's reputation was built on sand.'

'Plus if he harms the guvnor's missus, he'll jus' be the same as any other toerag who ends up being today's news and tomorrow's fish an' chips wrapping,' Noakes growled.

'I'm sure that's what Olivia will have told him,' Markham said. 'That he owes it to himself not to end up like any common or garden criminal and his polar scholarship needn't be over.'

'Yeah, they'd let him go on with that in the funny farm,' Doyle put in. 'He could still write stuff and, er, make a name for himself.' A thought struck him. 'The fact of him being the museum murderer is bound to whip up interest.'

Noakes shot the younger man a withering look.

'Somehow I don' see the Oxford University Press or any of those other poncy publishers rolling up to Broadmoor or Rampton or wherever he ends up.' The DS scowled. 'Any road, I ain't sure he's a proper barmpot . . . Okay, so he's got this hang-up about Scott an' Oates an' the rest of 'em, but he killed Colthurst cos he were jealous an' offed the others to make sure they couldn't tell . . . That's jus' downright *wickedness* an' nowt to do with any mental wotsit.'

Markham did not break stride as he absorbed this. 'Yes, Noakesy, but I think his self-identification with Scott and Co. was at the root of his jealousy. He had a possessiveness about them which meant he literally couldn't bear someone else to encroach on what he thought of as *his* territory.'

'He wasn't *that* flattering about them when all's said and done,' piped up Doyle. 'I mean, tying Captain Scott into this queer theory stuff isn't exactly kissing his arse.' At Burton's reproving glare, he hastily recollected himself, 'Sorry, sir. I meant to say, stuff like Kelleher came up with didn't exactly fit the heroic image.'

'It's alright, Doyle, I can see what you're getting at,' Markham replied. 'I gathered from Olivia that there's a kind of cottage industry around the explorers. In fact, she said there's this theory that Oates had an illicit relationship with a twelve-year-old girl and fathered an illegitimate child . . . You've got claims and counterclaims whizzing back and forth, the more sensational the better. As for the idea of the explorers being repressed homosexuals, that's quite respectable nowadays. Practically mainstream.'

Noakes snorted his contempt. 'Dirty-minded drivellers the lot of them.'

'Maybe so,' Markham said, 'but my point is that Captain Scott and his companions are still capable of generating intense passions a century or more after their deaths.'

They had reached the dell.

'Antarctica is a mysterious and wonderful place,' the DI continued softly. 'Dangerous too.'

'The Antarctic Treaty means no one country can dominate it.' Even at such a juncture, Kate Burton could not forbear to enlighten her colleagues.

'But no such treaty exists between academics and scholars, Kate,' Markham told her. 'And *that's* what lies at the heart of this case — a fight for Scott's legacy.'

The little castellated gatehouse was in front of them.

'It's like a toy fort or something,' Doyle said wonderingly. 'You kind of expect to see wooden knights lined up in front of it.'

But there was nothing mellow about its grey stone, and the college flag that had fluttered so jauntily from the roof on Markham's last visit drooped heavily on its pole.

There was no sign of anyone about, but they could hear the murmur of voices.

Markham pointed to the roof terrace, gesturing to the others to follow him up the spiral staircase on the right-hand side of the building. The wicket gate had yet to be installed by the phoney 'contractors', so access to the roof was clear.

The blood was pounding in his ears as he climbed, staying close to the wall since there was no balustrade. He felt light-headed too, as though from altitude sickness.

Most eerie of all, he seemed to hear a voice in his ear that whispered, '*Come up and be dead!*' With fierce resistance, he countered it. *No,* he told himself, *Get down to life!*

At the top of the stairs was an arch through which they emerged on to the blackened pavement of the roof whose low battlements were more ornamental than defensive.

Opposite them on the far side, Jonjo Kelleher waited with one arm round Olivia, holding her clamped to his side, the other hand in his pocket. Clive Ashworth stood a few paces distant, his eyes riveted on Kelleher's face as though no one else existed.

A crooked little smile played about the curator's mouth as he observed the detectives.

Without looking away, he said to Olivia, 'So you were in league with your handsome sleuth all along then, Liv.'

The familiar address jarred Markham, but he answered steadily enough, 'We were always going to find you out, Kelleher. It was just a matter of time.'

The curator's left hand emerged from his pocket and Markham felt his heart stop as he saw that it held an ice axe. With its stained wooden shaft and rusty metal tip, it looked very old, and he suddenly recognised it as an item on loan to the museum from the Scott Polar Research Institute.

Jonjo Kelleher meant to go down fighting.

Markham looked at Olivia, who was white to the lips, and then back to Kelleher.

'I know why you did it,' he said gently. 'And I can even understand. But what about the others? Why did *they* deserve to die?'

There was a hiss, like gas escaping, that cut off so suddenly Markham mistrusted the evidence of his own ears. But Jonjo Kelleher's pleasant tones were as agreeable as ever. It was only what he said that evoked horror.

'Yvonne wouldn't let well alone. A cufflink with dried blood on it came off my shirt the night I settled accounts with Tim.' There was something truly chilling in the curator's banking analogy. 'She found it and tried to pull my strings . . . wanted to wangle herself a better position at the museum in addition to sharing my bed.' A contemptuous smile. 'It was a "No" on both counts. Like a credulous fool, she agreed to meet me up here and . . . well, you know the rest.'

'An' that poor lad from Sherwin, what did *he* do wrong?' Noakes broke in hotly. 'Did *he* fancy being a notch on your bed post?'

Raising his eyebrows at such vehemence, Kelleher said lightly, 'He came to see me, full of insinuation . . . asked what he should say to the police about the Titus Oates Society and Des Milner — I think he'd somehow found out about that. We arranged to meet in the Hatton Library and,' he spat with a sudden viciousness, 'I shut his blabbing mouth for ever.'

'Did Freda Carrington have a loose mouth too?' Burton asked.

Colour rose in his cheeks. 'I had nothing to do with that.'

'Like we're gonna believe you,' Noakes jeered.

'It's the truth.' Now Kelleher's voice sounded ragged. 'And besides, she was my friend, not like the others . . . I'd never have hurt her.'

'*It was me.*'

If there had come a voice from the sky, they couldn't have been more surprised, as Clive Ashworth stepped forward.

The museum director removed his steel-rimmed spectacles and, with a shaking hand, put them into his jacket pocket as though he didn't wish to see too clearly.

'Freda rang me to say she'd found something that bothered her, something that implicated *you*, Jonjo. And she said that wasn't all . . .' A long pause during which the silence was so absolute it seemed as though the very walls were listening. 'She suggested we meet up at the river . . .' He ground to a halt.

'An' you saw your chance,' Noakes prompted.

'I had an idea what she was talking about, knew in my bones it could be lethal.' Almost pleadingly, he said, 'There'd been reports of a Peeping Tom scaring female rowers. I planned to make it look as though he'd suddenly escalated the violence.'

'You're five foot nothing!' Doyle exclaimed. 'Dr Carrington was taller and fitter. She'd have seen you off in no time.'

'I wore a ski mask and came for her when she was about to use the shower, so there was the element of surprise. She fell and smacked her head on a pipe, so in the end I didn't need to lay a finger on her. Not sure that I'd have been able to go ahead with it if it had come to that . . .' he added wretchedly.

'So she was concussed and you chased her into the river,' Doyle said levelly.

'Yes . . . I knew she couldn't swim and, you see, with the concussion . . .'

'You cowardly piece of shit,' Noakes said in disgust. 'You left her to drown. All to protect *that*.' He pointed at Kelleher who stood as though turned to stone.

'*Why*, Dr Ashworth?' Markham asked quietly.

'Why do you think?' came the bitter reply.

'I need to hear you say it,' the DI continued implacably.

'Isn't it obvious? I *care* for him.' Almost tenderly, he added, 'I couldn't have wished for a better assistant . . . one who feels the same way I do about *them*.'

'You mean Captain Scott and the Antarctic explorers?'

'Yes, Inspector.'

Suddenly, Olivia twisted violently in Kelleher's arms as though recoiling from someone advancing on her. 'Get away from me!' she screamed and wrenched herself out of his grasp.

Taken by surprise, Kelleher staggered, waving the ice axe in front of him, his eyes wide and dilated in terror, but with the low parapet behind him, there was no retreat.

In one swift sinuous movement, before anyone had time to react, he pivoted and launched himself over the battlements with the grace of an acrobat, the setting sun silhouetting his body as it traced a dark parabola through the air. There was one short, anguished cry of mingled fear and rage which was sharply cut off as though the thread of life had been snapped by an invisible hand.

Distantly from Ridley College the sound of the chapel bells reached them, tolling sonorously as though to offer up a dirge.

* * *

'Who was it you saw, luv?'

Never one to beat about the bush, Noakes was intensely curious about what had happened up there on the roof of Revenger's Folly. Even the restorative brandy organised by the Old Parsonage didn't deflect him.

The team and Olivia were gathered in the library which, once again, the hotel had made over for their exclusive use. In light of the horrific denouement to the museum murders, Markham found something almost unbearably poignant about the black and white portraits of 1960s Oxford.

'Didn't the rest of you see it?' Olivia asked, cradling her Remy Martin. 'Come on, you *must* have.'

'No, sweetheart,' Markham told her gently. 'Whoever it was, only you and Kelleher saw him.'

'Go on then,' Noakes urged. 'What was he like?'

'Thin and balding on top with mutton chop sideburns and pince-nez, wearing an old-fashioned frock coat with white stock at the neck . . . He looked like a clergyman from one of those television costume dramas,' Olivia said slowly. 'Like some actor on location at Ridley.' Her eyes moved from one to the other. 'But none of the rest of you saw him.'

Doyle shifted uneasily. '*Kelleher* saw him alright,' he said. 'You could tell from the way he freaked out at the end. His eyes were popping and he looked like he was shitting bricks. Sorry sir,' with an apologetic glance at Markham, 'but the bloke was definitely scared out of his wits.'

'Nathan says when people are around places where there's been a violent crime, they sometimes pick up psychic vibes from what happened,' Kate Burton told them, clearing her throat. 'ESP or something . . . especially if they're,' she hesitated, 'susceptible.'

'You mean loopy,' Olivia said bluntly.

Burton looked embarrassed. 'Oh no, not at all. It's a question of *receptivity*.'

Keen to head off any scientific BS courtesy of Shippers, Noakes cut in.

'Reckon it must've been the ghost of that mad geologist who clobbered Sir Whatshisface for nicking his stuff,' he said cheerfully. 'Came up trumps in the end an' saw to it that Kelleher got his comeuppance.'

'What d'you think Kelleher meant by saying Alex Mason had found out about him and Milner?' Doyle asked after an awkward pause. 'Were they having an affair then?'

'God knows,' Noakes retorted. 'One thing's for sure, though.' He took a huge gulp of his brandy as the rest braced themselves. 'They're all at it like knives here. It's a wonder they ever get any work done.'

'I'm not sure we'll ever have the answer to that, Sergeant,' Markham told Doyle. 'But clearly Alex Mason implied he knew something that Kelleher wasn't willing to risk becoming public knowledge.'

'Don' look as though we'll get owt out of poor ole Ashworth,' Noakes said. 'Jus' kept muttering in that weird sing-song voice like he's auditioning to be a wizard in *Harry Potter* or summat.'

'Yeah, totally bizarre,' Doyle agreed. 'He said something like . . . "for the infinity of a second Kelleher understood what had happened . . . he knew everything and then ceased to know".' The young detective raised his hands in bewilderment. 'Complete cobblers.'

'It's unlikely Dr Ashworth will ever be fit to plead to the manslaughter of Freda Carrington,' Markham said thoughtfully. 'His reason snapped.'

'Same as Kelleher's neck,' Noakes nodded with satisfaction. Then, 'D'you reckon him an' Kelleher had summat going?'

'I think it was platonic . . . a meeting of minds,' Olivia said emphatically. 'They loved their work at the museum and worked so well together.'

Markham remembered thinking that they made an impressive double act.

'I wonder if deep down Dr Ashworth suspected Jonjo murdered Tim Colthurst and the others,' she continued, 'but he just couldn't bear to face the truth. Poor man,' she added compassionately.

'Some tame trick cyclist'll come up with the usual bollocks about him not getting enough cuddles as a child an' he'll be out in ten, you'll see.' Noakes wasn't feeling very compassionate, though at Olivia's reproachful 'George?' he coloured to the tips of his ears.

Markham felt it was time to change topics.

'So, Noakesy,' he chaffed, 'What are you going to do about this plan to become Bromgrove's answer to Philip Marlowe?'

'Who's he, boss . . . another private dick?' the other asked anxiously.

'Just the nonpareil of investigators,' the DI replied, exchanging a glance of complicity with Olivia.

Noakes's expression cleared. 'Oh right, you mean some character in a book.'

Doyle was dumbstruck. 'Are you *serious*, sarge? I thought you were going to stay in CID and haunt Sidney till they carried you out feet first.'

'Reckon mebbe it's time to strike out for myself,' came the bashful reply. 'Be my own boss.'

As Burton and Doyle peppered their colleague with questions, Markham drew Olivia over to the charming old fireplace.

'A new chapter opens for DS George Noakes,' he murmured. 'I foresee interesting times ahead.'

She smiled up at him. 'It's a feather in your cap solving the museum murders, Gil . . . And one in the eye for Sidney!' Then, very softly, looking at the photographs of Oxford's *jeunesse dorée*, 'Poor Jonjo,' she said, 'poor deluded man. When I think of his glory days back in Manchester . . . *Golden lads and girls must, As chimney-sweepers come to dust.*'

'Noakesy's giving us the evils,' Markham told her. 'Time to forget philosophy and raise a glass to his new enterprise.'

Hand in hand, they turned their back on images of the dreaming spires and re-joined their friends.

THE END